KEEPING TIME

BROADWAY

New York

KEEPING TIME

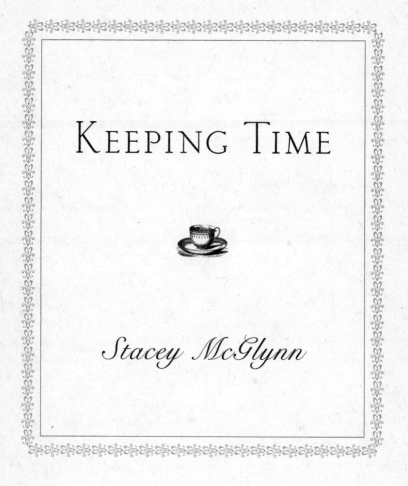

Stacey McGlynn

Copyright © 2010 by Stacey McGlynn

Reading Group Guide copyright © 2011 by Stacey McGlynn

All rights reserved.
Published in the United States by Broadway Paperbacks,
an imprint of the Crown Publishing Group,
a division of Random House, Inc., New York.
www.crownpublishing.com

Broadway Paperbacks and its logo, a letter B bisected on the diagonal,
are registered trademarks of Random House, Inc.

Originally published in slightly different form in the United States by Crown Publishers,
an imprint of the Crown Publishing Group,
a division of Random House, Inc., New York, in 2010.

Library of Congress Cataloging-in-Publication Data
McGlynn, Stacey.
Keeping time : a novel / Stacey McGlynn.
p. cm.
(alk. paper)
1. Older women—Fiction.   2. British—United States—Fiction.   I. Title.
PS3613.C4866K44 2010
813'.6—dc22

2010008925

ISBN 978-0-307-46441-5
eISBN 978-0-307-46442-2

Printed in the United States of America

BOOK DESIGN BY AMANDA DEWEY
COVER PHOTOGRAPHS © (WOMAN) MASAAKI TOYOURA/TAXI JAPAN/GETTY IMAGES;
(HOUSE) JACQUI HURST/DORLING KINDERSLEY/GETTY IMAGES;
(GATE) KARYN R. MILLER/GETTY IMAGES

1   3   5   7   9   10   8   6   4   2

First Paperback Edition

To Rob,
because of always

The character of Daisy Phillips was inspired by the incomparable
Dot Nicholson of Liverpool, England

KEEPING TIME

ONE

"COME ON, MUM. It's not as if you're being put out to pasture."
Words by Dennis. Aimed at Daisy. Tipping the evening on its
side.

Fifty-five-year-old Dennis, sitting on the taupe linen sofa, across
from the mahogany cocktail table. His new wife, Amanda, beside him,
not saying a word. Dennis, leaning forward, patiently waiting to hear all
the things Daisy wasn't saying. Then, hammering on. Forcing a smile.
"I hope you're not thinking that."

Actually, Daisy Phillips *was* thinking that.

Smelling the grass of the pasture.

Feeling the tickle of the blades under her nose.

Searching her son's face for some scrap of infanthood, a glimpse of
childhood, a shred of adolescence. Nothing. Silly to think there might
be, but Daisy was groping, thoroughly shaken.

Dennis, "I think, *we* think"—gesturing to include Amanda—
"you'd really like it there. It's crazy to go on like you've been." Meaning
to continue living in the house she had been born in and had inherited
from her parents. The house she had spent her whole life in. Dennis,
going on: "Life would be a permanent holiday."

Daisy, not replying. Too prim, too proper, with an elegance, a grace that never had to be taught, a perfectly straight back that did. Ironed into her by a mother who had spent a lifetime focused on the wrong things. Daisy, staring down at her hands clasped tightly in her lap. Adjusting her ring.

Dennis, thrusting the colorful glossy brochure into her eye line. Daisy, turning away. Dennis, holding it there for a moment, shaking it as though it needed shaking to get her attention. Not getting a response, Dennis, sighing. Putting it on the table next to him. Saying, "You can take the brochures home with you. Look through them when you're ready. Amanda and I think The Carillion would be perfect for you. There's a lot more to these senior homes than you know. At least think about it, okay?"

Daisy, looking at him. Meeting his eye. "I'd like to go home now." Standing up, smoothing her pleated beige skirt over her narrow hips.

Dennis, hoisting himself off the sofa. "I can take you right away if you'd like."

Daisy, "I'd like that." Nodding.

M INUTES LATER DENNIS, the top of his head glistening with rain from the trip out the front door to the car, driving his silent mother home, leaving the dark splashing streets of Merseyside for the dark splashy streets of Saint Helens, northeast of Liverpool. His wiper blades lashing noisily back and forth, rerunning the conversation in his head. He had not gotten nearly as far as he had hoped. Amanda would surely lay into him when he got home.

Pulling slowly into the driveway at 24 Rosemary Lane. Slipping the gear stick into neutral. Turning to his mother. "I hope you had a nice dinner."

"Yes. It was very nice, thank you." Stiffly.

"Look, Mum"—adjusting himself in the seat to face her—"I'm sorry, but it's been hard on me having two houses to maintain—two lawns to mow, two networks of pipes and wires to worry about. I appreciate that you try not to call me, but things always do seem to come up, and I'm not so young myself anymore. And you know Amanda wants to move to Chessex, to be nearer her family. And now that Gabriel's finishing school, there's really nothing keeping us here. We've already started looking at houses. Chessex is beautiful. You could have a cozy little apartment at The Carillion, with me and Amanda close by. Think of it as an adventure, a new chapter in your life."

Daisy, nodding her head. Slightly. Turmoil deep within.

Dennis, feeling a charge of relief. Maybe they were getting somewhere.

Her hand on the passenger side door catch. Leaning over. Kissing him. "Good night, Dennis."

"Good night, Mum." Dennis, watching her ease out of the car, before scurrying nimbly up the stone front walk, past the stone wall. Glimpsing her disappearing behind the cheerful yellow door, flanked by climbing red roses flush against white stucco, on her thatched-roof home half-timbered with exposed dark beams.

Not seeing what was on the other side of that cheerful yellow door: Daisy leaning heavily against it, her shaking frame pressing against its solid frame, surrendering to a fast-moving current of tears.

THE FOLLOWING SATURDAY, Dennis, calling. Daisy had been dreading his weekly call all morning. She had spent the whole intervening week in a closed-circuit loop over his recent proposal—locked in a cycle of ignoring it, denying it, being annoyed by it, irate over it, despairing because of it, hungering back to ignoring it again.

And now a ringing phone.

Daisy, picking it up. She had to. It was a responsibility growing stronger every day, knowing that Dennis wouldn't be thinking that she was busy in the kitchen, living room, or bath. He would be afraid that she was dead in the kitchen, living room, or bath. Sighing. Answering it.

An exchange of greetings. Brief pleasantries. Dennis, not getting to it right away. Saying first that he couldn't mow her lawn yet again because of the rain. Further discussion about the ceaseless rain. Then finally, the main point: asking if she had had a chance to look through the brochures.

Daisy, assuring him that she had—and she had, as they flew through the air into the wastepaper basket.

Dennis, asking what her thoughts were. About an apartment at The Carillion. About moving to Chessex.

Daisy, saying, "Oh my, what's that?" Saying sorry, she had to go. Someone was at the door. Pity they couldn't talk longer.

Partly true. Someone *was* at the door.

Daisy was at the door. Putting herself there, in the rain, with the portable phone. Saying their talk would have to wait until next Saturday, or until the rain finally let up and Dennis could come and mow the grass.

Hanging up, thin strands of guilt flowing through her. Pushing them aside. Hurrying to get ready to go to the club. A train to catch. An early lunch with friends, followed by shopping in the afternoon, and stopping for tea.

Daisy, standing at the gilded mirror above the bathroom sink, putting on makeup. Running a wide-toothed comb through her light brown hair. Applying lipstick. Taking a good hard look at herself. Her face, especially her chin—long, always had been, not brought on by the duplicities of aging. Her features small, delicate on a perfectly shaped head. Her nose, narrow. Big light blue eyes behind oval wire-rimmed glasses. Her cheekbones, not too crinkled, her forehead, not too smooth. Wavy hair, parted on the left side, thick clumps of bangs swooping off in both directions, forming a series of Cs and Js across her forehead. Her hair long enough to reach her eyebrows, short enough to reveal her earlobes, curling under at the collar in the back. A tiny, slender woman of seventy-seven. Gifted with an ever-present smile, an easy laugh.

Taking a deep breath. Standing as tall as she got. Confident, defiant, upbeat.

Ignoring a slow, steady dripping from the shower head.

H ER FRIENDS, GATHERED AROUND HER—Gladys, Marylin, Cate, Ellen, and her favorite, Dot. Umbrellas, drenched raincoats at the door.

Daisy liked these weekly luncheons. Taking the train into the city. Lunching, shopping at the rejuvenated Albert Dock. Feeling part of something with the city beating around her. Liverpool, recently voted Europe's cultural capital. The Merseyside Waterfront regional park and the whole waterfront area drew millions of visitors every year. The Cavern Club, the Beatles Museum, and the childhood homes of the former Beatles still attracted fans from all over the world. The cafés, pubs, heart-stopping architecture, cutting-edge theaters—all of it contributing to the energy Daisy loved.

If only the skies weren't consistently hosing the place down.

But that was Liverpool.

Daisy, feeling good. Wearing a new dress—navy with beige trim—that fell just below her knees. Sensible low-heeled navy shoes. Smiling during the conversation. Buttering her bread. Ordering the lamb. Ignoring nagging unpleasantries pecking away at her. Going over what she had lately been thinking about: hitting Dot up with a proposal.

Waiting for the appropriate lull in the conversation, then turning her attention to Dot, to get her idea out. Daisy, full of hope and slowly gathering excitement at spilling the words.

But then Dot blew her away, speaking first. Mentioning innocently that she was going on holiday for the summer. To Spain, where her daughter had a house. Shooting down Daisy's idea before it even got out of her mouth. Not giving Daisy the chance to say that she'd been thinking the two of them should go on holiday together. To Ireland. Or Scotland. Even Wales.

When Paul was alive, he and Daisy had traveled several times a year. Both loved exploring; together they had covered much of the globe. But Daisy hadn't been anywhere in the last four years—not since Paul died. She hadn't even thought of it. Until recently. Startling herself, imagining traveling again—on a much smaller scale, of course. Places she could drive to. She just had to figure out with whom. Dot's face had presented itself, and after thinking it over for some time, Daisy had concluded that Dot would indeed be the ideal travel companion. They liked the same things, needed their tea at precisely the same time, craved the same schedule of bed at night and waking in the morning, were equally active—which was to say they were unusually energetic for their ages—and were both devoted to the same evening ritual: Cointreau with mixers. Dot was as good a stand-in for Paul as Daisy could imagine.

But no sooner were the words "Dot, I've been thinking" out of Daisy's mouth than Dot dropped her bombshell. Daisy, nodding, smiling, wishing her well, her disappointed eyes sweeping around the table of faces to see if anyone else might be a candidate.

Dismissing each in turn. That creeping feeling again. Of walls closing in, of dreams swirling down drains, of possibilities not yet lived like dandelion seeds on wings of birds, launched, full of potential but never hitting the ground. Unable to shake the feeling that her best days were behind her. Paining her to find travel on that list, too—that great, sweeping list.

Sighing. When Paul went, everything went. Except her house, 24

Rosemary Lane. Still hers. It was not going to be stored away like short skirts, high heels, her passport—not if she could help it. Dennis and Amanda could go. Let them go to Chessex, but not with her.

She would hire someone to mow the lawn every week. Fix the shower head herself.

There. Problem solved.

TWO

WEDNESDAY, STILL RAINING. All of England under a deluge. People wondering if it would ever stop. Newspapers and television carrying stories of overflowing rivers, flooding streets, jammed motorways. Water, seemingly everywhere.

And where there wasn't water, there was dampness—lodged in houses, clothes, teeth, bones. People shaking their heads, trying to make the best of it. Citing how green the grass was, how happy the June flowers.

Daisy, at work. Seated behind the front desk at the local library, her part-time employment since Paul died. The shop had quickly become too much for her to manage by herself. She offered it, but neither son wanted it. Dennis was happy enough writing for the magazine *Artifacts, Archaeological Treasures, and Antiquities.* Talking about starting another book to follow up his last. And Lenny? Out-of-shape, overweight, never serious Lenny worked too hard at not working. A real job with real responsibilities would interfere with his minimalist freelance photography divorcé lifestyle. So Daisy rented the shop out, including the apartment above, and set about living on the income. The library job was just to be out and about in the world. To keep her head in the game.

To get the bestsellers before they hit the shelves.

Daisy, three pages into a home improvement manual. The plumbing chapter. An interruption, cutting into her concentration. She had been staring at the illustrations of shower heads and the pipes leading to them for more than thirty minutes, making every effort to prevent the black ink from diffusing into inscrutability. The interruption—a welcome hand on her shoulder—therefore, not at all perturbing. Turning to see Grace Parker looking down at her.

Daisy, preparing an answer as to why she was nose-deep in the mysteries of plumbing repair when Grace hit her with something else: "I'm leaving. I wanted to tell you personally."

"Leaving?" Daisy, wondering if she meant the room. The day? Forever? Hoping it wasn't the last.

It was. "I'm retiring."

Retiring! Sirens, bells, alarms, whistles. Daisy, not knowing what to say. Certain her mouth was hanging open, unable to close it. How old was Grace, anyway? She had to be younger, but by how much? Half a decade? A whole decade?

"Two weeks from today."

Daisy, focusing on Grace's ears. She had noticed them fleetingly in the past, but now she couldn't stop considering them. On this tall, attractive, statuesque, silver-haired, clear-skinned, minimally wrinkled woman hung the pointiest ears Daisy had ever seen. They stuck to the sides of her head as if a pavement artist or political cartoonist had created them for the comedic effect of exaggeration. Daisy could see that Grace tried to cover them with her hair, but at her age that was a tall order. She had probably been able to hide them easily enough in her younger years, but old age insisted on revealing things. Yanking away crutches when we needed them most.

Daisy, apparently, on the ears too long. Grace's hands speeding to their defense, patting her hair down over them.

Caught. Daisy, disgraced. Recovering quickly. Saying, "Oh, Grace, my Mondays and Wednesdays won't be the same without you. Of course I'm happy for you, very happy."

"Thank you. It's hard to leave after so many years, but Hal and I feel that it's time. We're selling the house, buying a flat, and traveling. We have four children scattered around the world. We might as well start enjoying life now while we're still healthy enough."

Daisy, nodding kindly. Voicing appropriate words and sentiments.

Very much wanting to go home.

D AISY COULDN'T REMEMBER the last time she had been in a hardware store.

Standing out on the pavement under her umbrella, gazing into the shop window, trying to remember. Concluding at last that it was probably with a grape lollipop in her hand and Mary Janes on her feet, on a Saturday afternoon generations ago with her father. Not wanting to delay the second foray any longer, in she went.

From what she could tell, sauntering through the aisles, not much had changed. Same musty, dusty attitude. Same lighting. Same sense of reassurance that they could fix life's problems. Armed with a digital camera loaded with pictures of her shower head, Daisy hurried to the back of the store to get assistance from the old man—older than she was, she was sure—behind the counter. He carefully studied the photographs of her shower head. Clutching her small silver camera in his wide red hand, he was able to diagnose the problem.

The shower stem valve, the portion behind the wall, must have a frayed washer. Replacing it was easy, nothing to it. Simply change the washer in the valve.

In no time at all, spread out before her on the counter, all she needed to replace the part. The man telling her how to do it—slowly, patiently, acting as if he had all the time in the world, which he probably did since she was the only customer in the shop. Assuring her the job could be done easily in less than an hour. Not expressing the slightest doubt about her ableness, which was something she would be forever grateful for.

And forever perplexed by. Assuming he must be either blind or crazy, but for the moment, anyway, his lack of doubt feeding her like nutrients.

THE FOLLOWING SATURDAY. Already. The rain, continuing. Dennis's call coming like clockwork. Ready for it, Daisy, picking up the phone, saying she had found someone else to mow her lawn and that he needn't worry about such things anymore. Thanking him for having done it for so long.

Her revelation, met with silence. Then sputtering, questions, apologies. Dennis, feeling his mother's words were an accusation. In time, however, reconsidering. Seeing how reasonable it was. Why not get some kid to mow, pay him a few pounds? Dennis, suddenly quite pleased with the news. Not saying a word about The Carillion. Talking instead about Gabriel's graduation party that was scheduled for the following day. Saying he would pick her up at three. Hanging up, his brain crowded with to-do lists.

Daisy, feeling both good and bad—good because she had managed to get the news out about the kid and the mowing. Good because Dennis had accepted it. Bad because it was totally made up. She hadn't actually done a thing about getting anyone to mow. Thank goodness for the rain. If it never stopped, she would never have to.

She headed into the bathroom, ignoring the increasing drip, to get ready for lunch at the club. Stepping over the neatly organized array of plumbing fixtures and tools that she had laid there three days earlier. Promising herself to do it first thing on Monday morning, before work and Grace Parker's retirement party.

THREE

NOTHING TO IT. Just unscrew the shower head from the wall, peek into the shower stem, find the frayed washer in the valve, pluck it out, replace it with the new one, put the shower head back on, and screw it on tightly.

Nothing to it.

First thing Monday morning. Daisy, thinking about her plumbing job during her tea and toast. Washing the plate and tea cup, deciding she needed more suitable work clothes.

Heading to the wardrobe. Peering into it. Nothing. Everything too fine. Certainly no plumber would put on good clothes to set out for a day of work. Turning to her chest of drawers. Rummaging through them, not sure what she was looking for but assuming she would know it when she saw it.

Nothing there sensible for shower repair, although she did find a pink sweater she hadn't seen in years and now remembered how much she had liked it. Remembered buying it for their trip to Spain. Had a fleeting image of an outdoor café in Barcelona—that sweater, big white sunglasses, and a sun hat with a pink sash. Taking the sweater out, thinking how unlucky it was that Dot would be summering in Spain, probably not only this summer but every summer thereafter, unknowingly robbing

Daisy of the only practical plan she had managed to come up with and relegating travel to the memories slot, not the upcoming events one.

Of course it was hardly Dot's fault. It was Daisy's, and she knew it. She should be looking into tours for singles. Thinking maybe she would.

Then thinking she most certainly would not. She had never traveled alone in her life and was unlikely to start now.

She put the sweater in her dry-cleaning pile. Then, Daisy, out of the room, heading for the cellar, admonishing herself not to fritter away any more of the morning searching for clothes to wear to do the repair. She had to actually do the repair, because if she could get some experience with such basics as screwdrivers, hammers, nails, and pliers, she could stay in the house, send Dennis and Amanda on their way, and decide on her own if and when it was time to go.

Down the stairs to the cellar, the old coal cellar that had been converted to laundry use and storage. Recalling a pair of old overalls that Paul used to wear. Thinking she probably would be able to find them, and use them, because they were held up by shoulder straps. It might feel good to wear something of his. He would be helping her change the frayed washer.

It was damp in the cellar. How could it be anything but, with constant rain?

She turned on the light and stood looking at the piles of boxes—some Paul's, some hers. Thinking it would be interesting to see what was in Paul's. He was not a hoarder. Seventy-eight years of life were distilled into a handful of boxes. Daisy, approaching the first of them, looking for some kind of label. Nothing was marked. Finding some that were hers, all her old treasures, but now she was not even sure what was in them—except one. She knew one. One that hadn't been opened since the day it was closed, one that contained a jewelry box.

Daisy, opening a box of Paul's. Bowling shoes. His and hers. Underneath, ice skates, a black pair, a white pair. And ski pants and ski jackets, plus random hats, scarves, gloves. Daisy, remembering skiing at Saint

Moritz, where they had bought them. Thinking it unlikely she would ever need anything in that box again. Donate it.

Closing that box, opening the next. Old Christmas decorations from years gone by. Daisy, lifting, inspecting, touching, lost for a time in memories. Closing it. Moving on, aware that time was ticking along. Old gardening tools, gardening gloves, packets of seeds never planted. No overalls.

Next box of Paul's, baby things. Tears springing to her eyes. He had kept their baby blankets! Daisy, gasping, running her fingers over first Lenny's, then Dennis's. How sentimental Paul had been. How lovely.

She had loved having babies. Never wanted those days to end. She may have been uncertain about marrying—and she was, terribly—but she had never held one single doubt about becoming a mother. Feeling tender inside, once again holding the blankets in her hands. Sniffing each one for some trace of baby scent. Nothing. Just a deep pungent mildew. Putting them back for the time being.

The next box, her own box, her wedding gown. How strange to see it again. Remembering how it had felt to wear it. The conflict. Her mother's impatience. Daisy, shuddering, her mother's face in her mind's eye.

Slowly lifting the gown out of the box, holding it up to her shoulders, leaning forward to see how it fell. She had loved the dress, the fake little pearls, and the high lace neck. Wondering if it would still fit. Thinking it possibly might.

Doing something she hadn't seen coming.

Trying it on, right there in that gloomy cellar. Stripping off her nightgown and stepping into it. From nightgown to wedding dress. Not even stopping to consider how silly it was. Just doing it. To feel it again.

Looking down at the drape of it; the hem reaching the cellar floor. Getting a glimpse of the back. Picturing her sons seeing her now. Laughing at what they would think.

Taking it off, replacing it neatly in the box, her mind drifting back to the one unopened box, the one housing the jewelry box. Returning to it.

Opening it. Peering inside. Seeing the jewelry box among other miscellaneous things, after almost sixty years. Reaching in. Lifting it out. Bringing it over to the stairs. Leaving it there to take up with her once she had found the overalls.

Seeing something at the stairs reminding her of what the old hardware store man had said to do. Doing what he had said. Turning the main water shutoff valve.

Feeling like a plumber.

Three boxes later, finding Paul's overalls. Bringing them upstairs with her along with the jewelry box—and something else: the baby blankets. Into her bedroom, her arms full of reclaimed booty. The overalls over the back of the chair, the jewelry box on the bedside table, the baby blankets laid lovingly on the bed.

Daisy, stepping back to admire the blankets. In their new home.

HALF AN HOUR LATER—overalls on. Shower head off. Frayed washer out. Stepping stool in. Daisy on it—one hand on the white shower tile for support, one finger probing around to make sure the new washer was placed correctly and smoothed out. Getting down to retrieve a flashlight, peering inside.

All looking good. Daisy excited, replacing the shower head again. Screwing it in.

She had done it. Off the stool again, back on the bathroom floor, looking up at the shower, congratulating herself. It looked perfect. And as the seconds passed, no drip!

Then, a humbling thought. She had turned the main water shutoff valve. Of course there was no drip. Quickly returning to the cellar to turn the water back on, then hurrying back to the shower to watch for water.

No drip! Now she could be proud.

Standing there, letting the minutes pass, enjoying herself. She *could* learn to do new things on her own. Eager to tell Dennis. She would call him right away and ask him to come over tomorrow evening to see her big accomplishment. Wouldn't he be surprised!

Feeling proud and happy, running into her bedroom to change out of her overalls and into her work clothes.

NOTHING COULD SHAKE Daisy's good mood because nothing had felt so good in a long time. When, during Grace Parker's retirement party, Grace appeared at Daisy's side to whisper and point out Grace's replacement, Daisy looked at the New Grace Parker and didn't worry. When Daisy heard the New Grace Parker—fifty years her junior—cheerfully and enthusiastically talking about the new technologies they would now be implementing to improve and update the library, Daisy didn't panic. And when she heard more about Grace's illustrious retirement plans, Daisy didn't feel a sharp pain in her side.

Instead, Daisy wanted to talk about her plumbing repair.

Imagining herself going back to the old hardware store man and discussing it with him. Maybe picking up some new tools or buying herself a little tool box. And asking him if he knew anyone who could cut her lawn. She was convinced now that it was true: Hardware stores really could fix life's problems.

But Daisy was too tired after the library to do anything but go home, and when she got there, she was too tired to do more than a simple meal, some TV, Cointreau, a little light reading, and early bed. Eyeing the jewelry box on her bedside table. Too tired to look. After all those years, it could wait another day.

Getting into bed, under her new blankets. Pulling the baby blankets up close. Holding them against her cheek. Ignoring the musty smell. Slowly drifting off to sleep under their warmth.

Reliving the feelings of being in a family of four—when she was the center of so many lives.

FOUR

IMPOSSIBLE TO KNOW exactly how long the sound of rushing water had incorporated itself into Daisy Phillips's dream, but one thing was certain: As far as rude awakenings went, this one would rank high on the list, because "gushing water" appears right after "incoming heavy artillery" and "ten-foot flames."

For the longest time she couldn't figure out what the sound was or where it was coming from. She lay in bed in the dark trying to decipher it. Thinking it was the torrential rains outside—as usual, there were torrential rains outside—before, tingling with trepidation, realizing it was more.

Torrential rains inside, too.

Feeling the heat of fear traveling up her body. Getting out of bed, putting on her slippers, drawing her robe around her. The sound of water was getting louder as she traveled down the hall, following the sound to the cellar door. Opening it. Stopping to listen. There was no mistaking it. Flipping the light switch on, starting down.

Water, everywhere, inches deep—several inches deep, clear across the floor, from wall to wall.

Gasping, on the bottom step. Trying to absorb the enormity of the situation. To get past the double whammy of not having Dennis to call. Of having to deal with it on her own. To figure out herself where the water was coming from. Inside? Outside? And what on earth she should do.

Spotting something: water, coming off one of the overhead beams. Why? Why from there? Was the beam leaking?

Daisy, seeing the ladder leaning against the wall on the other side of the deeply flooded floor. Not even hesitating. Stepping right down into the water—cold water up her calves, midway to her knees. Sloshing across the floor, retrieving the ladder. Setting it up under the wooden beam, under the splashing, cascading stream. Climbing up to the fourth step, peering overhead, looking for some kind of a hole in the beam or in the floor above it. Finding something unexpected.

The water was not coming *from* the beam. It was being shot *to* the beam. A forceful stream of water, hitting the beam from somewhere else, making it look as if the beam were leaking. Daisy, following the shooting water with her eye, tracing it to the washing machine. Water, shooting out from behind the washing machine, straight out at an angle and halfway across the room to the overhead beam.

Daisy, starting down the ladder, but not reaching the bottom.

Saving her life.

Because something was suddenly exploding.

Daisy, wobbly on the ladder. Clenching the sides. Her fingers pressing hard on the fiberglass, turning white at the tips. Watching in horror. Witnessing the fuse box shorting out. A horrifying riot of wild burning sparks shooting every which way. Daisy, afraid to breathe, afraid to move a hair. Watching in terror, the fuse box continuing its violent display.

At last, exhausting itself. Finally quiet. No sounds, except for the relentless flow of water descending from the beam, cascading down near her like a waterfall.

Daisy, not breathing. Not moving. Her brain, reviewing. Recognizing danger, the danger that lay around her. In the water. The water was not simply cold and unattractive anymore. It had gone up several notches on the scale of undesirability—to the top. To deadly.

The electricity in it could now kill her.

WHEN DENNIS FOUND Daisy after seven o'clock that night, she was barely recognizable.

He had let himself in when she didn't answer the bell, wondering why the house was dark, why all the lights were off, and what the "surprise" was. He heard the water immediately. Calling her. Following the curious sound to the cellar, assuming as he went that the dark and the sound were part of whatever "surprise" it was that she had promised him when she had called him the night before.

What Dennis encountered *was* a surprise, a terrible surprise, stunning him beyond anything he could have imagined. Never before in his life had his eyes called upon his brain to process such a bleak, dismal, utterly wretched scene.

The water was up to the fourth step of the cellar, and there was his mother, on a ladder, on the highest rung, her legs drawn up as close to her body as they could go, babbling. Babbling nonsensically through a quivering jaw and chattering teeth.

Dennis, calling her name, saying, "It's me, Dennis. Can you hear me?" Shouting at her. In panic. In near darkness. Again and again, shouting her name. Getting no response. The ladder was turned sideways; she was looking toward the opposite wall. He wouldn't be able to catch her eye even if he did jumping jacks. All he could do was stand there and yell and hope that she would snap out of it and tune into him so that he could reassure her it was over, that he was there and was going to get help.

Yanking his mobile phone out of his pocket. Quickly fumbling over the keypad, ringing the fire station.

The minutes waiting for their arrival, tedious. Dennis, spending them trying to piece together how this horror had come about, and trying to get his mother's attention, screaming her name in different tones of voice, hoping to jar her into coherence.

But she just kept babbling. Dennis, having trouble hearing her, unable to make sense of what she was saying. Thinking he might have heard her repeating a name, Michael. Who was Michael?

The firefighters arrived. A passel of uniformed men, bringing loud voices, hoses, masks, equipment. All forward motion ceasing when they saw the situation. Unanimously refusing to go down the steps until the electric company arrived. The water was "hot."

And so Dennis had to wait longer, standing by uselessly as they called the electric company and the ambulance. Pacing around, counting the long seconds of mayhem until the electric crew arrived and turned off the power to the house, finally enabling them to descend the stairs. And rescue his mother.

Daisy looked like a little wet rag doll in the big arms of the fireman. Carried across the water to the safety of the paramedics. Dennis, watching them putting her gently down on a waiting stretcher, sedating her, rolling her—adding insult to injury—through pouring rain to the idling ambulance at the curb.

Then Dennis, turning back to begin dealing with the "surprise" she had had for him.

D AISY PHILLIPS, SEVENTY-SEVEN, had spent eleven hours and twenty-seven minutes overlooking death from the top of a ladder.

Dennis Phillips, fifty-five, wasn't sure whether to laugh or cry. Once the paramedics, electric workers, and firemen had cleared out, once he had turned the main water off, once he was alone in the house, he sat on the top cellar steps and stared down at the water as black as oil, with the dark of the night gathering around him. He just couldn't get over it. His emotions were poking into corners so full of cobwebs that they couldn't have been visited in decades. He loved his mother, and at that moment was loving her more than he had in a long, long time. Feeling complete love, an utterly thorough love, an overwhelming resurgence. It was as if she had just died. Sitting on the steps, fresh love of her pumping through him. Layers of gratitude and relief.

When those layers of gratitude and relief began to fade, anger roared in. How could she have been so stupid? How could she have done whatever it was she had done? He didn't yet know what it was, but whatever it was, it had to be stupid.

But Dennis was also realizing that at least now she would sell the house. Maybe in some awful way the whole thing was just what she had needed—a big kick in the pants. Because, no question about it, he had to get out of Liverpool. It had become too expensive. The gap between what he was pulling in from his paycheck and his royalties from two nonfiction books—one a best seller—and his skyrocketing expenses had become unsustainable. Either his costs had to go down or his income had to go up, which wasn't likely. His invitations to speak had gone from baguettes to crumbs lately, leaving him grasping at hope that a move to Chessex would ease their financial problems, that a change of scenery would be the boost he needed to write another book, that there he would find again his lost intellectual energy.

Because Amanda was rather expensive—not that he had any regrets in marrying her. He had fallen in love with her by the end of their very first conversation, that day she had approached him after his talk, and their two years together had been wonderful. She showed him more love in a day—on a good day—than his first wife, selfish and self-important, had in the entire twenty-two years of their marriage. It was only that Amanda was so costly.

Her hair, for example. He had dreamed about touching it long before he was given the opportunity to, and he still never missed a chance to hold it, even while he slept. He liked to fall asleep with it covering his face. But the cost to maintain! He never could have imagined it. She tried to contribute, tried to pull in money teaching yoga, but there was no question that what she spent couldn't compare to what came in.

Dennis, taking his mobile phone out. Dialing Amanda to fill her in on all that had happened. Regretting that she was probably out there now. Somewhere. With credit cards.

FIVE

Daisy, three days in the hospital recovering.

Sleeping through the first two days.

The third day, Daisy sitting up. Feeling guilty, contrite, foolish. Her visitors: Dennis, Amanda, and Gabriel, and Lenny. He showed up three hours later than everyone else, full of good cheer, scooping Daisy up in his massive arms, planting a hearty kiss on both cheeks before lowering her softly back down on the stiff hospital pillow. And with him, someone new. A new girlfriend, Sarah. All eyes on Sarah during introductions; everyone silently wondering if Lenny realized he had broken the mold with this one—starting with her age, which was apparently in striking distance of his. And her hair color—a natural brown. And her clothes fitting as if they were picked for her current self, not her younger self. And her overall look—a smarter, warmer, more plainly attractive one than all his many previous girlfriends.

All of them kicking around in Daisy's private room, politely sharing the shortage of chairs, shuffling around one another, altering positions. Gabriel, claiming the foot of her bed.

Daisy started several conversations that went nowhere. Instead, the talk seemed to motor around in circles on wheels of its own, spiraling around a center that Daisy hoped would never bloom. It went like this:

GABRIEL: I think it's cool, Nan, that you hung in there all day on the top of that ladder.

A general nodding in agreement.

DAISY: I feel awful about having all those people come to the house. Can you imagine? Firemen, electric workers, ambulance people, all out in that pouring rain to rescue a simpleton stranded on a ladder in her own cellar.

LENNY: It wasn't your fault, Mum. It could have happened to anybody.

DENNIS: Except that the bubble in the washing machine hose probably burst when she turned the main water valve back on. The renewed pressure probably did it.

LENNY: So? All she did was turn the main water on and off like anybody else would have done. I'm proud of you, Mum, changing that washer successfully.

Daisy smiled. Proud of herself, too, until remembering where it got her.

DENNIS: I admit the wire that shorted out, the one that exploded the panel box, was a bit of simple bad luck, but none of this would have happened if the water main hadn't been touched. It was crazy of you, Mum, to think you could do this sort of thing on your own.

LENNY [shrugging]: You don't know that. Maybe the hose was going to burst at that moment regardless. We'll never know. It's not as if there's any special skill involved in turning on a water main.

GABRIEL: I think it's cool, Nan, that you hung in there all day on the top of that ladder.

A general nodding in agreement.

DENNIS: So, I guess we can all agree now that Mum shouldn't be on her own anymore. This is precisely the kind of thing we're seeking to avoid. And, at the risk of sounding like a broken record, bringing up Chessex again.

LENNY: Then don't. She doesn't want to go, do you, Mum?

"I, uh, well . . ." Daisy, scanning mental files, sifting through categories of polite, diplomatic answers. Refraining from shouting out that she didn't want it indeed. Feeling Amanda's eyes on her as if they actually had weight to them.

LENNY [continuing]: See, she doesn't. [Eyeing Daisy closely] Right? Senior apartments? That's not like you, Mum. You don't really want that, do you? And, besides, it's too far.

DENNIS: Far from what, Lenny?

LENNY: From me. [Simply put.]

DENNIS [exasperated]: Easy for you to champion her staying, Lenny. When's the last time you did anything for her? When's the last time she called *you* for help?

LENNY [a wide, guilty smile. Wiping his mouth with big, meaty fingers.] Must have been when Thatcher was PM.

DAISY: Those poor firemen will probably be telling the story forever, talking about the silly old woman on the top of the ladder.

GABRIEL: Maybe, but I think it's cool, Nan, that you hung in there all day on the top of that ladder.

A general nodding in agreement, and they would start around again. The same conversation playing through the long minutes of the afternoon, straight into the slowly dimming evening until, after Lenny, Sarah, and Gabriel had said their good-byes while Amanda, with her thick, glossy mahogany hair and amber eyes, her long and lanky body, her long slender nose on her long slender face, was glancing at a fashion magazine—the pictures, not the articles—a new topic of conversation popped up, breaking the pattern.

For Daisy, a doozy.

Dennis, staring blankly at the TV—the evening news on, suddenly turning to his mother, saying, "By the way, Mum, who's Michael?"

"Michael?" Daisy, blinking.

"You were talking about a Michael when you were babbling. When I found you. You were saying, 'Michael' and something about a box or a watch."

"Did I really?" Daisy, mystified.

Dennis, nodding. "Any idea who you might have meant?"

Daisy, shaking her head.

But of course she did.

She knew this: Michael Baker. 1945. Years before Paul.

A U.S. soldier. So handsome in an American way, like the movie stars. Like Gary Cooper. An easy, open, honest face, quick to reveal emotions. Surprising Daisy, this quality in a soldier, she had always thought they had faces made of stone. His uniform, dark green. Remembering the way it made him look: important, part of something essential. Capable, strong, smart, daring, brave. Ready for anything. Fearless, but not reckless.

Daisy, on the hospital bed, remembering the first time she saw him; she was convinced her heart had stopped, before resuming triple time. All he did was buy a newspaper, a cup of tea, a custard tart. To Daisy his every movement was miraculous. So tall. Broad shouldered. His hands and fingers strong, beautiful. Nothing at all like the boys she went to school with. Built nothing like the men in the village. Where did he get those shoulders? Those dark eyes? That chin? He had to be a movie star. That was her first thought. He had to be there filming a picture. She could feel her face burning red, part of her wanting to look away, to hide, to run, but unable to turn from him. His pull, too strong.

He wasn't there filming a picture. He was there with a friend, another American soldier, Gilbert Gilmore. They had been granted a few days' leave to make the trip involving a train, a bus, and a ferry—all the way from the American Burtonwood, Warrington Air Base, twenty-five miles outside Liverpool, on the other side of the River Mersey—to visit Gilbert's mother, who lived in Lancashire, where Daisy's parents' bakery was.

Gilbert had gone on to his mother's. Michael, into the shop.

Daisy couldn't help but stare. In all her eighteen years, she had never seen such a perfect individual, and he was right there! Her father was serving him! This man, this soldier, this artwork was sitting right there where other, more ordinary people usually sat. She pretended to be busy, was barely breathing, sneaking peeks as he ate.

Her father struck up a conversation with him. Daisy listened intently, not missing a word. The two had a lot of trouble understanding each other. It was all English, but their accents were so different that it might as well have been two distinct languages. They both had to slow their words to a crawl, pronounce each word carefully, and sometimes even spell them out. When he told her father his name, Daisy rolled the name, Michael Baker, slowly over her tongue as if it were candy, a sweet special treat reserved for Sundays.

Michael asked her father what there was to do in the town. He said he would be there for four days and that while he'd be lodging at Gilbert's mother's, he wanted to give his friend time alone with his family. He wondered if there was any good fishing around. He said he would like to stay outside, the weather was so nice.

Daisy's father told him he could set him up with all the gear he would need to fish, and that Daisy could walk him over to the best fishing around. Daisy felt her face, already red, get impossibly redder when Michael turned to look at her. She felt heat pricking around her neck and ears. Felt her insides melting like butter. Michael smiled and said thank you, said that that would be great.

Daisy cleared his plate and teacup while her father took him out back to the shed. She stared at the crumbs he had left behind, wanting to eat them, to inhale them. She did neither, only scraped them into the trash can and washed the plate clean. Daisy, remembering the difficult, awkward, stumbling conversation as they walked along to the lake. Remembering how he had asked her if she thought it would be all right to sit with him for a while while he fished. How she had nodded without speaking, and sat primly on the rocky bank under a tree.

How she was totally hooked long before that first fish was.

And Daisy, propped up on the hospital bed, was certain of this: He had loved her, too. He called her Little Nugget. He spent hours playing the piano for her, sitting side by side on the piano bench. He showed her card tricks, stowed cherry lollipops in the pockets of his uniform. Bought Maltesers to share with her. He divided the last malted milk ball in the bag in half, then divided his half again and slipped it into her mouth.

The war ended. Michael was going home. He came to her, knowing he shouldn't. He sneaked off base that last night and traveled the distance in the dark by a train, a bus, and a ferry, and got to her in the middle of the night. He tapped lightly on her bedroom window, careful to wake only her. Daisy opened it quietly, and in he climbed. He got down on one knee on the braided blue rug on her floor, took her hands in his, studied her fingers, and ran all his strong, gorgeous musical fingers over hers. Then he cleared his throat and said that there was no other like her on all the earth, not in his country or anyone else's, that he wanted nothing more in all the world than for her to be his wife, and that he was then and there pledging himself to her forever, whether she consented to be his wife or not.

Daisy, remembering him, his eyes, his breath on her neck. It was all coming back to her now. The spigot opened, and all manner of things rushed out. Remembering the way he had looked at her when he spoke those words—handsome, honest, strong. And his voice as he whispered, how it broke with emotion, and how she couldn't move, couldn't breathe.

There was an absence of sound. No rustling of starched bed linens or cotton pajamas. No creaking of the floorboards. From the moment those words left his mouth until she spoke, it was as though all was suspended in a vacuum.

Remembering how she had consented, of course, right then and there. His words were a dream come true. Falling back through time, from her hospital room into her old bedroom again. Landing on her bed. Feeling his arms wrapped around her. His body on hers. His breath on her neck. His joy repeated softly in her ear. Sensations of tingling and warmth behind both ears and deep, deep, deep in her stomach.

The plan: Michael would go back to New York, to Brooklyn, and get work. As a pianist. Performing and teaching on the side. Daisy, recalling the memory of his playing at her parents' house. There was no piano on the base, he'd used theirs. His fingers swept brilliantly over the keys, bringing that piano to life like no one else could—not before, nor since. Recollecting how worried he'd been about taking her overseas, away from her family, without being able to provide for her. And, of course, her mother wouldn't help. She was never nice to him. Coldly polite was all she could manage. She warned Daisy not to let it get serious. Her words fell on deaf ears. Daisy would have walked to the ends of the earth for him.

The last thing he did was take off his watch and slip it on her wrist, telling her that it would have to stand in for an engagement ring. He said his most important possession should be worn by his most important person.

He wrote every day, long passionate letters about her, about them, about his piano competitions, about his attempts to line up students, and how he was counting the hours until he could return to Liverpool to get her, bring her home, make her his wife, and be her husband.

Then he stopped writing, quite suddenly. He just stopped writing after months of daily letters, without a word of explanation. Daisy wrote letter after letter, begging for some word, but got nothing. Nothing ever came. She wrote constantly to his parents, Brooklyn town hall, the U.S. military. Nothing.

Daisy, on the hospital bed, knowing this: Part of her was still bothered that she had never received an explanation. And knowing this, too: She was glad that she still had the watch, and that it was at home now, waiting for her in that jewelry box on her bedside table.

SIX

THE HOUSE, UNINHABITABLE for two additional days after Daisy was released from the hospital. Dennis had to hire experts to clean out the cellar and restore the electrical panel. It was going to cost an ungodly sum, but he was hoping he would make it up on the sale, which he was now pretty sure was going to happen. His mother had not argued the point since her hospital stay, falling silent whenever it came up, listening to his plans and suggestions without a word of refusal.

Daisy, spending two nights at Dennis and Amanda's. Offering to make them a cup of tea every chance she got. Neither one ever accepting. After dinner the second night, when Dennis and Amanda went into the living room to watch television, Daisy excused herself to shower. Taking a new and particular interest in their shower head. Loving that she could picture the valves behind the wall.

After showering, getting ready for bed. Having to convert the sofa into a bed. Dennis, coming in as she was retrieving the linens from the closet.

"I'll set up the bed, Mum. It's heavy."

"Don't worry, Dennis. I'm fine. I've made up this sofa bed many times before." Putting the linens down on the arm of the sofa.

Dennis, moving to help her. Taking the seat cushions off on his side.

Daisy, stopping him, saying, "Please, Dennis. I'll do it."

Dennis, stepping back, watching her, thrusting his hands into his pants pockets.

Daisy, taking a deep breath. "I have to tell you something, Dennis. I've changed my mind, I'm not going with you tomorrow to look at The Carillion and houses for you and Amanda. It's good of you to want me to move to Chessex, but it's not necessary. You and Amanda can go. I'll be fine here on my own. As Gabriel said, not many people of any age could have lasted eleven hours in the position I was in." Watching his face, reading his barely concealed frustration. Removing the other sofa seat cushion, placing it neatly on the floor under the window.

Dennis, plunking himself down in the chair, his shoulders forward, rubbing his eyes. "You're making this awfully difficult for me."

"I don't mean to, but I'm keeping the house. I can't move, Dennis. I've been in it all my life. It's where I will stay till the end." Daisy, reaching down to pull the mattress out of its collapsed position. Tugging, but barely budging it. Throwing all her weight into it. Still, it hardly moved. "I could have died on Tuesday."

Dennis, watching her, resisting the urge to help. "I know that. It's exactly the point I'm trying to make."

Daisy, groaning. Straining herself—to no avail. Saying, "Right," through clenched teeth. "When I was up on that ladder"—a moan escaping from her—"I decided that if I ever got out of there alive, I was not going to move to a senior apartment. I don't need to take the easy road, Dennis. I want to live life, to really live life till the end."

Dennis, watching. Sympathizing with her mattress struggle. It pained him to watch her unwillingness to give up despite the impossibility of success. Having to make himself stay put. Saying, "I was hardly suggesting suicide. There's a great big space between senior living and throwing in the towel, but you are almost eighty years old. How am I going to move across the country and leave you in a house by yourself? And, besides, I thought you might welcome the chance to have an easier life."

Daisy, pulling. And pulling. Wanting so much to yank that mattress out, to show him that she could do it, but she couldn't. She was too weak to lift it out. Leaving her no choice but to admit defeat. Right there in front of him. Daisy, turning away, hiding tears.

Without a word Dennis, stepping over. Sliding the mattress out with one hand.

A FIVE-HOUR CAR TRIP, raining when they left Liverpool. Sunny in Chessex. That alone could make the trip worth taking. Daisy, in the back of the car, refusing to let the point of the journey weigh on her, refusing to be mad at herself for going. Telling herself that she had been wanting a bit of travel, and here it was.

Amanda, occupying herself with CDs, singing unself-consciously. Daisy, wondering, not for the first time, why this beautiful yoga teacher, still in her thirties with no children, had married this not bad looking but not exactly princely antiques expert and magazine writer, seventeen years her senior. Was being a mother to a twenty-two-year-old stepson enough for her? Or were more grandchildren on the way? And what would Dennis think of that? Did he want to become a father again at his age? Daisy would have loved to know, but of course she would never ask.

The tour of The Carillion going rather well. The apartments were clean, bright, and cheerful. Dennis's fears of listless people hanging around, more dead than alive, were unfounded. Daisy was genuinely surprised at finding it so pleasant. She was shown one- and two-bedroom apartments. The two-bedroom ones even had little terraces.

After, arranging themselves back in the car, Daisy with more piles of the colorful brochures. Stopping for a quick bite at a café. Talking about the merits of The Carillion. Amanda, eating quickly, excited about showing Dennis the houses she had picked out for him to see. Six had made the cut.

Finishing their plates. Daisy, taking out her purse to pay. Dennis, stopping her, saying it was his idea to take her across the country; the meal was on him. Daisy, saying no. Throwing money on the table. Dennis, pushing it away. Daisy, not picking it up. Repeating that she wouldn't.

She didn't. The money, temporarily forgotten. A controversy over the bill drawing their attention away. The waitress had charged them for a plate of sausages that had never come. Dennis, recounting the meal for the waitress. Daisy, watching Amanda quietly slipping the forgotten money into the palm of her hand.

Then into her wallet.

D AISY, IN THE BACKSEAT on the way back to Liverpool. After all six houses went bust. All much too expensive. Listening to Dennis's and Amanda's discussions, seeing them at opposite goalposts.

Daisy, humming quietly to herself. Happy because she had managed to saunter through The Carillion as though she were being shown a honeymoon suite, and it was Dennis and Amanda who had turned out to be pills.

SEVEN

Daisy, back at work. At the library—without Grace Parker. Missing Grace Parker.

The only one who had asked her about her sick days was the janitor, Old Joe, ninety-one years old, who never missed a day. His presence in the library was a continuing source of comfort to her.

Old Joe, while emptying wastepaper baskets, asking her why she had been out. Daisy, telling him the whole story of her basement flood. He listened, intrigued, his mouth hanging open. Really, it was worthy of a much larger audience, but there it was—he was it. It was lovely to have such an interested set of ears, but something even better came out of the morning's conversation.

Daisy, telling him about Dennis's pressure on her to move and about her recent wavering commitment to stay—how she had started out so sure of herself but Dennis's constant harping was beginning to chip away at her resolve. She was beginning to fear that he might be right. Telling him that she was now seriously considering a move she had always been so set against.

Old Joe's response: a booming, "Nonsense." Telling her she had years in front of her before she'd have to call it quits on her house, that there was nothing she couldn't handle.

Formulating a new plan: He would have his great-great-grandson, fifteen-year-old Patrick, mow her lawn. Daisy, suggesting that fifteen might be too young. Old Joe assuring her that by Patrick's age he had already been plowing whole fields, and, besides, Daisy was desperate. It had not rained today or yesterday—the first two-day break in more than a month—and the weather forecast was grim for tomorrow. Although Daisy had never paid any attention to such things as scheduling the mowing, or even noticing the regularity with which it got done, she did know enough to assume that after thirty-eight straight days of rain, a two-day break in the weather would have people hurrying to their mowers.

Old Joe, getting Patrick on the phone, arranging the whole thing.

Daisy, buoyant. Feeling confident again. Wanting to kiss Old Joe. Refraining.

D AISY, BACK HOME again after work.

Back for the first time since being removed by paramedics. Relieved to turn the key in the front door. Relieved to be home.

Readying the mower, leaving it out front for Patrick. Then going into her bedroom, changing out of her work clothes. Seeing the jewelry box on her bedside table. Reaching for it. With hands trembling slightly. Opening it.

Seeing the watch.

A ringing doorbell. Patrick.

Daisy, putting down the jewelry box. Hurrying to answer the doorbell. Seeing Patrick, so overjoyed that she almost kissed him. Quick hellos and a handshake, before happily leading him out to the lawnmower.

There really wasn't much to say. The boundaries of her lawn would be clear to anyone. Presuming he knew more about operating the self-propelled mower than she did—anyone would.

Relief tickling through her as she heard the sputter, the choke, then the roar of the machine—because it was Patrick doing it, not Dennis.

Standing for a moment, watching Patrick guide the mower through the tall grass. Seeing that it wasn't going to be easy, because of the ridiculous height of the grass, the soaking ground under it.

"I'm sorry the ground's so wet," Daisy, pleasantly, over the noise. "If the forecast didn't call for rain tomorrow, we could have put it off till it dried out a bit more."

Patrick, nodding. Pushing hard with his developing biceps. Concentrating too much to chatter.

"I'll just be in the house then, if you need me."

Patrick, nodding again. Ramming the mower through the tall wet grass.

Daisy, returning to the house, calculating how long the job was going to take, how much she should pay him—much more than she had originally planned. Crossing the threshold of her bedroom, Patrick and the problems of the grass evaporating from her mind, replaced by the jewelry box.

Opening it again. Seeing the watch. Surprising her that it didn't look familiar. Daisy, sitting on the bed, on the baby blankets, taking in every detail of the watch's face: the hands, the numbers, the band, the clasp. In her memory the face was small, in fact it was large; the band was leather, in fact it was silver; the numbers were just black lines, in fact they were roman numerals.

Examining it. Turning the watch over.

Causing a surge of emotion. Seeing an inscription on the back—a surprise so big that she couldn't wrap her mind around it. Rereading the inscription again and again, running her finger over it, tracing the words, touching them, testing herself that she was reading it correctly. How could she have forgotten something like this? How could she have forgotten such an inscription?

"To Michael, Good luck. Arthur Rubinstein." *Arthur Rubinstein!*

Her hands, shaking as her mind raced back over the hills and dales of the years. Trying desperately to trace when and where information like that could have gone. How could she have forgotten a fact so significant?

It was inscribed by Arthur Rubinstein! *The* Arthur Rubinstein!

Daisy, utterly floored. Puzzling over it intensely, only dimly aware that the former low-pitched drone of the lawn mower had changed to a high-pitched screeching. A terrible straining. Tearing through the great expanse of time, searching her head for clues, then beginning to tune into the very wrong sounds of the lawn mower. And that they were escalating. Finally reaching a crescendo with a sound not usually associated with a home gardening machine. A sound so bad that Daisy had to get up and look out the window.

To find Patrick no longer on the grass. Patrick, in her flower bed. The wheels of the mower were embedded in mud, turning without traction, spinning uselessly. Patrick, struggling mightily to get the mower out of the mud and back on the grass.

Daisy, watching him, wrapping the watch around her wrist, clasping it on, remembering when it was on her much younger wrist. Only half aware that she was doing it, her attention split between that and seeing that Patrick wouldn't be able to get the mower out of the mud. The mud was too deep, too thick, too sticky. The engine, revving like a turbo booster.

Daisy, running out of the house. Hurrying over to the flower bed. Patrick's face, a mess of emotions.

"Can't you get it out?" Daisy, calling. Making sure not to sound accusatory, though she had to yell over the sound.

Patrick, shaking his head. "It's really stuck, Mrs. Phillips."

Daisy, seeing that not only was it really stuck in the mud, but also stuck in brambles. The front wheels were deep into the bush, with twigs and gnarled branches sticking out from under the body of the mower. "Let me help you," Daisy, yelling.

"Maybe if you could take over for me at the back, I could lift the front and unjam it."

Daisy, nodding. Moving to take his spot. Noticing that he was sunk three inches into the mud, realizing that she would be, too. Looking down at her shoes. They were not a ratty old knockabout pair, but ones she cared about.

Doing what she had to do.

Stepping out of her shoes, into the mud. Taking over at the helm so he could move to the bow. Holding tight to the handlebar, her stockinged feet in the warm squishy mud, watching him sink down to his knees, trying to disengage the branches from under the mower. They were really jammed in; as hard as he tried to pull them free, they wouldn't come.

Daisy, trying to push down on the bar, thinking that lowering the back wheels would raise the front for him. Managing only to get the back wheels deeper into the mud. Daisy, trying to lift the handlebar, needing to unsink the back wheels she had just sunk farther. Finding that the only thing that lifting the handlebar did was sink *her* deeper into the mud. Her knobby anklebones joining her feet, disappearing deep into the mysteries of the soggy earth. If she lifted them, the wheels would sink farther; if she lifted the wheels, she would sink farther.

She had to laugh—almost—but wouldn't dare. Patrick was too overwrought, concentrating his efforts so absolutely. And getting nowhere.

Patrick, finally noticing that she was stuck, too. Getting up, his knees with soaking brown spots, dripping mud. Coming around to her side, saying, "I think I'm going to have to lift you out."

Daisy, laughing. Nodding. Giving him the go-ahead. Patrick, hoisting her up. Lucky for him that she was a tiny woman, but with both her feet firmly planted in the mud, she was much heavier. Patrick, lifting. Daisy, wanting to help, trying to pull herself up, instead knocking him over.

Both going down. In a flash. Into the mud. Scrambling to disentangle themselves from each other and the mess. Covering themselves in mud as they slipped, slopped, and crawled on their hands and knees over to the safety of the grass. The lawnmower, still revving. The back wheels, spinning, spraying mud at them.

Reaching the grass. Mud splattered on their hair, their faces, down the length of their bodies. To their feet. Both of them, laughing—at themselves and at the sight of the other. Laughing till tears ran down their faces. Patrick, pulling Daisy up, his hands under her armpits. Daisy, grabbing her shoes. The two of them stumbling out of the mud toward the house, leaving the lawn mower behind, its engine still running, its wheels spinning.

Daisy, saying to Patrick, "I'll get towels."

Patrick, nodding. Following her in.

Leaving her shoes at the door, hurrying down the hall. Patrick, standing in the doorway, afraid to track mud through the house. Daisy, returning with towels, handing him one. Patrick, drying himself off.

Daisy, asking him, "Can I make you a cup of tea? Nice and hot."

Patrick, shaking his head. "No, thank you."

"It's no problem. You could probably use one."

"No, really. Look, I'm sorry about all that." Wiping the mud off his face. "The grass was just impossible to get through. I had to push really, really hard." Shrugging helplessly. "I guess I slid. That's how I ended up in your flower bed. I'm really sorry."

Daisy, "Not to worry. Whatever was there will grow back." Her hair, soaking, mottled, sticking to her head. Her face, a mud bath. "I'm sorry the job was so impossible. You certainly didn't sign on for all this."

"No, I guess not." Sheepishly. Laughing a little as he compared what he had been expecting with what he got.

"Are you sure I can't get you a tea? It'll take only a minute. A cup would do you good."

"I don't think so." Shaking his head again. "I should be going. It's starting to rain again, and it's probably not going to let up. I'm sorry that I won't be able to finish the job."

"Won't you come back when it stops?"

"I can't. I'm going on holiday tomorrow. I'll be gone till August."

Daisy's face, falling. The lawn was looking worse than before; not even half done, a zigzagged line of mown grass amid high grass. Before it had looked like a slovenly, uncaring woman lived in the house, now it looked like a lunatic did.

"I'm sorry," Patrick, saying. "Really I am."

Daisy, "Let me get my purse." Hurrying off. Returning with a heap of cash.

Patrick, "Thank you. I guess I should go get the mower. I can't just leave it there."

"But it's stuck, remember?"

"Right."

The two of them standing there, thinking. Looking away from each other. Daisy, looking down. Catching sight of what she had forgotten.

The watch. Still on her wrist. Making her panic. Quickly inspecting it. Relieved to see it was still working. Daisy, suddenly clear about one thing: A watch inscribed by Arthur Rubinstein should not be rolling around in the mud. A watch inscribed by Arthur Rubinstein was too valuable to be treated with anything less than the utmost care. Daisy, marveling at what it had already been through. Awestruck that she had removed it, and the baby blankets, only one day before they would have been completely submerged under water, and although the baby blankets would have been able to recover such an assault, the watch could not have. Daisy, thinking, imagine after being boxed up for more than half a century, she had somehow managed to rescue it the very day before its ruin.

Patrick, waiting to be told what to do, but Daisy was no longer thinking about the lawn mower. She was thinking about the watch. And about a long, hot shower and clean, dry clothes. And a nice cup of hot tea. An early advance to Cointreau. Looking at him, guessing that he would probably fill the long, tedious hours of travel with his tale of crawling through the mud with a silly, barefoot, seventy-seven-year-old woman, her clothes, hands, feet and face dripping and slick, laughing until they cried.

Daisy, saying, "Just turn it off on your way past. Leave the darn thing right where it is."

EIGHT

Dennis, heading to his mother's house to explain all the things the electrician and repair crew had done. Getting there just as Patrick was leaving, before Daisy had a chance to clean up. As a result, seeing his mother dripping in mud. Seeing the zigzag of the cut grass. Seeing the lawn mower stuck in the flower garden. Seeing his mother giggling at the situation.

Leaving him flabbergasted, more certain than ever that he was right. Asking her if she now agreed that she was unable to manage the house on her own.

Daisy, laughing daintily. Saying, "Yes, I believe I do. I give up. You win. The Carillion wouldn't be so bad, really, so you can go ahead and sell the house." Turning away. Walking into the kitchen to put the kettle on. Wiping mud off her cheek and shoulders.

Dennis, following her in. Daisy, saying she would give up the house, but she didn't want any part of the selling. She didn't even want to be around while it was happening, but she had come up with a solution for that.

She had made up her mind.

She was going to the U.S. By herself.

Telling Dennis that much.

Not telling him the rest. Not saying that she was going to return the watch to Michael, or his children if he had any, and if it turned out he was dead. She had decided that the watch was too valuable to hang on to any longer. Now that she knew it had been engraved by Arthur Rubinstein, she couldn't keep it. It should never have been boxed up in her cellar for as long as it had been, and it never would have if she had known. But when Michael slipped it on her girlish wrist—amid kisses, tears, and vows—she'd had no idea who Arthur Rubinstein was. She had never even heard of him. She didn't know that he was one of the greatest piano virtuosos of the twentieth century. It was not until much later that she heard of him, but by then the watch was safely packed away, out of view and out of her mind. For the longest time after Michael's disappearance she had avoided anything to do with the piano—she couldn't even hear a chord without feeling ill—but she had kept the grand piano. She got it, not her sister, after her parents died. The very one that Michael had played remained in her living room to this day. The watch had waited a long time to be rediscovered, but now that it had been, she had to return it. It belonged with Michael and his family, not Dennis or Lenny.

"You're not talking sensibly, Mum. You can't go to the United States alone." Dennis, beside himself. "It's impossible."

Daisy, laughing lightly. "No, it's not." Wondering if he had always had so little faith in her. And, if not, when exactly it had begun. When had she crossed some unwritten threshold into an incompetent, doddering old age? Wondering, too, if Paul would have thought like him or if he would have been like Lenny—who, she was sure, was going to be happy when he heard.

That is if he ever got around to calling her back.

"Why? Why do you want to go?" Dennis, fully agitated. Both of his hands on the table, palms down, ten fingers thumping like pistons. "Where will you stay? What will you do?" Irritated. Frustrated. Totally thrown.

"I have a cousin in New York. On Long Island. I'll write and inquire whether I can stay with her."

"A cousin?"

"You must remember that my mother's sister married an American."

Dennis, blinking in rapid succession. "But you don't even know her."

"That's true." Daisy, nodding. "And it's high time I did." Hardly believing it herself. Proud and delighted that it had hit her. Perhaps she had needed that roll in the mud to free her.

And set her traveling again.

NINE

ANN PATTERSON, READING DAISY'S LETTER, standing in the kitchen, a field of noise and activity. Six of her seventeen grandchildren, the preschoolers, were on the loose. Two of the younger ones were using her thick legs as goalposts. Ann, rereading the letter twice. She would have read it again but a whiff from the oven reminded her that she had two trays of chicken nuggets and a tray of french fries ready to be pulled. Quickly refolding the letter, hurrying to rescue the food from near certain charring.

She didn't get another chance to look at the letter until around nine that night, settling down heavily in the recliner in the finally quiet house to watch TV, moments after the eldest of her five daughters, Elisabeth— harried and exhausted, rather more so than usual because her husband, Richard, was away on business, on top of which Elisabeth had had to work later than usual—had gone home after picking up her three youngest sons, Michael, Josh, and David. Ann, unfolding the letter, reading it again. Thinking.

A cousin Daisy. Her mother's sister's daughter, her aunt Meredith's daughter.

Ann, thinking hard, trying to find and gather crumbs of information about Cousin Daisy. Ann, knowing her mother had left England when she married Ann's father, knowing her mother had had a sister, Meredith, knowing Meredith had had two daughters, Doreen and Daisy. But Ann had only been to England on that one dreadful, fateful trip when she was six and had met her aunt Meredith—a trip she would never forget. She had never met Daisy or Doreen, who were teenagers at the time. After that trip, communications abruptly stopped. Ties, broken and forgotten. Her mother, gone now eleven years.

And here this Cousin Daisy was asking if it wouldn't be too much of an imposition to stay a few weeks while she took care of some very important business in New York. Saying she would come just as soon as Ann gave her the okay and would stay only long enough to complete the business. She hoped it wouldn't be more than a few weeks.

Ann, rereading the letter again, shuddering. Torn. In two even pieces, not shreds. On the one hand, she was sort of interested in meeting this cousin. It might be nice to try to resurrect family connections, to reconnect, to try again after all those decades.

On the other hand, it *would* be an imposition. It was hard for Ann to imagine another set of legs, another mouth emitting sounds, another belly to fill. The house was big enough, and there were plenty of spare bedrooms. It was just that there were already so many people using it as a home base. Usually by the time the various family members had cleared out for the day, it was almost time to head off to bed. She needed to be up early to receive the first round of grandchildren. How could she possibly have the time or energy for a houseguest? And how would a houseguest be able to stand the unrelenting noise, chaos, disorder, high volume, high voltage?

And what if Daisy was just like her mother?

Ann, sighing. She would just have to tell Daisy the truth. Write to her and explain that as much as she would like to meet her, she took care of seven grandchildren five days a week, and three more on top of that in the afternoons, and spent most of her days in the car, loading and unloading children, picking them up and dropping them off. She would tell this Cousin Daisy about the wall-sized bulletin board required to keep all the various schedules straight. Maybe she would even provide a photograph of it and say that while she was not trying to discourage Daisy from coming—although she was certainly doing exactly that, or at the very least encouraging some other kind of arrangement—a hotel stay maybe, or a briefer visit—she wanted her to know in advance that her available time for her would be quite limited.

Not to mention that the guest bathroom was out of commission until her son-in-law, Joe, got a chance to finish the renovation of it. Two women having to share a bathroom for several weeks? Well, Daisy might not like that.

Ann, leaning back, closing her eyes. Thinking she should get up and begin writing that letter, that she should get back to Daisy as quickly as possible, that it was the least she could do. Feeling terrible about disappointing her. But telling herself that she would be leaving the door partly open for Daisy to come if Daisy—after knowing what the situation would be—still wanted to.

But what a problem it would be if she did.

Ann, remaining heavily settled in the recliner with her eyes closed. Picturing herself getting up and moving into the study to find her note cards. Picturing herself rifling through the desk drawers until she found the box. Picturing herself sitting down at the desk to begin writing.

Falling fast asleep.

TEN

DAISY WAS SPARED. She never would hear that Ann didn't want her because Ann never did get around to writing that letter. She put it out of her mind, the letter and all the conflicting emotions that went with it, until it was discovered more than a week later by her eldest daughter, Elisabeth.

The day after Elisabeth got formally placed in a new category proclaimed by her gynecologist to explain a host of irritating symptoms. Irregularities stretching back at least half a year. No longer deniable. Elisabeth's new status: perimenopause. Up at dawn after another lousy night of sleep. Sweating in her pajamas again. Her bed sheets. The word lolling around her mind all night. A distasteful word that invaded her thoughts day and night.

Still, she had a job to do. Up by 6:30. Showered and dressed by 7:30 in a beige suit, a size or two larger than she would care to admit, not yet having come to terms with even the smaller size she had recently blown through. Throwing on a copper-colored silk blouse, a string of pearls; her fine, light brown hair quickly blown dry and tied back. Her serious, if tired, expression combined with the way she carried herself made her look every bit the successful CPA she was—even down to the way the wrinkles were forming around her eyes from years of peering at numbers on narrow lines of tax returns, spreadsheets, IRS regulations, computer screens.

Preparing a quick breakfast for four of her five sons; the fifth, Steve, away at college. Fantasizing about having Richard home to help instead of on the 6:00 a.m. train to the city every day. She cleared the table, loaded the dishwasher. Ready to hit the road by 8:15 when her middle son, thirteen-and-a-half-year-old Michael, realized he couldn't find his flash drive which he needed for his European History class. It not only had his project on it—he said he didn't care about that, which was no surprise to Elisabeth who had neither seen him do it nor heard him mention it—but had his best friend's project on it, too.

Elisabeth and the boys turned the house upside down before her youngest, nine-year-old David, located it. For some reason found on the fireplace mantel instead of in an ordinary place such as the countless shirts, pants, jackets, or backpack pockets they'd check.

The whole drama caused the boys to miss their buses, compelling Elisabeth to drive them to school, two separate schools. David, eleven-year-old Josh, and seventeen-year-old Pete—all except Michael, the guilty one—jabbering anxiously about being late, begging Elisabeth to go faster although she was locked in immovable traffic while the clock sped on, making her late for her meeting. In the tension, knocking over her coffee, spilling it all over the front seat of the SUV, covering everything within a two-foot radius, including her new suit, old shoes, and open briefcase. Several files, dozens of tax returns, and the tan leather would carry the smell of stale coffee till the end of their days.

Elisabeth, arriving at work frazzled, harried, mentally jammed. As difficult as the early morning hours had been, finding there that things could get worse. Having been late to the meeting, her boss, Palmer, had injudiciously offered to cover for her. Apparently in no shape to do it. A liquid breakfast.

Palmer's boss had to deal with it. Once the clients had gone and Palmer had been sent home, Elisabeth was called in on the carpet. Asked to please close the door. Her heart, sinking fast at those words. A stern reprimand for being late. Followed by a general discussion regarding Palmer, what to do about him, and a thorough rundown of her upcoming deadlines and any of Palmer's deadlines that she was aware of.

Finally, Elisabeth, chastised, returned to her office, obediently getting busy behind her large desk, surrounded by pictures of Richard and the boys. None more recent than five years ago, in frames of various worth. Wondering if this was it.

Was it? Was this it? Was this all there was?

Chin on her palm on her elbow on her desk. Longing for something to cheer her up. Giving in to her usual quick pick-me-up. Doing what she often did: logging onto PuppyFinder.com. To stare at the sweet faces of puppies. Today Yorkshire terriers; yesterday it had been beagles, before that collies. A brief run through all the puppies before reluctantly X'ing out. Forcing her way back into the grind of the day.

In the meantime, Ann was at home with her grandchildren. All five of her daughters left one or more of their children with her—the preschoolers during the morning and Elisabeth's David, Josh, and Michael after school.

Ann spent the morning as she always did: entertaining, reading to, painting with, coloring with, allowing thirty minutes of TV time to, and otherwise feeding, diapering, and occupying all seven children. She fed them breakfast at nine—each got cinnamon toast and a glass of juice— and then let them discover life on their own in the playroom while she had her tall coffee, the third of the day, and three pieces of whole wheat toast. Ready to act in a heartbeat if she needed to. Watching carefully over the children from her kitchen table. Admiring the way they interacted with one another at such young ages and how intently they focused on something they had never seen before.

Lunch was macaroni and cheese in seven small bowls, one large one for her, and broccoli, which—and this always surprised her—they all liked. She took hers with melted butter; theirs was plain. Each child got a cup of milk.

Ann had another tall coffee.

At 3:15, David and Josh arrived and started their homework, enjoying the cookies and milk she gave them while she had another coffee, her fifth and last for the day. At 4:00, because it was a Tuesday, she piled the two grandkids she still had left into the Chrysler minivan—the others had already been picked up—to drive David and Josh to their piano lessons, dropping off one of the two other grandkids at home on the way.

Ann, playing with four-year-old Brandon during the piano lessons, doing her best to keep him from getting too bored and out of control. Pulling a bag of pretzels out when all else started to fail. Keeping him happy until they piled back into the minivan and headed home, a full thirty-five-minute drive when traffic was not a problem—which never happened on Long Island. First swinging by the school to pick up Elisabeth's Michael from baseball practice. He greeted her with a nonchalant wave, climbed into the minivan, remaining hooked up to his iPod—as usual. Lately.

They got back to her house after six, pulling into the driveway just minutes before her daughter Lynn got there to take Brandon home. Elisabeth would be there to get David, Josh, and Michael as soon as she got back from taking Pete to the eye doctor for new contact lenses.

Spaghetti, meatballs, and salad for dinner. Together at the table—Ann, David, Josh, and Michael. David and Josh chattering at length about teachers, friends, sports, whatever. Ann, wondering, as she often did, if fear of eating alone kept her going as she did.

Michael, not part of the conversation. Plugged into his iPod. In a world of his own despite hitting elbows with her every time he lifted his fork to his mouth. Ann, wishing he would unplug his ears and talk to them, but she was never one to enforce rules if the behavior wasn't hurting anyone. More than anything she wanted her grandsons to be happy there with their grandma.

Elisabeth got there at 7:30, her copper-colored blouse untucked on one side, her hair falling haphazardly out of the holder, her lipstick long faded. A worried, wary look in her eyes. Because of something she had just heard on the car radio.

Ann, loading the dishwasher. Elisabeth, sending the boys off to gather their things, scowling at Michael as he passed. Saying, "How about saying thanks for this morning? I missed a meeting because of your misplaced flash drive."

"Thanks for this morning." With absolutely no expression.

"Do you have to dress like that?" Elisabeth, yanking one of his ear buds out.

Michael, looking at her. Scowling. Saying, "What's wrong with what I'm wearing?" Jamming the ear bud back in before hearing the answer.

Elisabeth saying loudly, "Only everything." Staring in disgust at the back of his jeans as he headed out of the kitchen and into the living room to get his backpack. His pants were riding ridiculously low below his waist, weakly fighting gravity and the ten pounds of extra denim hanging around his legs. His belt was midway across his butt revealing four inches of plaid boxer shorts above them.

"What makes him think the whole world wants to see his underwear?" Elisabeth, asking Ann. "It's so arrogant, really." Wondering, not for the first time, how he would feel if *she* went around exposing the top four inches of *her* panties.

"Oh, he's all right," Ann, saying. "It is a stupid fashion, but we partook of stupid fashions in our day, too."

Elisabeth, thinking her mother was probably right. Feeling rattled by what she had just heard on the car radio. What should have been nothing more than a typical news snippet had unnerved her into having even less patience with Michael and his iPod than usual. A familiar litany running through her head: She would never let Josh and David, both talented classical musicians—almost as talented as Michael—follow in Michael's footsteps. She would never let them quit piano. She was still regretting every day that she had caved in to Michael's demands to quit after nine years and thousands of dollars of lessons. Look where it had got him.

"Everything all right?" Ann, asking. "How was your day?"

"Hectic. Ridiculous." Elisabeth, watching her mother sponge off the table. Then, not that she had planned to bring it up, "By any chance have you been following the news about this guy they're calling Dart Man?"

Ann, shaking her head.

"Well, there's this guy in Manhattan riding around on a bicycle, shooting darts at the butts of women."

"What?" Ann's face, scrunching up. Was there no end to the perversions of the human race?

"I'm not making this up," Elisabeth, saying. "He's hit five women in the last three weeks and one today. I just heard it on the car radio. The darts are not fatal, but obviously it hurts to get shot in the butt, and the police can't figure out who's doing it and why."

"Crazy." Ann, shaking her head. Returning the sponge to its cradle at the sink. Thinking about getting the vacuum—the floor, its usual mess. She had to vacuum every night, at least the playroom and kitchen. The rest of the house could usually go longer.

Elisabeth, "Here's the thing. I think Richard might be Dart Man."

Ann, looking at Elisabeth, surprised to see that she was saying this with a straight face. No longer thinking about getting the vacuum. Thinking her daughter had gone off the deep end. Saying, "Elisabeth, you can't be serious."

"I am."

You can't be."

"I am."

"You think your husband is Dart Man?"

"He could be. He might be." Elisabeth, nodding her head.

"Where would you get such an idea?"

"Well, listen. First"—Elisabeth, ticking the following off on her fingers—"they say he must be smart to be getting away with it. Richard's really smart. They say it's probably someone with no prior record. Richard has no prior record. They say it's probably someone with no impulses to violent crime. I don't think Richard has any impulses to violent crime. They think it's someone just seeking attention. Richard likes attention. He has attacked only on Mondays and Thursdays for some reason. They don't know why. What days does Richard ride his bike downtown? Mondays and Thursdays! What kind of bike does Dart Man ride? He's been seen on what's described as a red mountain bike. What kind does Richard have? A red mountain bike!" Spitting this last bit out with emphasis. Then regrouping for even more: "And here's the real clincher. What does Richard love doing? Playing darts! Remember back in the days when he actually had a life outside of work? What did he do? He played darts! Remember? He loved darts! Remember how good he was?"

Ann, standing there staring at her daughter, her forty-four-year-old, successful, businesswoman daughter. Looking for signs on her broad, pale face that she was joking. Maybe a twinkle in her green eyes? A smirk on her thin lips? Waiting for Elisabeth to break into a smile. But it never came. Elisabeth was in earnest. Ann wasn't sure where to begin. Preschoolers were so much less complicated.

"Okay, Lizzie, a reality check here, please. Your husband's not Dart Man. He's a lawyer, a successful lawyer in a big firm, a partner. Hardly the type to be wanted by the police for anything, much less shooting darts at women."

Elisabeth, nodding but not convinced. "I know. It does seem hard to believe, but you never know. Isn't it possible that a totally stressed-out, pushed-to-the-edge man could end up committing this kind of act? You hear stories all the time about people suddenly snapping. And what do these people do when they snap? Something they're good at. Darts. He played at Yale. He was on the team!" Elisabeth, all worked up, her voice picking up speed and intensity. "You hear stories about women finding out all kinds of outrageous things about their husbands all the time. There are stories like this in the paper just about every day."

"Yes, but you're not one of them. You're not going to find this out about *your* husband." Looking long and hard at her daughter. "You need to go home and get a good night's sleep. You'll probably laugh at yourself in the morning."

Elisabeth, nodding, hoping her mother was right. Hurrying into the playroom to gather the boys. Get them home. Josh and David still had their piano practice, an hour each. And Michael had a European History final plus math and chemistry and other year-end finals and state Regents exams in a week. He couldn't afford any more subpar grades. He should be home studying. Elisabeth, imagining that it was going to be a struggle to get him out of his iPod stupor and into his textbook. Thinking back with longing to the time when he was the most cooperative of all her boys, to the days when her word was everything. What had happened? When? No answer.

Checking her watch, telling them to hustle. Worrying about later tonight when Richard got home from work. What if she couldn't look at him? What if all she could see were darts?

Pushing the image aside. "Come on, boys." Shaking her keys, surveying the room for any of their things. "Let's get a move on."

Yawning. Then noticing the overseas envelope. Picking it up.

The boys filing out, one after the other. "Bye, Grandma," in chorus.

"Bye, boys. See you tomorrow."

"What's this?" Elisabeth, asking her mother, watching recognition click in her eyes, followed by tension. "Who's Daisy Phillips?"

"A cousin. From England. Her mother was my aunt Meredith."

"Why is she writing you?"

"She's planning a trip to New York. She asked if she could stay with me."

"How nice!" Elisabeth, smiling, the idea of someone flying in from England breezing over her like a current of fresh air. "When is she coming?"

Ann, frowning. "I didn't exactly tell her she could."

"What? Why not?"

"Mom!" Michael, screaming from the porch steps. "What's taking you so long?"

Calling back, "I'm coming." Turning back to her mother. "Why didn't you tell her she could?"

"I was afraid I wouldn't have time to entertain her." Coming clean with only part of the truth.

"Does she need to be entertained?"

"Well, no. She said she's coming to take care of business. But once she's here, I'm sure she'll need at least *some* attention. She'll have *some* requirements. I'm afraid I just won't have the time or energy to devote to her."

"Mom, that's crazy. Did you tell her not to come?"

"No. But I didn't tell her *to* come either. I didn't write back."

"Mom! Come on!" Josh, yelling from the front door. "I've got to start practicing."

"Get in the car. I'll be right there." Elisabeth, turning back to her mother. "Mom, you've got to write to her and tell her she can come. If you think she'll be too much, she can stay with me. I'd love to get to know her. We never get to see any of your English family."

"Really?" Ann, sensing a possible solution. "She can stay with you?"

"Sure she can. The boys will love her."

"Really? You'll put her up? Richard won't mind?"

"Of course he won't," Elisabeth, answering. Hoping it was true. Hoping, after twenty-one years of marriage, that she still knew him well enough to say it.

Hoping he wasn't Dart Man.

ELEVEN

Daisy, MAKING HER way into the house, barely fitting through the front door, struggling with two overly full shopping bags in each hand, containing shoes, two new pairs; three new skirt sets; a pretty pale pink robe with matching slippers. She hadn't felt so thrilled in a long time. Enjoying every aspect of the preparation for her trip, ignoring worries that she still hadn't heard back from Ann. Preparing herself so that when she did hear back, she would be ready to hop on the first available flight.

To New York, of all places, a place she had never been. She had never wanted to go after the disappearance of Michael. Whenever Paul had suggested going, and he had many times over the years, Daisy always came up with an excuse not to.

Pushing through the doorway with visions of New York, Manhattan, the skyline, the Empire State Building, Times Square, Broadway swirling in her head. Hoping she'd have a chance to see all those things while she was there. Needing to check how far Long Island was from Manhattan and where exactly Port Washington was, the town Ann lived in.

Hurrying to her bedroom. To start packing.

* * *

Dennis, pulling into his mother's driveway. Hurrying up the front path to her rose–framed yellow door. Her roses, consistently thriving, healthy. Rain was beginning to fall, the first in two days. The weather forecast once again predicting a deluge.

Up her front steps two at a time. Ringing the bell, shielding the papers in his hand from the rain. Hunching his shoulders forward. Protecting them. They were the reason for the visit.

The door opening. Daisy, smiling as she let him in. She knew why he was there; the smile was a put-on. Inside she was sick, sick, sick. Starting to lose her resolve again. Starting to think she really couldn't do it. She couldn't sell the house.

"Come in, Dennis. I'll make you a tea. I see the rain is starting again."

"No, no thanks. I only have a few minutes. I have to get back to work. We have some deadlines that are going to be murder to meet."

Following her into the kitchen. Taking a seat at the table. Placing the papers in front of him. Lining them up tidily.

Daisy, putting the kettle on. "Lucky we had those two dry days. I was able to get the grass cut." Thinking, finally it looked like a sane woman lived there.

"Who'd you get to do it?"

"No one," Daisy, saying, proudly. "I did it myself. It was no trouble at all." No trouble if you didn't count all that had happened before yesterday, and didn't count that it had taken her more than six hours, on her hands and knees on the ground with a pair of household scissors clipping the grass almost blade by blade before getting the lawn mower to do its job.

"Really?" Dennis, unbelieving. "No trouble at all?" Naturally thinking of all that had happened before yesterday. Wondering how she could honestly claim it was no trouble at all. "Now, Mum—"

"Perhaps you can do it while I'm gone," Daisy, breaking in. "Just once or twice—if the rain lets up."

Dennis, running his hand over his eyes, rubbing them. "You're not still thinking of going to New York, are you?"

"Indeed I am."

Dennis, sighing, "When?"

Daisy, not answering at once. She had still not heard back from Ann, but was determined to go with or without her cousin's house to stay in. "Soon." The water starting to boil, the kettle to whistle. Daisy, turning off the heat, carefully pouring the water into her teacup. "Are you sure you wouldn't like a nice hot cup of tea? It'll do you good."

Dennis, shaking his head. "How soon? Do you have dates worked out? What does your cousin say?"

"My passport is in good order, and I've done all my shopping and packing. I imagine I'll be gone a month." Putting the kettle back on the hob, sitting down to her tea.

"A month? Really? That long?"

"I imagine so. Yes. Perhaps even longer." She had no idea where Michael Baker lived; she had only his return address from letters sixty years old. She had no idea whether he was dead or alive or how to find him. Or how to find any children he may have had. "I'm buying an open-ended ticket." Stirring a teaspoon of sugar into her tea. The spoon making its familiar, cozy, homey sound as it hit the inside of the teacup on every rotation.

Dennis, "It seems like a crazy time for you to be planning an open-ended trip, but I don't suppose I can change your mind."

"No, I don't think you could, Dennis. My mind is quite made up." Wishing she had received a positive word from Ann.

"Well, now then." Dennis, clearing his throat, realigning the papers in front of him on the table. "On to the reason I'm here. These are the papers the agent needs to show your house. You just have to sign in a few places." His finger targeting the first blank line.

Daisy, stirring her tea. The silver spoon sound ringing out merrily— *tink, tink*—in a nice little rhythm.

"Mum, I hate to be an insensitive boar, but I really haven't got much time. Just sign here and one other place so I can get going. Please."

Daisy, unable to take the pen from him. Staring at the forms, unable to move.

The phone, ringing.

So startling, Daisy jumped. Racing to pick up the phone.

Hearing, "Hello? Are you Daisy?" An unfamiliar voice. An American voice! Daisy's heart, leaping with joy.

"Yes, this is Daisy."

"Daisy, this is your cousin Ann. How are you?"

"Oh, Ann! Fine, I'm fine. How are you?" Daisy, giddy with glee. No time to worry that the news might not be good, that right there in front of Dennis she might hear that she couldn't stay with her. Feeling only one thing: relief. Relief that Ann wasn't dead and that she had called.

Looking at Dennis sitting stiff-backed at her table, showing equal parts exasperation and curiosity.

Ann, "I thought calling might be better than writing. I wanted to respond to you as soon as I could, not to keep you waiting."

"Yes. Gorgeous. Thank you."

"I'm sorry to say that, well, the situation is, well, I'll just get right to it. I'm afraid that it would be very difficult for you to stay with me, but my daughter Elisabeth would love to have you. She has an extra room. She lives only five miles from me."

Daisy, thrilled. Relieved. "Gorgeous."

"Just let us know the date and time of your arrival. We'll be happy to pick you up at the airport."

"Gorgeous," Daisy, repeating, barely thinking straight. "I was hoping to come in a few days if that would be okay." Stumbling over her words. Turning back to face Dennis. Seeing him sitting at attention, tuned into her every word.

Ann, saying, "That would be fine. Take my telephone number, call me when you have the tickets and the times all sorted out."

"Gorgeous," Daisy, repeating, worrying that Ann was thinking she was a simpleton who knew only one word.

Ann was thinking no such thing, of course. She was thinking she should get off the phone to break up the fight brewing between Matthew and Brandon over a purple crayon—before one or both ended up in tears.

Daisy, taking the number, thanking Ann. A whole new Daisy returning to the table. Picking up her tea, sipping it happily, filling Dennis in on Ann's end of the conversation.

Despite himself, Dennis, totally interested. He vaguely knew he had American cousins—his mother had mentioned it from time to time through the years—but he had never given them any thought. Now they suddenly had names: Ann, Elisabeth. They had just become real. He had to pull himself back to the reason he was there, finding that he would rather be thinking about these new cousins, this Ann and her daughter Elisabeth and to imagine them and their lives in New York. On Long Island.

But he had a job to do—two jobs to do: One in Liverpool, where he was desperately behind. The other right there in that kitchen, where he was also desperately behind. Pointing to the line on the contract. Saying, "Mum, can we get this over with? Then you can go back to planning your trip, and I can get back to work." Holding out the pen to her.

Daisy, not taking it. Saying, "I've changed my mind, Dennis." Boldly. "I'm sorry. I'm not selling the house." Suddenly realizing, Why should she? Never once in her life had she gone back on her word, but there are times when one should. "I'm sorry to do this to you again, Dennis, but you and Amanda should go on without me. I mean it." Squeezing his hand.

Dennis, staring at her. Despite Amanda's certain reaction, he didn't care. His head filled with thoughts of his unknown cousins in New York. He would deal with Amanda later. Maybe stop at the jeweler's on his way home from work. A little something always went a long way.

TWELVE

DART MAN STRIKES AGAIN!

Ann, hearing it on the nightly news. On TV. While preparing a steak, salad, and mashed potatoes for herself, David, Josh, Michael and Pete for dinner. Suddenly wondering if it really *could* be Richard. Chastising herself immediately. No way. It was ludicrous. He was and always had been a model husband and father, hardworking, responsible, and kind, with never a bad word to say about anyone. Ann had no idea what had gotten into her daughter's head—where and why this flight of fancy had taken hold—but she was sure she didn't need it nesting in her own head, too.

Plopping a heap of mashed potatoes on each plate, wondering if Elisabeth had heard the news and, if she had, what she had thought. Hoping that by now she had found it completely irrelevant to her life.

She hadn't.

When Elisabeth saw the news on the Internet, she was knee-deep in a corporate tax return that was days behind; four and a half minutes into a telephone conversation with Michael's European History teacher, Mrs. Caulfield, about his latest frightening grade; and her concern about what he was going to get on the state Regents exam. The teacher was mystified as to why her top student had tanked so thoroughly and so quickly.

"Has something been going on at home recently, Mrs. Jetty, that could be affecting him?" Mrs. Caulfield, asking politely. Afraid to pry.

"Now let me think," Elisabeth, stalling for time. "Um." Could it be that his father was Dart Man? Could that turn an A student into a nincompoop? "Well," Elisabeth, saying. Thinking that even before Richard might have started shooting darts at women, he hadn't been home before Michael went to bed more than three times since Christmas. It's June now. Could that be it? Or was it that Richard, who once coached Michael's baseball games, had gone to exactly one of them all season? Or that Richard had his nose glued to his BlackBerry every weekend? Or that when he wasn't staring at the BlackBerry, he was staring at the TV? Could that be what had been turning Michael, the former ace student, into a dolt? The former gifted classical pianist into a pop music iPod-addicted groupie? The former history buff into a pop culture devotee? The former healthy, happy family participant, who had always had time for his younger brothers, into an antisocial lockbox?

Or could it be that Elisabeth was stretched so thin that she was afraid shredded wheat was more together than she was? Was that what might be troubling Michael? Long ago when she and Richard had started having all their children, he had been working reasonable hours and she had been part time, but as the family costs increased—college tuitions, music lessons, property taxes, and so on—Richard had had to join the frenzied rat race of law firm partnership, and Elisabeth had had to go back to working full time. And to make matters worse, she hated her job—now more than ever, because they had just fired Palmer and handed her all his clients. If she had to do another one of his tax returns, she'd die. She was sure of it.

She should have gone to art school. It was her mother's fault that she didn't. But who could blame her mother? Her father abandoned his family when Ann was six. And Ann's husband went and died on her, leaving her with five daughters to raise on her own. Naturally, she had advised her daughters to take the safest paths.

"Um," Elisabeth, aware the teacher was waiting, aware that she had to say something. "I don't know." Feebly. Thinking, "I don't know where to *begin*." Feeling so tired. Sleep had become a luxury for the young. It was as if she had grown out of it, leaving her with drenched night garments.

"I just don't know what to do here," Mrs. Caulfield, scratching her head.

Elisabeth, thinking that that made two of them.

"Other than scheduling a mandatory meeting between him and the school psychiatrist, which I've already done, and allowing him to retake the final. I've never done that before, not once in my twenty-two years of teaching, but I've never seen this before, either. On Monday I'll let him retake the final, a different one."

"Thank you," Elisabeth, holding her head in her hands.

"You're welcome. Now, the Regents is next week. What he gets on it can't be undone. It will be on his high school transcript permanently. And a fifty-nine going in? A fifty-nine on his final exam? I've spoken to his other teachers. They all report the same thing. Something must be going on with him. You must have noticed it at home."

Elisabeth, looking down at the half-finished overdue corporate tax return on her desk, the one she was supposed to have finished three days ago. Closing her eyes, wanting it all to go away, or back to where it once was. To freeze the time when all her boys were still small and their problems were small, too. To a time when she had had all the answers.

"You must have noticed a widespread falling off of all his grades."

A kaleidoscope of tests, rushing into Elisabeth's head: fifth-grade tests, seventh-grade tests, ninth-grade tests, twelfth-grade tests; Josh's, David's, Michael's, Pete's; math, science, language arts, reading, Spanish, French, history. All of them swirling around at a dizzying pace.

"Well," Elisabeth, struggling to say something that would belie the obvious conclusion this teacher must be drawing, that she was a totally checked-out parent, "you see . . ." feeling very much the forty-four-year-old she had become, perimenopausal, period-skipping. This must be it, she thought. The slow decline, rapidly accelerating. Wishing that someone else would step in and do the talking. How about Richard, for example? He would do a much better job. "Let me see . . . his last math test—" Her eyes falling upon her computer screen, stopping her in her tracks. The headline news: Dart Man struck again.

Mrs. Caulfield's voice cutting into her thoughts. "Okay." Sounding exasperated. "We must come up with a strategy to get through to him the importance of the Regents exams and getting his grades back to where they should be. He has a math and English Regents, too, I understand."

"I, uh . . ." Elisabeth, scanning the news story to see when and where Dart Man had struck. Incapable of pulling her eyes from the screen. Unable to focus on the telephone in her hand. Reading that the police were seeking any information regarding this elusive criminal who had struck again this afternoon on East Forty-eighth Street and Lexington Avenue, hitting a woman in her mid-thirties while waiting for the light to change.

Elisabeth's mind flying through the facts. It couldn't be Richard. He rode his bike only on Mondays and Thursdays, and today was Wednesday! A feeling of relief washing over her. It was finished—all her silly Dart Man fears, just because Richard liked darts and rode his bike in the city twice a week. She really needed a vacation. Thank goodness school and all the attendant parental duties were finally ending, bringing on the relative relaxation of summer.

"Mrs. Jetty?" The voice again, interrupting her.

Elisabeth, snapping out of it. Trying to backtrack to the last question, the one she was supposedly busy working out an answer for.

"I, uh—" groping for a response. Suddenly it didn't seem like such a big problem anymore. Nothing she couldn't handle. "Mrs. Caulfield, Michael will be all right. I'll see to it that he studies for the new final you are so generously letting him retake on Monday. And he'll do fine on the Regents. I'm confident he will."

"I hope you're right." Mrs. Caulfield, barely concealing her doubt.

Cordial good-byes. Hanging up. Elisabeth, leaning back in her chair.

Inhaling, exhaling calmly. All tension regarding Richard dissolving. Regaining her footing—not as confident as she had led Mrs. Caulfield to believe, but confident enough. She would find the strength and persistence to whip Michael into shape. She would stay on top of her other boys, too. Cracks only got bigger.

Now, on to other pressing things: the past-due tax return in front of her, a thought about preparing for the houseguest, this cousin, Daisy Phillips, who was coming tomorrow, the many, many school year-end parties, summer league tryouts, piano recitals and concerts on the calendar for the next two weeks.

Her desk chair, springing noisily back to its usual position. Elisabeth, leaning forward over the desk, her eyes blurring on the tax return. Needing another minute before getting back into it. Logging back onto the puppy Web site. Today, golden retrievers.

An email coming in. From the head of the firm. Reminding her that she was late on a tax return. Three days late. It was due Monday. Today was Thursday.

Her blood, chilling. And not about the tax return—about the day. It wasn't a Wednesday.

It was a Thursday.

THIRTEEN

THE NIGHT BEFORE Daisy's trip to New York, her fingers and toes, tingling with excitement. Two red suitcases lay open side by side on her bed. Daisy, sitting quietly next to them, her hands in her lap. Reviewing things again.

She had packed and repacked several times. Sometimes the baby blankets made the cut; sometimes they didn't. Sometimes she thought it was stupid to take them; sometimes she thought it would be nice to have them. Sometimes she didn't have the space for them; sometimes she did.

Checking her passport, tickets, flight information, U.S. currency. She had gone to the hairdresser. She had called her friends to say good-bye. She talked to her new boss at the library and explained that she would be gone for a month or more. The new boss smiled sweetly and suggested that Daisy needn't call when she got back, thanking her for her past services. Daisy didn't mind. Without Grace Parker she no longer had the same appetite for the job.

Going over all the travel plans in her head. The baby blankets—for the moment, anyway—omitted. Daisy, looking at the clock. Only seven. Wanting a good night's sleep before traveling, but seven was ridiculous. And, besides, there was something else that needed doing.

Getting up, pouring herself a Cointreau, taking it into the bedroom with her. Thinking about Paul, picturing him getting ready. She had seen it so many times that it was not hard to imagine. It calmed her to think of him—or maybe that was the Cointreau. Or maybe both.

Back on the bed, thoughts of Paul leading to thoughts of Michael. The reason for the trip. Finishing her drink, deciding not to put it off any longer. Picking up the shoe box from her bedside table that had been brought up earlier from the cellar, before the flood. The shoe box containing Michael's letters—letters that she hadn't seen in almost six decades.

Carrying the shoe box tightly against her body to the piano, the grand piano where Michael had played, thirsting for it as if it were life-providing water, so parched were his days on the military base.

Daisy, down at the piano, allowing herself to remember sitting beside him on the very same bench, watching the flight of his fingers over the keyboard, marveling at their speed and touch, delighting in the miraculous sounds they produced. In love with his face—the knit brows, taut jaw, hair flung back off his forehead, penetrating eyes deep in concentration. All of it, all of him, channeling into deep, mysterious reservoirs of passion. For the music, for life, for her. When he played, Daisy could feel his every heartbeat merging with hers.

Lifting her hand, running her fingers slowly over the keys. Paul had often suggested that the boys study piano, but she had always found a reason to dissuade him. She just couldn't bear to see them tinkering with it. Couldn't bear to have it have a place in her life or cause her to think about what could have been.

Taking a deep breath, opening the shoe box. His handwriting, there. Until this moment she would not have been able to bring his handwriting to mind, but now that she saw it, she recognized it immediately. A nostalgic warmth passed through her, gazing into the box at the dozens of letters in there. She would read them all.

Picking up the first one, relieved to see that it had a return address on it: Michael Baker, 11440 Second Street, Apt. 2, Brooklyn, New York.

This was her starting point: step one in tracking him down.

Gingerly opening the envelope, musty, threatening disintegration.

Daisy, reading—slowly at first, because they were just words, but as she continued, a certain rhythm, a particular way of speaking, an American accent, beginning to reawaken in her—the way he had called her Little Nugget.

By the end of the third letter it was his voice, not hers, that she heard.

D AISY, REREADING EACH LETTER TWICE, eighty-seven in all. Each one as well written and full of feeling as the others.

Rereading the letters, an unreal experience. It was like a book, someone else's life, someone she knew intimately. She was so absorbed by the letters that she almost didn't hear the doorbell.

Lenny. Lenny and Sarah. Lenny, throwing himself around Daisy, planting a heavy kiss on her cheek, saying, "We're just coming from Dennis's. He tells me you're off to New York. Are you?"

Daisy, laughing happily, stepping back to let them enter. A piece of her, still in the letters.

"Come in," Daisy, cheerily. "How about a nice hot cup of tea?"

"No, thanks. We're not going to stay long." Following Daisy into the kitchen. "We just wanted to stop by, wish you well."

"Oh, have a quick cup. It won't take long." Daisy, putting the kettle on.

Lenny and Sarah pulling out chairs, seating themselves at the table. "So what's all this about New York?"

Daisy, spilling everything, except anything about the watch.

Lenny, leaning back in his chair, hands clasped over his stomach, listening, smiling. "Maybe we'll go too, someday, huh, Sarah?" Sarah, glowing at the thought, saying she'd love to. "You go lay out the groundwork, blaze the trail. Sarah and I can follow in your footsteps."

Daisy, smiling, studying Sarah. Delighted to take in her warm eyes and other features. Happy that this one seemed different in looks, in manner.

Lenny, "And I hear that when you come back, this house might be sold."

The water, reaching its boiling point. The kettle, screeching. Daisy, jumping up, turning off the heat. Standing there, kettle in hand. Puzzled. "Who told you that?"

"Dennis just did." Lenny, pushing away the teacup she had laid out for him.

Daisy, carefully pouring water into her cup. Sarah, waving a hand over her cup, saying, "No, thank you." Daisy, returning the kettle to the stovetop. Asking, "Just now? What exactly did he say?"

"He said you've signed the papers. The two of them are practically spending your profits already, about to close the deal on a house in Chessex as if you were already dead and gone."

Daisy, lips pressed together, staring at Lenny.

"If I might say," Sarah, speaking up, "it was his wife. It was Amanda who was doing all the talking. If you ask me, Dennis looked as surprised to hear about them close to settling on a new house as you were, Lenny."

"Could be, could be," Lenny, agreeing.

Daisy, feisty. "Well, there's not going to be any sale of this house. Dennis knows that. I never signed the papers. There's not going to be any profits, so there's not going to be any big house for Amanda—at least not till I'm dead and buried." Crossing her arms over her chest.

"Good. I never did like the talk of it. Dennis was probably just afraid to tell Amanda the truth. She seems to have got way ahead of herself."

Daisy, nodding. Leaving it at that. Lenny, steering the conversation back to New York, wishing his mother a lovely trip. Then sliding his chair out from under the table, declaring that they must go. Kisses, hugs, good wishes all around, then they were gone.

Leaving Daisy back with her letters again—and the photograph, the one photograph, the military picture. Daisy, in quiet contemplation, gazing deeply at it, attempting unsuccessfully to invoke new memories. Reading through the letters again before stuffing them into a manila envelope, packing them. Returning to the kitchen to wash her teacup. Off to the bedroom.

Picking up Lenny's baby blanket from the bed, placing it in the canvas suitcase. Closing the zipper.

Getting into bed. Turning off the light.

Turning on the light. Opening the zipper.

Dennis's blanket going in, too.

FOURTEEN

THE NIGHT BEFORE DAISY'S ARRIVAL, the house, quiet. Everyone asleep.

Except Elisabeth—again. Lying in bed, her nightgown clammy, damp, matching the sheets beneath her, listening to Richard snore, as she had done so many nights before. But unlike any other night, this time quietly slipping out from under the covers. Creeping silently out of the room, down the stairs to the powder room where she had left a change of clothes. Still not fully sure that she would actually go through with it. It would be, arguably, the craziest thing she had ever done. Moving forward with the plan, brewing coffee in the dimly lit kitchen of the dark, silent house, asking herself again about the wisdom of her quest.

Deciding that crazy or not, she was going to do it.

Pouring the steaming hot coffee into her well-worn stainless steel travel mug. Unable to remember the last time she had had coffee from a regular ceramic mug while sitting at her kitchen table. Who didn't only have coffee on the go anymore? Adding skim milk, a no-calorie sweetener. Grabbing a box of cookies, a can of peanuts, not wanting to get sidetracked by hunger or exhaustion. Slinking soundlessly out of the kitchen into the cool night air, down the front path, and onto the paved driveway.

Slowly opening her car door, noiselessly. Placing her coffee in the cup holder, the food and her handbag on the passenger seat. About to get in, stopping herself, with one foot in and one out. Deciding to check his car first.

Over to it, his brand-new silver BMW. Kneeling on the driver's seat. Her palms surfing the upholstery, the carpeting, under the seats. Scanning the whole interior.

For darts.

If he was Dart Man, he would have darts.

Scouring the inside, coming up empty. Relieved but not surprised. It would be foolish of him to keep them in there. Their absence proved nothing. They would be too easily detected in his car, stashed under a seat or in a glove compartment. The boys could go into his car on a whim, and so could she. Elisabeth, out of his car, closing the door softly.

Slipping into her leased black Mercedes SUV. Heading out.

To Manhattan. To Richard's office. To check for darts.

Knowing it was crazy but going all the same—through the dark and empty Port Washington streets, along the harbor and around the curve to Main Street, past the hardware store and the library, past the many restaurants, gas stations, pubs, delis, and bagel stores toward the highway.

Daisy was coming tomorrow. Elisabeth needed to know if she had invited this old cousin to Dart Man's house.

I T WAS NO TROUBLE for Elisabeth to get into Richard's building through revolving doors into a vast lobby at 1:30 in the morning. All it took was her driver's license. The security guards tended not to mess with partners' spouses.

The elevator, opening into the ultramodern, high-tech reception room of his thirty-sixth floor office. Elisabeth, checking the long hallways, right and left, relieved to find them free of people. She hadn't exactly figured out what she would say.

Although she hadn't visited it in years, she had no trouble remembering the way to Richard's office. When Steve and Pete were small she used to take them to Richard's office every Christmas. They would all go together to see the tree at Rockefeller Center before elbowing their way through FAO Schwarz and joining the line of people inching past the wonderful store windows: Macy's at Herald Square, Lord & Taylor, and Saks on Fifth Avenue. Elisabeth loved the boys' rosy-cheeked faces peering keenly at the creative, beautifully crafted, mechanically operated moving displays.

But they hadn't made the Christmas trek to the city in years. Elisabeth, promising herself then and there, creeping down the artwork-lined, plush-carpeted hallway, that despite whatever insanity was going on at the time, come hell or high water she would take her boys in next Christmas—David, Josh, and even difficult Michael who was still defiantly refusing to study, claiming not to care about school or grades.

Another blowout earlier in the evening. She had to hide his iPod, send him to his room, imprison him all night, not knowing what he was doing in there. He was asleep before she was; that much she knew.

Elisabeth, switching on the light in Richard's office, stepping inside. Feeling sneaky and creepy.

And guilty—because of the first noticeable things: all over his desk and credenza, pictures of her and the boys, pictures she didn't even know he had. Elisabeth, staring at them, her heart beating faster, picking one up, holding it. Seeing her life objectively just as any visitor to Richard's desk might. Her life looking mighty good. Smiling faces of her handsome sons on vacations. She and Richard through the years, starting with the wedding photo, tracking time through to this past Christmas. A picture she didn't even know he had, of them hugging in front of the decorated tree, in a rare moment when they were both home and awake and unoccupied enough to pose for a picture. Steve, home from college, had taken it. She remembered that. And here it was, framed, on his desk.

When had Richard done that? When had he selected the picture, bought the frame, and framed it without even mentioning it to her?

Overcome with tenderness for him. Seeing that nothing had really changed. They had gotten older. They had gotten busier. She had gotten crazier. Holding the framed photo in her hand, feeling tears forming in her eyes, wishing herself back together with him in bed in the quiet of their room. So she could listen to his breathing and try to imagine his dreams as she always used to do.

And she would apologize to him—not aloud, of course. He didn't even know he was accused. She would apologize to him in her head for even thinking that this steady, responsible, wonderful husband, father, and man could ever have done what she had seriously been thinking about.

Elisabeth, putting the picture back on the desk. Sitting down, not in his chair but in a facing chair. To take just a moment. To summarize where she had been and where she was now. To run through the medley of her emotions. Getting up, going around his massive desk to sit in his chair—to reconnect on some level. To put herself back squarely where she had always been with him. Seating herself in the high-backed black leather chair, her arms on the armrest. Planting her feet and swiveling the way her boys would have done. Picturing Richard in it, holding a meeting. Allowing herself a surge of pride in him. Look at the size of his office. Look at his view. That was Central Park out there, thirty-six floors below. He had done very well for himself. He had gone to Yale, on scholarship, both undergraduate and law school. His father had been a New York City bus driver; his mother, a medical secretary.

Elisabeth, feeling better than she had in some time. It was 1:45; she had a long drive ahead of her. She had better get going, and she would—without even looking in a single drawer. It was over. She would tuck this little episode away.

Standing up. Starting out of his office.

Stopping dead in her tracks.

There, on the back of his door, a dartboard. Four darts in the bull's-eye.

E LISABETH, HURRYING BACK to her car, telling herself to stay calm. All the way down Fifth Avenue, telling herself that dartboards had been hanging on the backs of office doors since the beginning of time. That it had probably always been there on his. That it meant nothing. Wanting to get herself back into her former place: loving and trusting her husband.

Forcing herself to stop thinking about it. Turning on the radio, fumbling around. Switching the station from her daytime public radio station. Moving up the dial to one playing songs. Adjusting the volume. Way up. Blasting out lyrics.

By the time she got to the Williamsburg Bridge she was thinking about nothing but the lyrics, the music, the beat. Songs from her youth. Singing out strong. No fear of being overheard. Only a few other cars on the bridge, a lone taxi or two. Elisabeth, driving over the speed limit, relishing the rare openness of the road.

Hitting the empty highway, hitting the gas. Moving further over the speed limit, further up the volume, songs sung even louder. Recapturing something: exhilaration. Feeling positively charged. Liberated and alive.

Unable to remember the last time she had felt so free. Flying along the highway toward home like someone out of an old hippie movie, thinking it was even better than gazing at puppies' faces on the Internet and the most fun she had had since her gynecologist spoke those dreadful words.

Sleeping better that night than she had in months.

FIFTEEN

DENNIS, ON THE WAY to the airport. Almost crashing the car.
It was true that the cabbie in the next lane was driving as
though he fully believed in the promise of a rich afterlife.

It was also true that Dennis was not entirely without blame. Swerving back into his own lane, taxi horns blaring. "Did you see that?" Running his hand nervously through his hair. A bead of sweat being born on his left temple. "He should have his license revoked."

"Yes." Daisy, calm as could be, hands folded neatly in her lap, her leather purse straps thread through them. Although she hated to, asking, "Incidentally, did you tell Amanda that I'm not selling my house?"

Dennis's face, darkening. "Yes. Yes, I did. She knows."

"Fine, then. I just wanted to be sure."

Dennis, thinking that she could be sure. Remembering the huge row it had caused.

The cabbie pulling alongside their little blue Audi, waving his fist at Dennis. Cursing in a foreign language.

"Maniac," Dennis, muttering, regaining his composure.

Daisy, "Any new thoughts on a move for you two?"

Dennis, sighing. "We're still going. Amanda is dead set on it. I'm sorry to say we could be moved by the time you get back, in which case Lenny will have to pick you up from the airport."

"That's no problem. I hope you'll be happy in your new home."

Dennis, hoping the same. "Now, do you have everything you'll need?"

"Yes, dear."

"Passport?"

"You asked me that already. Yes, passport and tickets are right here." Calmly tapping her bag.

A car horn blasting. Dennis had drifted into the wrong lane again. He swerved back, feeling apologetic. "Oh, dear, I seem to be all over the place today. I don't know what's with me."

Daisy did. He was a basket of nerves. She was relieved when he finally parked the car. He hurried to the back, pulling out her suitcases—two of them, a big one and a medium-sized canvas one. Both were on wheels. She had her purse and her carry-on. Together they entered the terminal.

Daisy, feeling a thrill just being there. So many people from all over the world, momentarily drawn together on invisible intersecting paths. Quickly scattering in different directions, feeding off one another's energy and creating new energy, spiraling onward and away. Most were hurrying, rolling suitcases swiftly behind them, eyes focused ahead. A small grungy group in their early twenties sat stupefied in corners on the floor, staring blankly, sipping coffee from plastic cups with covers, their overstuffed backpacks sprawled out beside them. Barely speaking, as if they had run out of things to say a few countries back and were too tired to care.

Daisy and Dennis, walking over the smooth floor to the check-in counter. The line of travelers ahead of them snaked a distance away from the counter, reaching all the way to the end of the roped area where a large sign was posted that displayed universal symbols of what was no longer being permitted in carry-on luggage.

Daisy, stopping at the sign. Good feelings vanishing. Because nobody had told her—or maybe they had and she had forgotten—that she couldn't bring any liquids on board, including toothpaste, shampoo, and makeup, none of which she had. But if those things were prohibited, certainly other similar things would be, too, things she did have.

Dennis, stepping past the sign to take their place at the end of the queue behind a businessman. Looking back at Daisy to see why she had stopped. Seeing her looking troubled. A couple with three small children, lining up behind them, a sprawl of suitcases and attendant accoutrements.

Daisy, nervously, "Dennis, I have a problem."

Dennis, "What is it?" Eyes swiftly scanning her in search of something obvious. Casting a worried glance at the family behind them, all craning their necks to see if the line ahead was moving along without him.

It was. A gap. Opening between him and the businessman.

Daisy, pointing at the sign. "Look what can't be brought on board."

Dennis, looking. "Okay. Do you have any of that?"

Shaking her head. "No, not quite that."

"Well, then good." Slightly exasperated, sidling up behind the businessman.

Daisy, not sidling up with him. Glued to the floor in front of the sign. "Orange marmalade." Apologetically. "I have six jars of orange marmalade."

"Orange marmalade! In your carry-on?"

Confirming it. "A gift. Three jars for Ann. Three for Elisabeth."

"They can't get marmalade in New York?"

The family behind, as if on cue, making their way around Daisy and Dennis, pushing and pulling and dragging dozens of suitcases in various sizes—first the father, then the mother, then the three small children. Behind them, another group immediately forming. And a messy group behind them, folding in.

"I don't know," Daisy, her voice cracking. "I don't know if they can get marmalade in New York. They probably can, but not from Dunkirk's.

I wanted to bring them marmalade from the oldest original marmalade factory in Liverpool."

Dennis, looking past his mother, anchored in front of the sign, to the group of tense, impatient travelers behind her. "You're sure it's in your carry-on?"

Daisy, nodding.

"Well, then, we'd better get it out. You'll have to put it in your suitcase and check it through." Poorly concealing a scowl. Giving up his place in line. Setting out, with Daisy following fast behind him, to find an available uncrowded area to make the transfer. Walking across the concourse, weaving through hassled crowds.

Daisy, making an effort to recapture some of her initial excitement, but it was gone. All she felt was dumb—for biting off more than she could chew and for undertaking such a foolhardy journey. And nervous because any minute now she and Dennis would be making their good-byes. He would leave her all on her own in this great big anonymous, uncaring world. And what if she couldn't do it? What if she had made other orange marmalade mistakes? Now that she had had enough time to think about it, she remembered that she had been told about the carry-on restrictions. And she had forgotten. It was true that she sometimes forgot things.

Suddenly feeling her age, self-doubt coming on strong. Should she cancel the trip? Plead with the airlines? Try to recover what money she could? Call the cousins, thank them, and invite them to Liverpool? Go back home to enjoy the quiet routine of her life?

Looking at the back of Dennis's head as he steadily navigated across the crowded concourse. Even the back of his head looked piqued, the way his hair was falling to his collar.

His annoyance, bracing her. Riling her up, restarting the belief that she could do it. After all, Dennis forgot things, too, all the time. And Lenny? What didn't he forget? Either one could have forgotten the carry-on restrictions. Anyone could have, at any age. She could have done the same thing twenty, thirty, forty, fifty years earlier.

She would not be so easily shaken. She was going forward. She was going to New York. Come what may.

Tapping him on the shoulder. "Look, Dennis, there's a spot." Pointing to a small, unoccupied alcove in a waiting area to her left.

Dennis, looking. Approving. Making his way toward it. Six jars, out of the carry-on, tucked neatly into one of the suitcases destined for the cargo bay. Dennis and Daisy back on their way to the check-in line.

Daisy in the lead.

BUCKLED IN, READY FOR TAKEOFF.

Daisy, deep in her seat, engines revving. Closing her eyes, the plane picking up speed down the runway. Squeezing her fists as the nose lifted off, her fingernails into soft palm tissue. The plane tilting upward with a great big thrust of engine power.

Imagining Paul's hand in hers. As it always used to be.

SIXTEEN

WHILE DAISY WAS BOARDING, carefully stepping in from the connecting tube to the inside of the plane, her hand lightly patting the exterior first, something she and Paul did before every takeoff—Ann was thinking about who should go to the airport to get her.

Elisabeth, knowing her mother's aversion to highways, had already assumed she would be the one picking up Daisy. Richard and Pete were still sleeping. David and Josh were downstairs watching TV. Elisabeth, leaning inside Michael's door in her bathrobe and slippers, guarding it. Blocking his escape. Fondly remembering her last night's secret drive. Saying, "Monday, you got it? Mrs. Caulfield's being really nice letting you retake the final, and you're going to reward her kindness by getting a hundred. And the only way to do that is by studying. And the only way I can be sure that you're studying is to watch you. Yesterday you accomplished nothing. I am not taking my eyes off you from now till then. You can't go to baseball practice, you can't listen to your iPod, you can't play with your Xbox or your Wii or your computer. You are studying all day today and tomorrow. Got it, Michael?"

Michael, looking so much younger in his pajamas. So early in the morning. Still warm from sleep. Hair ruffled. He had no fight in him, no teenage attitude—just a blank look.

Elisabeth, "And you're coming with me to the airport."

Michael, yawning. "For what?"

"For what. For Cousin Daisy, that's what."

Michael, groaning. "Do I have to?"

Elisabeth, nodding. "You do. We're leaving here at noon, so you'd better get up now, come down to breakfast, then start hitting the books."

Without waiting for an argument, turning and heading downstairs to begin breakfast. Moments and memories of her magical midnight ride threading through her, providing her with little mini boosts of fresh life, energy, outlook. Pushing away the image of the dartboard on the back of Richard's door, switching instead to the glorious driving portion of her secret night. Wondering half-jokingly if it was too late to become a long-haul truck driver.

Getting Richard out of bed with the news that he had to take David to a bowling party at ten and get Josh to a laser-tag party at eleven, and then be back at noon to pick up David and back to the laser-tag party at one to get Josh. Elisabeth, telling him that the parties were in opposite directions, and with the usual weekend morning traffic, they were probably an hour apart. Reminding him that their houseguest was on her way and that they were having all her sisters and their families for dinner to welcome her.

Richard, in a blue T-shirt, plaid flannel drawstring pants, looking at her very unlawyerlike. Unshaven and nubby, with dark eyebrows and hair tossed wildly, the muscles and skin around his jaw, tense. Totally dazed while she said all this, slipping a mug of coffee into his hand—a gesture of kindness to help jump-start his day. Elisabeth, witnessing long beats of confusion swirling around him before they gave way to his murky recollection of having heard it all before.

Five to twelve, Elisabeth and Michael alone in the house. Elisabeth, appearing in Michael's bedroom door. Finding him at his desk, where he had been for the last hour and a half. Wondering if he'd actually gotten anything done. Thinking she might have seen him closing a desk drawer when she got there.

"Time to go." Elisabeth. Way upbeat.

"Go without me." Murmuring. Without hope.

"Uh-uh. No way. Let's go welcome my long-lost cousin." Making it sound adventurous.

"Like I've got anything to say to an old lady." Closing his book. Caving fairly easily. Actually, he had been reasonably cooperative all morning, going through gestures of defiance without any real passion. Making Elisabeth feel guilty. Obviously he was enjoying her full attention, her being focused on him and only him, holding him on her radar. Elisabeth, even joking with him a little, like she used to. Wondering if that was all there was to it, if that was all it was going to take, and, if so, how long she would be able to keep it up.

Michael, getting up. They were almost of equal heights now. His denim jeans, struggling to hang on well below his hips, boxers puffing out above.

Elisabeth, scowling. She didn't want to—the morning had been so calm—but she couldn't help it. Saying, "Oh, come on," in a nice enough voice. "You're not really going to wear that, are you?" Keeping her cool.

Michael, looking down at himself, feigning incomprehension. "Why? What's wrong with what I'm wearing?" As if they hadn't been through this a million times before.

"You're not going to greet an old English woman in pants that don't reach much higher than the tops of your socks, are you?" Keeping it light, jokey.

"Why not? Why should an old lady care what I'm wearing?" Starting to take it seriously. Old defenses recurring.

Elisabeth, looking long at him, trying to remember herself at age thirteen. Wondering if she had ever thought like that. And wondering if he was right. Why should Daisy care? Wondering if she should let it go or send them both trudging down the same well-worn unpleasant path again. After such a smooth morning.

"Just change, please." A slightly begging tone.

"No. I like it." Smoothing down the front of his orange T-shirt. "I think I look nice."

"Do you?" Elisabeth, asking. He wasn't giving in. He was standing his ground, making things difficult. And what if he was being genuine? Elisabeth, looking at him another long moment. Considering something. Considering going through with something she had thought up during her midnight ride last night. While gleefully speeding along with her fellow speeding highway drivers on the Long Island Expressway. Somewhere in Queens. A vision—one of many—had wafted through her head. This one concerning Michael.

"Fine." Elisabeth, deciding firmly not to let it disintegrate into the same old unwinnable roles. Thinking she would try something new. A new approach. A totally different tactic. "Go ahead and grab something from the kitchen. You might get hungry on the way. I'll be right there." Turning, leaving his room.

A few minutes later, Elisabeth, in the kitchen, saying, "Ready to go?"

Michael, rummaging around in the refrigerator. Turning to answer, a jar of pickles and several stacked plastic-wrapped pounds of cold cuts balancing in his hands. Seeing her. Staring, frozen in position.

"Let's go, buddy." Elisabeth, casually. "We don't want to keep an old lady waiting."

Michael, unable to move. Shocked by her appearance, no idea how to react.

"Let's go." Elisabeth, repeating herself, sailing out of the kitchen. "You don't have time to make a sandwich. Just grab an apple or a banana."

Michael, staring after her, getting a view of her from the back. Seeing his mother in his father's jeans, wearing them like Michael did: loose, riding barely above the tops of his thighs, and held up weakly by a belt that transversed the lower portion of her butt. Brightly colored flowered old-lady panties—she had pulled an old hideous pair of maternity underwear out of a box at the bottom of the closet. They stretched a good five inches high above the waist of the pants, over the contours of her middle-aged belly. Wearing a short blouse so as not to block any of it from view.

Michael, watching her go, horrorstruck. Fumbling clumsily in attempts at getting the unopened food back into the refrigerator. Then quickly chasing after her.

"Mom," catching up on the front porch, "you're not really going out like that."

"Why not?" Elisabeth, innocently. "I think I look nice."

"No, you don't! You look horrible!" Scanning the street, making sure no neighbors were watching. Holding his ground on the porch while she got in the car.

"Come on. We've got to hurry now." A singsong voice.

"You're not really going to do this." Holding his textbook flat against his chest like a shield. "You're not really going to meet your cousin dressed like that. You're just doing this to get me."

"If you change, I will," Elisabeth, putting the key into the ignition, her car door open. One leg was out of the car, sneaker flat down on the driveway.

Staring each other down. Michael, tense on the porch. Elisabeth, giddy in the driver's seat. Finding that, surprisingly, being dressed like Michael did not leave her embarrassed at all. It made her feel goofy and silly and fun and unburdened. Maybe there *was* something to not caring what other people thought. And, besides, at forty-four it wasn't as if she was going to look good anymore, only good for her age.

"But what's your cousin going to think?" Michael, actually pleading.

"She'll think you and I dress alike. Now make up your mind: Either go change and I will, or get in the car." Cool as a cucumber.

Michael, stalled on the porch. Undecided. Overwhelmed. Not sure if he was being toyed with and should be mad and refuse to change, or if he should protect his reputation, his mother's, his whole family's for that matter, or if he should be proud of his mother for not caring what other people thought.

Elisabeth, "Come on, buddy. Make a choice."

Michael, sputtering, "Just change, Mom. Come on. It's not the same for me as it is for you. Don't try to pretend it is."

Elisabeth, starting the car, revving the engine, reviving whiffs of the Williamsburg Bridge, a scent of the Long Island Expressway, the essence of the long stretch of the left lane. "Why shouldn't it be? If you don't care about showing everyone your underwear, why should I? Didn't you ever hear of the goose and the gander?"

"That's about gender. This is about age."

"Whatever. Now let's get going. It's already too late to change. Just get in."

A tall, thin neighbor, Mr. Toomey, with a beard and a runner's body, dressed inappropriately for the hot weather in a long-sleeved New York Mets baseball sweatshirt, walked past, his little brown pencil-legged Chihuahua leading him. Elisabeth greeted him from the driver's seat. He waved back.

Michael, red in the face, horrified at what Mr. Toomey must be thinking, notwithstanding that Mr. Toomey should be the last person on earth to cast aspersions on anyone else's wardrobe choices. Michael, reluctantly going, dragging his feet all the way to the car. Elisabeth, watching him in the rearview mirror, buckling himself in. The car shifting into reverse, slowly backing out of the driveway.

Out of nowhere, a car, careening into the driveway, screeching to a halt beside them, missing them by a hair. Leaving Elisabeth and Michael jointly jolted, having to straighten themselves out, to right themselves.

Ann. Turning off her car, heaving herself out with an effort.

"Mom!"

"Grandma!"

Both, "What are you doing here?"

"I'm coming." Ann, hurrying around to the passenger seat. "Goodness, I was so afraid I'd miss you."

"Really?" Elisabeth. "You're coming? This *is* a shocker."

Ann, opening the car door. "I was afraid of what she'd think if I wasn't there, how bad it would look." Getting in, pulling the door closed. "You know what they say: You never get a second chance to make a first impression."

"Yeah, Mom." Michael.

WHAT'S SHE GOING to be like, do you think?" Elisabeth, asking her mother on the notoriously unpleasant Belt Parkway, cutting across Queens.

Michael, in the back, supposedly studying the book on his lap. Instead studying the highway and the houses and city parks that flanked it.

"I don't know." Ann, considering.

"It's amazing that you've never met her."

Muscles on Ann's face, tensing. "I met only her mother—when I was small. That one trip my mother and I made to England in 1945. After that trip, my mother no longer had any appetite for England, and nobody ever came here to see her. Her family never forgave her for marrying a foreigner, a New Yorker—an acrobat in vaudeville, no less—and skipping off to America. They didn't trust him. They said no good could come of it. The worst part is that they were right."

"Well, not entirely." Elisabeth, her left elbow resting on the windowsill of the car door, her fingers in her hair. "They did have you. That's something good."

"They used to dance together." Ann, immersed in thought. "My mother and Daisy's mother, Meredith, before my mother got married, before their falling out. Meredith was nine years older than my mother. They toured England and Europe. That's how my mother met my father—in Dublin. It's funny that those two, a dancer and an acrobat, should produce me, klutzy, with two left feet. I must have been very disappointing to them."

Elisabeth, a sideways glance at her mother, surprised that she was talking so much on a topic she rarely touched on. Noticing pain on her face. Elisabeth, recognizing that even after forty-four years you could still find something new about people you thought you knew entirely.

SEVENTEEN

THE LANDING, TOTALLY SMOOTH. Like sliding across glass.

Daisy, in the middle seat, darting her head from side to side, trying to get around the man's big beefy head on her right, eager to snatch her first view of New York, JFK International Airport. Her stomach, hosting all manner of activity.

The plane slowly taxiing in, coming to a final halt. The unmistakable sound of hundreds of seat belts unbuckling in unison skirting around in the enclosed air. People from front to rear popping out of their seats as though orchestrated.

Daisy, remaining seated. No use getting up; the aisle completely clogged. The man with the big beefy head getting up, standing entirely too close, leaning over her in a failed attempt to get his things from the overhead bin. His round stomach bouncing off her head. Daisy, trying to flatten herself against her seat back. The man on her left, a trim business type who had spent the whole flight tapping away on his computer, standing quietly, patiently, waiting for the river of people in the aisle to start flowing.

Daisy, in no hurry to get going. As long as she was in the plane, she was still somehow tethered to home. As soon as she stepped out of it, she would be on her own—utterly dependent on strangers and near strangers for everything. Once again worrying that she wasn't up to it. A million what-ifs harvesting in her brain.

The aisle showing signs of movement, an easing of the congestion, a little breathing room, a slight widening of the spaces between those assembled. Daisy, sensing that if she didn't hightail it out of there right behind the trim man with the trim laptop, the beefy-headed man would run her right over. Gathering her stuff in her lap. Not missing her cue to join the queue.

EIGHTEEN

ELISABETH, FINDING A PARKING SPOT.

Michael, not wanting to join them in the terminal. Sitting in the back of the SUV, not unbuckling. His long legs and big clumsy feet were spread out before him, his arms folded across his narrow chest, his facial muscles set firmly over smooth pink skin. Declaring, "I'll wait here. I'll study."

"No, come in." Elisabeth. "We may need you. There's no telling how much luggage she brought." Lifting the latch to open her door.

Ann, getting out. Stretching her back in the parking lot. The day, sticky hot, the strong midday sun high overhead, the skies, a perfect clear blue.

"So now I'm your pack mule?" Michael, irritated.

"You've always been." Elisabeth, smiling. The waistband of her panties, riding high, her jeans low. Elisabeth, scanning the stretch of terminals in front of her, looking for British Airways.

Michael, "I thought I was supposed to be studying."

"You are. But since you didn't study the whole way here when there was nothing else to do, I don't see the point of starting now when there is."

Michael, deliberately huffing and puffing, loudly. Stumbling out of the SUV, squinting in the bright light. "So let's go." Grumbling.

Starting toward the terminal.

"I do believe I'm getting a little nervous." Ann, before preceding their one-at-a-time entrance through the revolving doors into the arrivals section.

Elisabeth, "I am, too. I mean, did she say how long she's staying?"

"She didn't."

Michael, moving slowly along behind them, doing his best to show them how much he didn't want to be there—even before the horror of his mother's attire. In shock that she had actually gone through with it.

Ann, eventually noticing—while standing at the arrival gate. Her eyes on Elisabeth's clothes, blinking twice. Comprehension, rapid. Quick perusal of Elisabeth's face. A hurried shifting to Michael's. Michael was looking at her, his eyes urging a definitive reprimand from mother to daughter.

Ann, uncertain where she should fall, whose side she should be on.

Michael, "Doesn't she look stupid?"

Elisabeth, looking down at herself. Having to laugh. She had almost forgotten what she was wearing. "I'm thinking of wearing it all the time." Enjoying her newfound wackiness. Big CPA. Big partner's wife.

Michael, turning away, to the stream of travelers beginning to make their way through the arrival's gate.

"What does Daisy look like?" Elisabeth.

"I have no idea." Ann. "She could look like anything."

The number of people coming through the gate increasing.

"We know she's old." Ann, again. "There can't be too many old women traveling alone."

Elisabeth and Michael, agreeing without comment. Watching arrivals coming through the gate, passing them on their way to the baggage claim section.

Minutes passing. Throngs of people winnowing down to a trickle. Still no old lady. Shifting uncomfortably, the beginnings of worry.

And then, at last, Daisy.

NINETEEN

From Liverpool, known for its maritime history, its great shipping ports, its industrial center, its sports stadium, and, of course the Beatles, came Daisy, marching along as if to a beat, rolling along a red carry-on, bright, cheerful, curious eyes on everything. Taking it all in.

Ann's heart, skipping a beat, seeing in Daisy the very image of her own mother—as if her mother, gone now all those years, had returned.

Daisy, spotting them, hurrying over. The minute she had laid eyes on the three of them, she knew they were the ones. The short, heavy woman in the dark blue pants suit with brushed back hair, guarded light brown eyes, soft round nose, lightly wrinkled tan skin, looking nothing like anyone else in the family. The younger, forty-something woman—and here Daisy had to blink; her clothes were indescribable—making Daisy rethink her presuppositions that New Yorkers would be as fashionable as Europeans. And the teenager—tall, slim, stretched, gangly, displaying all the arrogance of youth.

Daisy, wheeling her carry-on toward them. Ann and Elisabeth, welcoming her movement in their direction; summoning her, gathering her with their eyes. Elisabeth liked her immediately—the way she carried herself, her diminutive frame, the curious and accepting air about her.

Ann, finding everything about her familiar. Seeing in Daisy all the things Ann's mother had been and had hoped for in a daughter but never got. Instead she got a squat, broad, heavy daughter with the body-type genes that were handed down from her grandfather on her father's side. Disappointing her mother and crushing Ann, humbling her for life.

"Ann?" Daisy, when she got a respectable distance to speak.

Ann, nodding. The two women standing there, gazing at each other. Neither one reaching out to touch.

"Daisy," Elisabeth, stepping forward. "How nice to meet you. I'm Elisabeth, her daughter. Did you have a nice flight?" Reaching over to gently pat Daisy's arm.

"Gorgeous." Daisy.

"Great." Elisabeth. "We're all very much looking forward to your staying with us." Quelling the cacophony of dissenting voices in her head—her own and those of her children.

Fortunately, Richard had not dissented. He had merely said, "Fine," and had then fallen off to sleep, making Elisabeth wish again that she could have more of his time, because by the time she got finished briefly summarizing Michael's recent attitude and hastily updating him on the lives of their other boys, Elisabeth had less than a minute of Richard's consciousness to cover everything else.

"This is my son, Michael." Elisabeth, pressuring Michael forward with her hand on his back, moving him toward Daisy for the introduction.

"Glad to meet you, Michael." Daisy, cheerfully, thinking about the name.

Michael, nodding, looking hard at the floor, thinking, generic old lady; they're all the same.

"Let's get your suitcases. Baggage claim is this way," Elisabeth, suggesting. The group falling in line with the remaining stragglers going in that direction.

A massive crowd had huddled around the baggage carousel. Daisy, taking a deep breath. Tired all of a sudden. She had hardly slept on the plane—nerves—and she was hungry; she had only picked at her food—nerves again. Everything suddenly seemed so daunting: getting her luggage, getting to the house, the strangeness of where she was. Maybe she had taken on too much. Maybe she should get the next plane back, not remove the bags, just carousel them over to the next flight back across the Atlantic.

A churning of gears from beyond; the belt beginning to move. Suitcases, appearing. The crowd rustling, individuals from the back pushing forward, roughly parting the thick wall of shoulder-to-shoulder people to get at their things. Daisy's heart pumping anxiously, waiting to spot hers. Ann and Elisabeth, busy stealing peeks at her, sizing her up. Michael, not even bothering. He had already seen what he needed to see. She was a little old lady, and little old ladies were about as interesting as historic house tours where they talked at length about the materials used in the draperies, tapestries, throw pillows.

Elisabeth, trying to gauge how much time and help Daisy would need, and whether she would be all right on her own all day. Wondering what she had planned. Remembering her mother saying that Daisy had some business she wanted to take care of—but what? And would it involve Elisabeth? Did Daisy drive? Could she manage the other side of the road thing? What if she thought that Elisabeth would be free to drive her around everywhere? Did Daisy know that Elisabeth worked full time? Had Ann mentioned that? Now was a fine time to be thinking about such things, she knew, but like everything else in her life, she didn't focus on it until it was right under her nose.

Elisabeth wasn't the only one wondering what Daisy's trip would require. Ann was wondering, too. Both women were dwelling on the same thing when Daisy spotted her luggage.

Daisy, tapping Ann on her shoulder before beginning her struggle through the crowd that had loosened and thinned somewhat but was still large enough to pose a challenge. Daisy, going ahead, politely tapping people on the shoulders, excusing herself through the reluctantly parting crowd. Ann and Elisabeth in her wake. Elisabeth, grabbing Michael by the sleeve. Michael, muttering complaints.

Daisy, in the front, pointing out her suitcase. In the meantime, a very loud murmur was springing up. People, reacting to something coming toward them on the conveyor belt. Pointing. Others craning their necks to see. Everyone ready to laugh at the dummy who had done it—the person who had put orange marmalade in a canvas suitcase. There it was, orange marmalade leaking out of every seam of the bag. Dunkirk's orange marmalade, oozing across the conveyor belt, dripping over the cold metallic sides to the floor.

Michael, "What kind of a moron would do that?"

Daisy, aghast, pushing away a trickle of sadness. They would never get their Dunkirk's. Then stifling a laugh. Wishing Dennis and Lenny were there. Maybe Dennis wouldn't find it funny, but Lenny would. He would be roaring with laughter.

Daisy, hearing Elisabeth saying, "How embarrassing to have to own up to that."

Michael, "Whoever did it is probably too dumb to feel embarrassed."

Daisy, watching her mistake approaching, about to be in front of them. Despising that she was going to have to admit it was hers. How could she ask Michael to pick up such a mess? They would probably try to lose her in the parking lot.

The crowd, watching, all eyes on the suitcase, waiting to see who would claim it. Daisy, quickly trying to recollect what was in the bag, thinking maybe she could just walk away, leaving it there to rotate forever.

No such luck. Remembering: toiletries—expendable; nightgowns—expendable; a second pair of shoes—expendable; books and maps of New York—expendable; Dennis's and Lenny's baby blankets—not.

Her moment of reckoning. The canvas suitcase, two feet away.

Should she let it go around again? Daisy, feeling herself heating up, blushing all over her face. Her skin awake in a way that hadn't happened in a long time. In her earlier days, blushing—the vibrant red, the intense heat—had chronically plagued her, but it hadn't in recent decades. Suddenly here it was again—and sort of sweet. Making Daisy feel younger, delighted that blushing was still possible.

The suitcase. On the belt right in front of her. Daisy, newly alive, reaching past Ann, bending over to lift it, aware of gasps of surprise behind her. The suitcase was sticking to the belt. Daisy, tugging to wrench it free.

Peeling it off with a loud sucking sound. The bag, swinging, dripping. Daisy, drawing it closer in, stopping the swinging with her body. Feeling dozens of eyes on her as she turned to her gaping American cousins, saying, "I'm afraid it's my bag. Terribly sorry about the mess. I'll clean it before I put it in your car, of course, if we can find a loo. I can see my unfortunate mistake in packing. I'll never do that again, I tell you." Giggling. "And let others learn a lesson about last-minute packing. It was the no-liquids-on-board sign I encountered only minutes before checking bags that led to this."

Breathlessly finishing her explanation, holding the bag far enough away that the dripping jam hit the floor, not her. Expecting some reaction. She wasn't sure what, but there should be something in the wake of her confession. Instead, three completely blank faces looking back at her without a shred of comprehension.

"Was that English?" Michael.

"It must be." Elisabeth.

"I didn't catch a word of it." Ann.

"Was that just her accent?" Michael. "Because I don't think it was even English."

"I'm afraid we're not getting you," Elisabeth, saying, talking to Daisy as if she were deaf. "We don't understand your accent."

Daisy smiling, not getting Elisabeth, either. Standing there awkwardly, holding the bag, looking into the faces of her cousins. For some seconds nobody speaking, then Daisy hoisting the straps of the offensive bag on her forearm, almost to her elbow. Her hand, at a right angle to her body in a rather regal fashion, her head held high, her nose tipped upward, dignified. Turning, moving through the crowd, which parted quickly, afraid of getting smeared. Daisy, carrying herself as if showcasing the finest luggage the world over.

The cousins, slowly following, avoiding the sticky drops landing on the floor.

"Goodness." Ann.

"Holy shit." Elisabeth.

"Maybe not generic," Michael, "but totally weird."

The three following Daisy and her trail of orange marmalade in search of the bathroom.

D AISY, IN THE BATHROOM nearly twenty minutes dealing with the mess. Carefully pulling open the zipper top. Cautiously reaching in to pick out and throw away the six metal covers of the jars, the many large pieces of thick, marmalade-covered curved glass. All going into the enormous plastic trash bin overflowing with crumpled wet paper towels.

The others waiting for her outside. Daisy, not daring to guess what they were thinking. Concentrating on cleaning up and on the knowledge that she was there. The uncertainties and exhaustion of travel mostly behind her, with cousins who seemed like nice people even if one of them dressed funny. She was soon to get in their car and be taken to a house on Long Island where she would be able to stay. She would meet new people, see new things, and take care of old business. Maybe she would even see a Broadway show, the Statue of Liberty, the Empire State Building, Ground Zero, and Wall Street, if she could manage it. If not, that was fine, too. She was in New York!

Finishing in the bathroom. Rejoining them. Saying few words, following them out of the terminal to the parking lot where it wasn't raining. Not even a wisp of cloud blemishing a crystal-clear sky.

TWENTY

*T*HWACK!

An arrow hitting, not the yellow bull's-eye but the next ring, the red one surrounding it. Following it, three more arrows, all farther from the bull's-eye. Disappointing. Frustrating.

The next arrow, getting closer to the target.

Elisabeth, pulling into the gravel driveway of their well-tended house with red shutters, a red front door, elegant front porch, impressive lawns, impeccable flower gardens, mature specimen trees. Their house, not unlike others in this typically "gold coast" north shore town. Daisy had noticed that the farther north they went from the highway, the more impressive the houses had become. This one was no exception; it was out of eyesight of any neighbors and, she was told, only a short distance from the Port Washington harbor with its picturesque sailboats.

Elisabeth, shifting into park with a cheery singsong "Here we are."

The four, getting out. Elisabeth, scurrying to help Daisy. Ann, starting into the house. Michael, trying to escape, until caught. Elisabeth, calling him back to help with the luggage.

Michael, responding with "I'll get Josh and David." Slipping away into the house.

"Right," Elisabeth, murmuring, looking toward the house to see if anyone was coming to help and greet the houseguest.

Nobody.

"Daisy, why don't you come inside to meet the family. Richard can get your things in a few minutes."

"Fine, fine," Daisy, saying. "That would be fine." Straightening herself up, her dress, her hair. Walking with the others up the bluestone path to the front door, delighting in all she saw, euphoric at the sensation of sun on her cheeks.

Elisabeth, hurrying ahead through the house, calling the others. Looking for them. No one was coming. Ann, going off to the bathroom.

Daisy, hurrying to keep up with Elisabeth, following her into the kitchen, noticing top-of-the-line appliances and that everything was oversized. Thinking that like America itself, everything in it was *so* big.

Elisabeth, showing her a seat at the long oak table, asking, "Can I get you anything?"

"I'm fine, thank you." But thinking what she wouldn't give for a cup of tea.

"Are you sure?" Elisabeth, asking. "Not even a cup of tea?" Teasing. "You know what they say about Brits here, right? That you're all tea freaks."

Daisy, speechless. Wondering how she could request one now. Her taste buds standing erect, eager for the next tide of tea to wash over them. What time was it anyway?

A quick peek at her watch. Sounds of children's laughter from outside. It was nearing eleven at night her time, though just five there in the kitchen. Feeling suddenly tired. Normally she would be asleep by then. Thinking maybe she could just ask Elisabeth to be shown to her room and be allowed to sleep.

Hearing instead: "We're having a big welcoming dinner for you tonight." Elisabeth, standing across the table, pushing stray hair behind her ear. "My sisters are all coming. There are four of them. They should start trickling in the next hour or so with their husbands and children. Everyone wants to meet you."

Daisy, thinking, oh no, but saying, "Oh, how lovely. Gorgeous." Wondering how she would ever get through it. It was starting in an hour or so? Wondering if she had misunderstood the American accent. Hoping she had.

"Now where are Richard and the boys?" Elisabeth, to herself. "I'll just be a minute." Feeling awkward leaving Daisy alone at the table. "Will you be all right for just a moment?"

"Oh, fine," said Daisy. "I'll be just fine. You take your time."

Elisabeth, blinking, not getting that, not more than a word. But seeing that Daisy was nodding. Elisabeth, scooting out of the kitchen and through the living room, heading for the sliding glass doors. Stepping out into the brilliant sunshine. Stopping dead in her tracks on the deck. Because of what she saw: a large archery target on a stand. Brand new. Yellow arrows sticking out.

Elisabeth, staring at Richard in a perfect archer's position, looking quite expert as he pulled back the bow cable, stretching it to its maximum tautness with the arrow. Releasing. He, Josh, David, Pete, and now Michael, all watching the arrow shooting through space, hitting the target, almost a bull's-eye.

"Whoo hoo!" The boys cheering deliriously at having their father home and awake and doing something they could do.

"Your best shot yet." David, his face gleaming with pride.

Richard, turning to Elisabeth. "Did you see that? Total control of an object moving 333 feet per second. I'd like to see anyone beat that."

Elisabeth, standing where she was, her jaw slinging so far down that it was nearing the waist of her pants.

"You want to try, Lizzie?" Richard, asking her. "Come here. I'll show you how."

"I want to try," the boys all crying, moving en masse to the target to pluck the arrows out, fighting over who got to go next every step of the way.

Elisabeth, stunned, stuttering, "Where did you get that?"

"The sporting goods store. I got to the laser-tag party a few minutes early. I had time to run next door. I thought it would be good for me to rehone my skills after all these years. You didn't know I was an archer, huh?"

Wiping the film of sweat off his face, handing the bow to Pete. Starting toward her. The boys, racing to the starting line, to the spot where Richard had shot from, arguing over the arrows.

"I was good in college." Richard, not noticing Elisabeth's stunned reaction. "Most of us on the dart team did archery, too. I must say it doesn't look like I lost much." Standing in front of her, reveling in the memory of it before breaking back to the present and taking a quick deep breath. "So, where's your houseguest?"

Elisabeth, trying to absorb the image of her husband hitting bull's-eyes. What was he picturing when he lined the arrow up? Swallowing hard. Not answering his question. She didn't have to because Ann was coming out onto the deck with Daisy in tow.

Richard, stepping forward, wiping the last bead of sweat off his temple with the inside of his upper arm, adjusting his black rectangular glasses, taking Daisy's hand in his. "Good to meet you, Daisy." Cupping her hand warmly, noticing how delicate her wrists were. He had never seen such wrists before. "How was your flight?"

Daisy, nodding, comforted by the warmth of his greeting. "Fine. Just fine." Her hand, cozy in his, making her long for more coziness, for bed.

"Mom," Elisabeth, asking, "did you see that Richard is shooting arrows?" Using her eyes to signal the underlying point. "He's a real marksman." Added for emphasis.

Ann, blinking, slowly getting the implication. Turning to look at the target. "Archery, Richard?" Asking, her voice steady, conversational, pleasant, but inside her a case was creaking open. Worries creeping out like garden snakes. Suddenly taking Elisabeth's fears seriously. Then quickly discarding them. They were ridiculous, weren't they?

Richard, unaware of this exchange between his wife and his mother-in-law, continuing with Daisy, "Has Elisabeth shown you your room? You must be tired. It has to be close to midnight your time."

Daisy, almost falling into him in relief. Somebody understood. Answering that she would appreciate being shown her room. Richard, prodding Elisabeth to take Daisy while he went to the car to get her luggage.

Ann, remaining on the deck after the three had gone, surveying her grandsons' attempts at archery. Tamping down questions.

TONGS, PRESSING SIDEWAYS into one of the three thick slabs of steak. Flames below, rising, enveloping the meat, spitting noisily as fat dripped to feed them. A group of them, camped in a circle around the flames. Daisy, back from being shown her room, insisted on joining the real American barbecue, soldierly taking part, fighting drooping eyelids, stifling yawns. Everyone watching the spectacle of meat over flame, titillating olfactory sensations.

Richard, moving the tongs to apply pressure on the other two steaks, muttering aloud, "Tender, like a woman's behind."

Everybody around the grill suddenly staring at him. Surprised to hear him say such a thing in front of their guest, upsetting the sensibilities of an old English lady.

"Richard!" Elisabeth, exclaiming. Who would say such a thing? Answering her own question: Dart Man.

Richard, "Oh, sorry. I can explain."

Elisabeth, hearing his words repeating themselves in her head. Feeling sick.

Richard, chuckling. Turning to Daisy. "I do apologize. I'm just repeating something that happened at work. We have this legal assistant, a guy in his early twenties who wants to be an actor. Apparently—I wasn't there, but I heard about it—one of the senior partners asked him to make up a contract involving legal tender, and this legal assistant says, "Tender, like a woman's behind." Richard, smiling. "Apparently it was very funny."

Daisy, giggling.

Elisabeth, not.

Daisy, looking around, changing the subject. Admiring the expansive lush lawn. "It must take you ages to mow." Picturing herself back in Paul's overalls, picturing her lawn mower.

"Oh, I don't do it. We have gardeners come in. Right, Liz?" Noticing that she seemed far away in her thoughts. Wanting to bring her back into the picture. Wanting her to jump in, to join the conversation.

But she didn't. She was too deep in thought, working out whether she would really call the police on her husband of twenty-one years— and, if she did, what she would say.

And what they would say.

And what they would do.

"ENGLAND HAS *the* most awful weather. For the life of me I don't know why people come," Daisy, looking at the faces around her, trying, despite her exhaustion, to engage them, "but they do. They just keep coming."

Daisy, seated not far from the Olympic-sized built-in swimming pool at a marble-topped cast-iron picnic table, part of a fabulously expensive outdoor garden set that came complete with an outrageously costly woven couch and loveseat, both of which exploded with bright orange-striped pillows, all of high-quality fabrics. Low-hanging candlelight. They were all elbow to elbow—Ann, her five daughters, their husbands, and their children. Daisy, doing her best to remember names and faces.

Most couldn't make heads or tails of Daisy's accent and had broken into private conversations. Ann, Elisabeth, her sisters, and her brothers-in-law couldn't, not really; they were successful only to narrowly vary-ing degrees. Daisy, commenting on the landscaping, knew the names and characteristics of every last thing growing in the garden.

Richard had little trouble with her accent, having the advantage of English clients, even some from western England who had similar ac-cents. He understood Daisy, became her translator, and was charmed by her. Listening intently to all she said. Impressed by her wide knowledge of the plants—his trees, shrubs, bushes, and flowers. Abashed that he couldn't tell a daffodil from a tulip and that he barely ever looked at his gardens. Asking her questions about home. About family.

"We all have long, miserable faces in our family." Daisy, using her hands to pull her cheeks down to demonstrate. "We're not miserable people. We only look like we are."

Mosquitoes and lightning bugs moving in, taking over territory. Grown-ups lathering children in mosquito repellent. Daisy, mentioning that there were no mosquitoes in Liverpool. It went unheard. No one was listening, everyone buzzing around like the insects they were trying to avoid.

The grown-ups, moving indoors. The sisters and Ann, in the kitchen. Their husbands, except Richard who was cleaning the grill, standing in the living room in a circle, beer in hand, discussing the Mets. Records swapped, plays analyzed. Their backs to Daisy who sat unno-ticed on the sofa, mostly forgotten.

Exhausted amid the chaos, noise, and boisterous activity of the chil-dren running in and out of the house, she had found a comfortable spot to settle in. Josh and David, in drying bathing suits, scratching fresh mos-quito bites, and settling down on the other end of the sofa to play Game Boy Advance SP, their heads touching so that both could see the small screen.

Daisy, without warning, fell fast asleep. Her head, thrown unflatter-ingly back on the sofa; her mouth, wide open, facing the ceiling. Snoring.

The husbands noticing, turning away. Elisabeth and her sisters, after finishing in the kitchen, drifting back into the living room, seeing Daisy. Turning away, averting their eyes. Ann, sighing, feeling strangely impatient at the sight.

Michael, "Looks like she's trying to catch dust from the ceiling fan."

David, hunched over Josh's shoulder, saying to Michael, "That's not nice."

Richard, just entering the room, standing in the doorway, greasy barbecue tools in hand, noticing Daisy. Outraged, shooting an accusatory glance at his wife. "You're just going to leave her like that?"

Elisabeth, seeing his point, feeling horribly guilty, realizing she was consumed by thoughts of nothing but him, unable to stop herself from picturing him doing archery.

Richard, sweeping up to the sofa, crouching down in front of Daisy. Gently nudging her awake, calling softly, "Daisy, come on. It's been a long day. Let's get you off to a proper bed."

Daisy, jolted awake, her eyes blinking at the crowd of unfamiliar faces gawking at her. Richard, leaning forward, putting his strong hand under her upper arm, helping her up off the sofa.

"Oh, goodness. I'm terribly sorry." Daisy, embarrassed. "I'm so sorry I dozed off."

"Don't worry about it, Daisy. We understand." Guiding her gently along to the guest room, annoyed to find himself wondering if the others in fact really did.

TWENTY-ONE

Later, deep in the night. Daisy's internal clock telling her it was dawn. Time to get up.

Sitting up in bed with darkness all around. For the first few seconds, confusion. Patching together reality. Spotting a clock: 1:30 a.m. She had been asleep about three hours. Remembering how she had been brought to the room by Richard. What a nice man. Remembered sinking into the pillow. That was all.

Wondering where her toiletries were. Wanting to brush her teeth and use the loo. Spying the bag, pulling back the covers of the bed. Going to the canvas bag, the marmalade bag. It was better now but not perfect. Some areas were still sticky, but they were certainly better. Finding what she needed, trying to remember where the bathroom was. Richard had shown her. It was at the end of the hall, wasn't it? But which way? Right or left? Hoping she wouldn't have to creep around opening wrong doors before she found it.

Putting her hand on the doorknob, admiring it—an old round cut-glass knob that was unlike anything from home. A very nice doorknob. Turning it, pulling open the door. Standing, listening to the quiet, sleeping sounds of the house.

Peeking out into the dim light, looking for a memorable marker.

Padding, barefoot, silently, in her lightweight robe, making no noise as she crept along, not wanting to wake anybody. Three doors down she found it.

Then, creeping back to her room. Listening to her own quiet breath and to the night's stillness in the house. But, hearing a sound in the quiet, a rustling of cotton. It was not her robe, she was sure. It was a sound from behind, from another hall.

Daisy, listening. Sure enough, hushed movement. Not wanting to have a conversation at that hour, hurrying noiselessly back to her room, closing the door with great care. Listening for sounds from the hallway.

Surprised instead to hear noises from outside, from the driveway. A car door, slowly opening. Daisy, crossing the room to the window. Peering out.

Elisabeth, slipping into the car, pulling quietly out of the driveway, backing into the deserted street. Driving away.

Daisy, wondering as she watched, until the red taillights piercing the blackness disappeared.

E LISABETH WASN'T SURE herself what had motivated her to crawl out of bed in the middle of the night, get in her car, go back over the Triboro Bridge, cross Central Park at Ninety-seventh Street, cruise down Broadway to Houston Street, then head east to the Williamsburg Bridge. But she had, and now she was gliding onto the bridge, a traffic-free bridge with wide-open lanes, oldies blasting on the radio, singing her head off, loud and proud at deafening volumes, the center lane all to herself. The glow of city lights was behind her, she had taken part in the mystery of city nights, had become part of its nightly playing out in the dark. Now that she had done it and was heading home again, she knew what had motivated her to crawl out of bed in the middle of the night and into her car.

It was glorious, just glorious.

Releasing inner aspects that had been holed up too long. Drawing something from the inside out like a salve, something from her earlier self, from a time brimming with self-confidence and self-assurance. Reconnecting with another Elisabeth Jetty. One she liked better.

N̲O ONE HAD ASKED DAISY why she'd come to New York. She had expected they would. If they didn't soon, she would have to bring it up herself. Eager to get started.

Sunday seemed too hectic. In the morning they all skittered off to church, except Richard, who was stuck on back-to-back business calls in his home office, from which he emerged yawning, tousled, and hassled. Rubbing his red-ringed eyes, giving Daisy a hasty "Good morning" before fleeing to make his appointment at the car garage for a mandatory annual New York State inspection due no later than today and a well-overdue oil change.

Elisabeth, bags under her eyes, wearing the same strange pants as before. The house was whirring. At one o'clock was Josh and David's year-end piano recital. David would be playing Beethoven; Josh, Chopin. Elisabeth, ironing their white button-down shirts. Searching for two ties. Tracking down four black socks. Praying their shoes still fit since the last recital in January.

Pete had a baseball game; he wouldn't be able to make his brothers' recitals. Ann wouldn't be there for the same reason. Elisabeth, hustling around the house looking for this and that, answering the phone that rang endlessly, making plans for the whole family, which she jotted down on the giant bulletin board in the kitchen. Distracted by everything that crossed her path, shouting orders to study to Michael every time she passed him.

Michael, looking up from his game saying, "You're not really going to wear that to the piano recital."

Elisabeth, looking down at her clothes, which were the same as before except a new shirt. Pleased that he had commented. Richard hadn't said a word. Elisabeth, repeating her mantra: "When you change, Michael, I'll change." Hurrying off with a laundry basket riding her hip.

Daisy, sitting awkwardly, was clear now, at least, as to why Elisabeth was dressed the way she was. Pretending to read her book amid all the activity. Feeling unseen. Thrown a bit because no one had asked her what her business was and why she had come. Hoping someone would. Needing their input. Deciding to talk to Michael, alone on the sofa, across from where she sat. Asking pleasantly about school.

Michael, barely looking her way, saying, "It stinks," rubbing his nose. His eyes on the screen, involved in a battle between his clones and the attacking enemy.

Daisy, trying again. "Are you performing in today's recital?"

Michael, "Nah. I quit piano." Groaning inwardly, anticipating the obligatory speech about regret or grabbing second chances. Strangely, it didn't come. Daisy just turned away, humming quietly to herself. Michael waited a few seconds, but still it didn't come.

Because Daisy wasn't thinking about his decision regarding piano. She was wondering if this Michael would have any good ideas about how to find the other Michael. Wondering what this Michael would do, how he would find someone not seen or heard from in sixty years. Young people usually had good ideas. They knew things. But he seemed reluctant to talk. Daisy, thinking she would try again later.

Lunch—all were called to the table. Daisy, truly hungry. She had missed some meals since she left. She ate heartily what was offered: a bowl of macaroni and cheese with the boys. Elisabeth was too busy hustling around the kitchen to sit and eat—emptying the dishwasher, scrubbing pots, cleaning countertops.

Daisy, uncomfortable doing nothing while Elisabeth was a whirlwind of great magnitude in close proximity. Looking over, watching her a moment, then asking, "Can I make you a cup of tea?"

Elisabeth, looking up from scrubbing maple syrup off the maple cabinetry. Blinking at Daisy quizzically, as if she were parsing some foreign language. But this time it wasn't the language, it was the concept. She smiled, relaxing her shoulders.

Saying, "No, thanks. I wouldn't have time to enjoy it. But you go right ahead if you like. I think I have tea bags." Throwing the sponge into the sink. Heading for the cupboard to explore.

Daisy, bounding to her feet. "Please, Elisabeth, let me. I know where they are. I found them this morning."

Elisabeth, halting. Surprised.

"I hope you don't mind," Daisy, quick to add, "I was up early. I found all I needed."

Elisabeth, feeling admonished. "How thoughtless of me not to show you last night. I'm sorry you had to rummage around in here on your own."

"Oh, that's okay. I was fine. I don't want to be a bother."

"You're no bother," Elisabeth, pleasantly, thinking that that was the understatement of the year. No one, it seemed, had bothered with her one whit. Time to correct that blunder. She would sort through how and why it had occurred at some later time. Perhaps. "Is there anything else you need? Anything else I can show you or get you?" Seeing herself and her family through Daisy's eyes. Feeling like crap.

"Oh, no, I'm fine." Daisy, involuntarily picturing a bottle of Cointreau.

Elisabeth, suddenly noticing the volume of the computer games in the family room. "I'm sorry. The boys can't be out of my sight for a minute." Flying out of the room.

Daisy could hear the shouting. Elisabeth, yelling at David and Josh to stop watching Michael's video games, to get to the piano and run through their pieces. The boys, racing for the piano, arguing about who would go first. Elisabeth, screaming at Michael to start studying. Following him up the stairs, reminding him about a test he should be studying for, one he would be having the next day.

Daisy, picking up her lunch bowl, washing it. Hearing someone at the piano playing Chopin. Stopping. Listening. Such exquisite music. Whoever it was played beautifully. Stealing a peek at who was playing.

Josh. Eleven years old and playing like that. David, pacing the floor behind him, waiting for his turn to practice. Daisy, standing in the doorway, soaking up the moment; the music flowing through her.

When Elisabeth returned, Daisy was sitting near the piano, rapt as Josh played. Elisabeth, asking Daisy if she would like to join them at the piano recital. Doubting she would, but not sure what else to do with her. Elisabeth had been watching to see if Daisy was making any plans, hoping Daisy would ask about trains to the city, tours, information about shows or other Manhattan attractions, or maybe ask to use the phone, but she didn't. She was simply sitting here or there, looking content, hands clasped neatly in her lap—leaving Elisabeth confused.

Daisy, saying yes, she would love to go to the recital, that it would be gorgeous. Certain it would be. These boys could really play. Daisy, more than content to be a part of the musical equation: the vital receiving end. Plus, the boys looked adorable in their suits.

Daisy, also supposing it was possible they might pass a shop along the way that sold Cointreau.

T HE PIANO RECITAL was in a local church. Elisabeth parked, popped out, and hurried inside. She had had to return home for David's music. Before he had left the house he insisted he didn't need the music, that he had the piece memorized. Three blocks from the church he changed his mind.

Elisabeth had to drop Daisy and the boys off and then turn back into choking traffic and roads loaded with mobs of Sunday afternoon shoppers.

Mere seconds before the recital was to begin, she made it back to the church. Searching the rows until she found them. Only seconds before, Richard had hurried in, having gotten held up at the garage with his inspection and oil change. Elisabeth sank into the empty seat next to him, relieved that she had made it in time—that *they* had made it in time, because she had not come back alone.

When she went into the house for David's music, she found Michael splayed out on the couch playing video games, as far from studying at his desk as she was from being an astronaut. As a result, here he was now, sitting three seats from Daisy, his textbook opened, ready to be ignored, whispering to his mother, "Doesn't she have anything better to do?"

Elisabeth, seated between Michael and Richard. Richard next to Daisy.

Michael, saying, "Like she came to New York for this." Looking over at Daisy, with her back erect, hands clasped primly on her lap. Rolling his eyes. "What *did* she come for anyway?"

"Darned if I know." Elisabeth.

"You didn't even ask?"

"It's not my place." Elisabeth, thinking, Where *is* Mom anyway? Elisabeth understood that Ann didn't want a houseguest, but she had assumed that she'd be all over Daisy once she got here. How could she not be? This was her long-lost relative, her first cousin, her mother's niece. How could it be that Ann seemed the least interested of them all? Why was it that she had barely spoken to Daisy last night and had not even called this morning to ask Daisy what she would be doing for the day?

It was very hot in the room. No air-conditioning. Several fans, both ceiling and upright, spun at top speeds, a rapidly clicking metronome. The pianists playing slow pieces could well be doomed. The fans brought no relief. They were not up to the monumental task of cooling the room that had upward of one hundred people and a temperature upward of one hundred degrees.

The audience sweltering, swooning around her. Elisabeth, drowsy, but Daisy—the least accustomed to soaring temperatures—barely noticing. Delighted to be there. Tracing back how she came to be in attendance at an American piano recital, a New York event. Little more than a day ago she didn't even know these boys existed. Now she was ready to root for them, to lay claim to them.

She looked at the program, scanning for their names. They were near the end; a good thirty-five kids were before them. Daisy, settling down, eagerly waiting for the program to begin. Stealing a glance at Michael, wondering if he was studying. She had to lean forward to peer past the chests of Richard and Elisabeth, who were both busy futzing with cameras—Elisabeth with the camcorder, Richard with the digital—connecting attachments, manually focusing. Neither noticing that Michael was staring at the ceiling.

The head of the music school, presenting opening comments. Followed by a line of performers—very young children, four- and five-year-olds. Proud, nervous parents hovered in the aisles to record their first recital. Every heart in the place opened wide to the children. Elisabeth could remember when she was one of those parents, when it was all so new. Michael was the first in the family to take piano, taking the audience by storm. Elisabeth, remembering his first recital: His head barely topped the keyboard, and he had the audience eating out of the palm of his hand. Nobody could come close to matching his visceral connection to the instrument, his ease at the keys. Nobody.

But he was willing to throw it all away.

Heating up again, the cauldron of unresolved anger stirred anew. Elisabeth, turning to look at him. Maybe it was a good thing he was there, and not just so she and Richard could keep an eye on him. Maybe seeing the little children perform would reawaken something in him. Maybe, just maybe, he would go back.

After one look at him, Elisabeth dismissing it. She couldn't miss it. He was totally disconnected. Not even looking at the children, not the little boy playing "Twinkle, Twinkle Little Star" or at the others nervously awaiting their turns, sitting up front in their suits and party dresses and the black leather, faux leather, or patent leather shoes on their little feet that didn't reach the floor. He wasn't reading his book, either. He was staring like a dunce out the window.

Elisabeth, sighing. Yawning. It was so hot in there that it was making her sleepy. Telling herself that she should have forgone the pleasures of her midnight ride. But happy that she hadn't. Putting the backs of her hands on her cheeks to cool them, breathing deeply, thinking again about Richard. Wondering if she should just ask him, broach the subject. But how? "Richard, dear, have you recently discovered any new hobbies? New activities to blow off steam?" Or "So, how do you choose your targets? Must they be tender, like a woman's behind?" Sighing. It was hopeless. Turning her low-level attention back to the little boy at the piano.

For Daisy it was different. She was hanging on to every note. Cherishing the faces of the children. Their little bent wrists, bowed heads, small fingers at work. One after another after another, long past people began shifting in their seats, long past the first sighs of boredom began to be audible, long past when Richard seriously began stifling yawns, hot under his collar, daydreaming of a solid night's sleep, scrolling through his email, the BlackBerry back in position in his left hand, answering urgent emails despite his exhaustion, long after Elisabeth, slumped low in her chair, with continuing deliberations about her Dart Man problem, long after the others in the room had bowed out, Daisy hung in with gusto. Extending the same level of interest to each student that she had given those who had gone before. Clapping just as hard after the sixteenth "Twinkle" as the first. Others may have been bored—clearly they were; others may have been dreaming thoughts a million miles away—clearly they were. Most grown-ups stared blankly ahead, but not Daisy. This was indeed a treat for her.

When at last the time came, she watched keenly. David, stepping up to the piano, his thick dark brown hair untamable like his father's, his face round like his mother's, but the freckles on his nose and cheeks and the dimples around his mouth were all his own. He bowed, sat on the bench, and then inched across to center himself. He adjusted his fingers, lining them up with the middle C. Not a sound in the room as he began.

Daisy, concentrating intently on every note, gently swaying with him, barely breathing, sharing his tight, restrained breaths. Listening closely, hoping before each note, chord, and rest that he would nail it.

He did. A flawless performance, not one mistake, not even a little one.

The audience, impressed. Clapping loudly. Daisy, surprisingly clamorous for one with such small hands. Turning to Richard and Elisabeth to share their excitement, to applaud with them, to partake in their pride at David's unquestionable achievement.

Instead, horrified at what she saw.

Elisabeth and Richard, both snoozing. Dozing. Snoring. Lids closed, chins on chests—the two of them, mother and father, side by side, in seats eleven and twelve in row J. Richard had deep rumbling breaths, Elisabeth had a high-pitched wheeze.

Daisy, clapping with all her might through the arthritic pain it caused. Catching Michael's eye on the other side of them. Reading his look that more or less said, "See what I mean?"

Daisy's eyes, back on David who was standing beside the piano bench, about to take his bow, scanning the room for his family somewhere in the applauding audience. Daisy running defense, refusing to allow him to see what he would see if he located them. Doing two things: Reaching past Richard, slamming Elisabeth in the stomach. Then elbowing Richard hard in his mild paunch.

Michael, watching. Seeing what she did. Totally shocked. He had never seen anyone lay a hand on his parents before. He had never seen anyone treat them with anything other than the greatest respect. Who would ever have expected such a move from this little old lady? Could it be that the woman who had stowed marmalade jam in a canvas suitcase to cross the Atlantic in the cargo bay, the little old woman who had fallen asleep at a welcoming dinner made for her—with her head tilted back and her mouth wide open—wasn't so bad after all?

Michael, processing her through new eyes. Resizing her. Rethinking. He admired those moves: the slam given his mother, the elbowing of his father. There was more to this Daisy than he would have given her credit for.

And even more still: She was whistling! She had two fingers in her mouth—like a man! Paul had taught her. She hadn't whistled in years, not since the boys were young and they used to go to the rugby stadium. But there she was whistling, cheering, turning heads while Richard and Elisabeth sputtered back to consciousness, quickly catching up. Distressed to see that it was David up there taking the bow, that they had dozed through their son's entire performance.

Realizing that they owed Daisy big time.

TWENTY-TWO

AFTER DINNER, MICHAEL." Elisabeth, the evening of the recital. Seated at the rectangular kitchen table with Richard, Daisy, Ann, and all the boys. Piles of Chinese food were spread out before them. Chopsticks, clicking. Hands, reaching simultaneously with giant spoons to scoop out mounds of fried rice, sesame chicken, beef in orange flavor, shrimp in black bean sauce. "You have to study right after dinner. Right, Richard?" Looking across the table at him, seeking support. Trying not to think of darts.

Richard, nodding. "Absolutely. I'll be watching." Hoping it was true. He had a memo to write by morning. He needed it for an 8:00 a.m. meeting downtown.

"I'll be watching, too," Elisabeth, adding. Also hoping it was true. She had their own tax return to do; they had an extension only until Tuesday. There was no time tomorrow; back-to-back meetings were scheduled for all those other people with June 15 deadlines. Dreading the piles of paperwork and forms she had to pore over. It was going to be a long night. Wishing she weren't a CPA.

"Actually, I don't think I need to study," Michael, announcing, sitting back in his chair.

"Really." Elisabeth, trying to remain calm. "Why is that?"

"Studying is a waste of time."

"You're studying." Richard, firmly.

"How about a nice hot pot of tea?" Daisy.

"Not for me." Richard, thinking of cognac.

"Not me, either, thanks," Elisabeth saying. "But if you want one, I hope you'll help yourself. Feel free to make yourself at home." Shooting a glance across the table at her mother, trying to wake her up because, shockingly, Ann was displaying no interest in Daisy whatsoever and hadn't been all evening. Elisabeth had to push her into coming to dinner at all, and since then she and the boys had been locked in a noisy conversation at the other end of the table.

Since the embarrassment of the recital, Richard and Elisabeth had been treating Daisy like royalty. Hanging on to her every word. Making the supreme effort—by Elisabeth, anyway—of struggling through Daisy's formerly inscrutable but now slowly becoming comprehensible accent.

"Well, then, perhaps instead of tea . . ." Daisy, starting.

Richard, getting it. "Would you care for an after-dinner drink?"

Daisy, giggling delicately. "Perhaps I could do with a bit."

"A bit of what?"

"Oh, I don't know. I don't suppose you have any Cointreau?"

"I believe we do." Getting up from the table, knees stiff.

"Lovely. Thank you."

Richard returning with Daisy's drink, standing beside her, slowly sipping his scotch. Checking the time, thinking he should be starting the memo.

Daisy, with the familiar taste on her tongue, comforted. Peering down the long table at Michael. "What is it you have to study, Michael?"

"European history." As if the words themselves were toxic.

"He used to love history," Elisabeth, slipping a plate into a slot in the dishwasher, letting the water run uselessly down the drain in the sink.

Ann, collecting leftovers, spooning them into plastic bins.

Michael, his young voice strident. "What difference does history make? It's not like we ever learn from it. Knowing about World War I didn't stop World War II."

"I wish it had," Daisy, saying, "I could have done without being bombed."

"You were bombed?" Michael's eyes lighting up. "You actually saw bombs falling?"

Daisy, nodding. "Too many to count. We were bombed very heavily. Liverpool was second heaviest in England behind London because of our large ports on the River Mersey, ports that were easily accessible to the United States. We had loads of naval ships stationed there, and we also used the ports for import and export. More than ninety percent of the materials used during the war passed through those eleven miles of quays."

"Really? And you were right there?" Josh, jumping in.

"Right there, all hunkered down. And your great-great-grandmother, our grandmother"—gesturing to include Ann, who was leaning so far inside the refrigerator that she had almost disappeared—"spent the war in her car." Chuckling. "She was a tough old thing, our nana. She had a new car. She was one of the first in the village to own one and certainly the first in the family. Oh, she was so proud—so proud that when the sirens went off, sending us all diving into air-raid shelters, she wouldn't go. She wouldn't get out of her car. She didn't want to leave it unattended, unprotected, afraid it might get bombed. So she sat in it. Everyone yelled for her to get inside. Even the Air Raid Wardens screamed at her. But she ignored them all and just sat there in her car, bombs falling all around her." Daisy, laughing again. "She was a character all right."

For a moment, nobody speaking. Richard, reseating himself at the table, telling himself that the memo could wait. Elisabeth, too, joining them. Those few sentences suddenly opened a whole new family to her, a whole new ancestral history. And for her boys, who sat staring wide-eyed at Daisy, a whole new world.

D AISY WAS OVERJOYED that they liked her stories. They must have, because they sat huddled around the table, plumbing her for more memories. They all got past her accent—except Ann.

Normally, Daisy would have assumed that the distance, which was made painstakingly clear, was just Ann's way, that she was simply a remote person. But Daisy thought she perceived reactions to it from Elisabeth: raised eyebrows, curious sideways glances, puzzled expressions, making her think that it was something new, and darned if Daisy—or Elisabeth, for that matter—knew why.

Elisabeth had to tear everyone away from Daisy's stories, making everyone get on their way, sternly reminding them, over their protests, that it was a school night and that Josh and David still had homework. Pete and Michael had studying, and she and Richard had work. Daisy scurried off to her bedroom to gather her things for the bathroom. Longing for a shower. Relieved to find the bathroom unoccupied. Hoping she wasn't inconveniencing anyone by being there. Deciding to make the shower brief. But that wasn't likely to happen because she couldn't even get it going. Arthritis in her hands and fingers. Making it impossible to turn the shower knob.

Standing at the lip of the tub, staring down at the white-tiled wall in despair, cursing the fixtures. Getting them to turn with her mind, willing it.

Trying again.

This time getting the cold on. The icy water descending fast and furious into the tub, but what was the good of that when she couldn't get the hot water on? Looking around the room to see if there might be something she could use. Lifting her nightgown off the sink, placing it on the knob, wrapping the nightgown around it, making the fixture grippable. Trying to join her fingers to the plumbing, to bring them into perfect harmony like ballroom dancers.

No luck. The nightgown, back in a loose ball on the sink. Daisy, sinking down, shoulders hunched forward, on the porcelain edge of the tub, trying to figure out what to do. There was only one thing. Surrender.

Standing up, turning off the cold water, opening the bathroom door, heading down the hall in search of one of the boys.

The first bedroom door was closed, but there was a light on behind it. Daisy, knocking, startling Michael. Surprised to see Daisy standing there. He had been certain at the knock that it would be one of his parents checking on him, making sure he was studying—which, as it turned out, he was not.

Behind his back, his iPod. Still playing. A discernible beat.

"Can you help me with the bath?" Daisy, asking.

"The birth?" Michael.

"The bath, the shower."

"Oh, sure." Slinking past her and into the hall.

Daisy, following him into the bathroom. "Because of my arthritis I can't turn the knobs."

"No prob." Thinking that anything was better than his parents noticing he still hadn't opened his textbook. He pulled back the shower curtain and easily got the water running. Looking at Daisy over his shoulder, adjusting the temperature. "So, did you really black out your windows?"

"Of course we did," Daisy, saying. "We didn't want to get bombed."

Michael, smiling. Working the knobs, adjusting the temperature and pressure. Daisy, watching him with grateful eyes.

"And did you really have rations?"

"Oh, yes." Daisy, tired of standing, seating herself on the closed lid of the toilet.

Michael, noticing that she was getting comfortable, doing the same, sitting down on the side of the bathtub, his hand remaining under the running shower water.

"It was terrible." Daisy, seeing that he wanted her to go on. "My parents had a bakery, and they had a terrible time trying to keep it going. They had to make do with so little. We were always running out of ingredients. Thank goodness for your great-grandmother, your grandmother Ann's mother. She saved us by sending us food from America—rice, flour, and sugar mainly, things that wouldn't go bad. It could take months for the shipment to get to us.

"Once, I remember, she sent us these bags that were almost as big as you are, one of sugar and one of rice, and everything got mixed together. All the rice was in the sugar bag. Oh, my goodness, it was awful. My father was so distressed. My mother cried for days. I wanted to help, so at night I would sneak out to that bag. It had been dumped into the pantry and forgotten. I dragged my sister Doreen with me, and we worked a few hours while our parents slept. Doreen gave up after the third night, but not me, I kept at it. It took more than two weeks for me to finish picking every single grain of rice out of that sugar bag."

Michael, silent, picturing it. "Cool," he finally said. "What else?"

"I'll tell you what. I'll tell you more tomorrow if you put away that iPod you shoved into your pocket and start your studying."

Michael, smiling, saying, "I'll tell *you* what. I'll study and wait until tomorrow for more stories if *you* promise that one of them is why you came here, what your business is in New York."

Daisy, surprised. Pleased. "You want to know what brought me here?"

"We all do, including my mother. But she thinks it's not her place to ask."

"Well, I'm glad you did, and I think you're going to love it. Do you like detective stories? Because if you do, you're going to love why I came, and you may even be able to help me track someone down." Her eyes, getting big. "Does that sound good?"

Nodding. "Cool."

"Good. Then it's a deal, but only if you get a good grade on your European History test and all your tests after that."

Michael, nodding. Smiling. Pulling his hand out from under the shower water. "Shake on it."

Daisy, smiling, taking his wet hand in hers. Such a nice lad.

TWENTY-THREE

HOURS LATER. THE HOUSE, QUIET. The boys, in bed. Daisy, too. Elisabeth, bleary-eyed and half dead, was like a zombie as she went through her nightly ablutions after her four-hour stint at her home office desk, sifting through a year's worth of W2s, 1099s, interest and dividend statements, monthly bank statements, mortgage statements, crumbled business receipts, checks to charities, and barely legible scrap paper containing information about business investments. Robotically brushing her teeth. Surprised to find two hands cupping her butt.

Richard had crept up from behind. In the bathroom without knocking—at almost one in the morning, on a work night, and after spending his day yawning, zoning out, and sleeping through his sons' recitals. His day, his week, his month, his half year. His life since January. His job constantly pushed him harder with unrelenting stress and ever-increasing hours.

Elisabeth, tingling at his presence. Trying not to picture her five-time baby-bearing torso seeking refuge under her frumpy cotton nightgown, her ever-expanding waistline that was no longer the twist in the Tootsie Roll wrapper but was now the Tootsie Roll, or her sad breasts losing their fight with gravity. Perimenopause. Would he be able to tell? Skipped periods, two in a row after months of more frequent, heavier-than-usual activity.

Her skin nonetheless blinking awake, in full agreement that a twenty-minute suspension from drudgery was welcome indeed. Feeling her stance softening. Her breath, shifting. Her head, falling back in his direction, forgetting that the Crest toothpaste was foaming in her mouth and her toothbrush poised midair.

Remembering. Clumsily finishing her teeth, Richard's hands caressing the contours of her back, hips, butt, waking cells one at a time. Delighting her that her exhaustion was quickly seeping away like water into soil. Turning to him, holding each other with kisses, mapping the course to the bed. Murmurings transporting them there. Anticipation sweeping through their soft landing. Palms, fingers, lips, mouths, packed with pent-up agendas, now unleashed, following unspoken orders, relishing the journey, prizing the finish.

But Elisabeth's quest unexpectedly ended. Too early and certainly not to be prized. Her hopes, ruthlessly dashed, her expectations quashed, her satisfaction left unclaimed.

Because of what he said. And when he said it.

When all was in place, all set for the big finish. Everything, just right, words, whispered: "Tender like a woman's behind."

She could hear the smile in his voice. The words, ousting her from the place she had been, ripping her away so thoroughly that there was no way back.

Elisabeth, hobbling to the finish.

Richard, sprinting mightily.

Elisabeth, rolling away, hollow.

Richard, sleeping, spent.

ELISABETH, MINUTES LATER IN BED, blinking into the dark night—thinking, sweating, listening to Richard's deep slumber. Reaching a decision. Once again, creeping out of bed. Once again, down the long hallway silently in the dark. Down the creaky old stairs, holding her breath until she was out the door and on the driveway.

Completely unaware that Daisy, who was still not entirely on U.S. time, was wide awake behind the guest room door, watching quizzically. Wondering if all Americans didn't sleep at night or just this family. She watched as Elisabeth got in her car and headed out into the darkness, not knowing that someone else was awake in the house.

Michael, his forehead resting on the palm of his hand, was heavily involved in his European History textbook, devouring the history of England during World War II so deeply that he didn't even hear his mother go.

E LISABETH HAD NO TROUBLE finding Richard's bike. He had been locking it in the same garage—a block from his office—for decades. She recognized the red mountain bike at first glance. The only bike there, it was chained to an old, dented, rusty rack.

She got the lock's combination right on the third try. It wasn't his birthday; she had tried that first. It wasn't their anniversary; she had tried that second. It was what she had considered the longest shot and found exceedingly touching: her birthday.

The lock sliding open. Elizabeth, breathing very calmly, inhaling the smell of grease, oil, tires, exhaust. A car horn, blaring angrily on Fifty-seventh Street, just outside the wide garage entranceway. Elisabeth, trying to look convincing, as if she were accustomed to unlocking her husband's bike at 2:15 on a Sunday morning. Eyeing the attendant. Waiting, crouched, breathing evenly, until he was otherwise engaged and had drifted off into the bowels of the cavernous, echoey garage. Elisabeth, pocketing the chain and lock, wheeling the bike to the SUV, hoisting it up, shoving it inside. Closing the door calmly, moving in a way that would not draw attention.

Pulling away from the garage slowly, checking the rearview mirror for any signs of distress. Nothing. The attendant was just walking back into his little booth, not having noticed a thing, flipping a coin in the air, whistling.

Elisabeth, feeling her lips curve into a smile. Heading west, toward Central Park.

CERTAINLY ELISABETH NEVER would have believed that some hot summer night in mid-June, at age forty-four, she would be wheeling her husband's bike into Central Park at East Sixty-seventh Street. Moving quickly along a path to a playground situated not far from her illegally parked, emergency-flashing SUV. The playground had a black metal fence around it with a gate. It was empty, naturally, at that hour.

Perfect.

Checking for possible thugs or rats, surprisingly unafraid, making sure not to lose sight of her car. Wheeling the bike quickly over to the shiny, black, three-foot fence that was spiked on top. Leaning the bike there. Leaving it.

Turning and stepping away from it. Back up the path. Noticing she had somehow broken a fingernail. Tearing the hanging piece off with her teeth, spitting it out, smoothing the jagged edge with her thumbnail. Thinking about Richard discovering his missing bike. Hurrying along the concrete path, turning back to take one last look. Paying her last respects, mumbling good-byes.

Boom! Crashing headfirst into something hard. The sound of bodies colliding, of clothes shifting. A cool metallic edge of something nicking the corner of her eye.

Spinning around to see a badge with the name of a lieutenant, one of the two New York City police officers blocking her way.

"Good evening." One of them.

Elisabeth, completely shocked, murmuring in kind.

"That your bike?" The other, gesturing over her shoulder with his chin.

Elisabeth, turning around to look at Richard's bike. Struck dumb, dumb and worried. They must have seen her leaving it there. They had to have. It would be better not to feign surprise.

Her insides churning; a destructive storm blowing through, whipping her organs around in different directions. Every part of her was drenched in adrenaline. Her heart pumping triple time. Afraid to hesitate for too long, fearing that she wouldn't have a voice when her mouth opened. She nodded and tried to look normal even though her tongue was overturned and stuck halfway down her throat. Looking past them to their car with its lights blazing, pulled alongside hers, emergency flashers calling out in the night. A young couple, arm in arm, passing on the sidewalk, heads and shoulders touching, fingers interlocked. Elisabeth, eyes returning back to the cops, but unable to look them in the eye. Swallowing hard. Her jagged fingernail forgotten.

"You mind telling us why you're leaving your bike there?"

Unfortunately, Elisabeth *did* mind telling them. Wanting to ignore the question, get back in her car, and hit the road, but evidently they wanted an answer. They stood waiting, staring her down, more than idly curious.

Elisabeth, snickering. All of a sudden the whole thing was so stupid that it was funny. She had been wondering for weeks whether she should call the cops, confess her suspicions, and throw her husband's name into the mix. Also wondering whether she would really be able to do it, rat out her faithful husband of twenty-one years, and if there really was anything to rat out. And now here she was being handed all this on a silver platter. She could feel the cops' eyes penetrating her, reading her openly. She had to answer; that much was clear. But how? That much was not.

"I don't want it." Elisabeth, dimly hoping that would be enough. Of course it was not.

"What's your name?"

Elisabeth, telling them.

"You live around here?"

Her response causing four eyebrows to rise upon both cops: the tall, barrel-shaped, thirtysomething, red-lipped, dark-eyed, round-jawed, Hispanic-looking one and his shorter, wide-handed, big-footed, light-brown-haired, late-twenties, Irish-looking partner.

"Port Washington, Long Island? And you drove all this way at two in the morning to leave a bike at a Central Park playground?"

This wasn't going well. Elisabeth was no longer snickering. Actually, she was slightly panicked. Did they have the right to haul her off to the police station? This might not turn out to be such a funny story after all.

"Actually, it's my husband's. He keeps it at his office." Her voice, wavering slightly. Attempting to stop it from doing that. "I've been wanting him to get rid of it for years. It's such an old piece of crap. It must be dangerous riding downtown on it. But he's attached to the old hunk of junk, so what I did was . . . well, you can see what I did. He'll think it was stolen. He'll have to buy a new one." Finishing with a chuckle. Thrown in for good measure.

Then standing there like a schoolgirl: feet together, pointed forward; hands at her sides; head held high. She could feel them continuing to size her up, looking from her to the bike and back again, going through her words and sniffing around for a lie, a hole, a discrepancy.

She saw it. It was small, almost imperceptible, but still she saw it—a slight shoulder movement, the slightest, by the Hispanic-looking one. There was the smallest letting go, a loosening, a guard going down, shoulders dropping, lowering by a hair, a degree, nothing more. But for Elisabeth, enough to buck her up. Not home free yet but perhaps on the way.

"Where's your husband's office?" The Irish-looking one with jaw thrust forward and eyes slightly narrowed, looking skeptical.

"He's a lawyer, a partner at a law firm on Fifty-seventh Street."

The Irish-looking one, now even more skeptical. Sniffing the air—he actually did sniff the air—with an upward movement of his face.

"Your husband's a partner in a law firm?"

"Yes." Elisabeth, chuckling lightly as if sharing their incredulousness. Mutually agreeing that she was some kind of a kook. "He'd die if he knew I was here in Central Park in the middle of the night, leaving his bike."

"You know, we've been looking for someone who's been riding around on a bike like that. Dart Man." The Irish-looking one.

Elisabeth, feeling his intense gaze, trying not to blink. Did she? Did she blanche or stiffen? Were signs surfacing all over her face?

"Have you heard of him?" The Hispanic-looking one, looking into her eyes. Could he see into her? Read her fear?

In a way this was the moment she had been waiting for, the moment that would crack open the lid and squeeze out the truth. It would force her to conclude, to confront what it was she really thought—force fantasy into fact or fact into fact. It would make her come to an understanding, admit to herself what it was she really thought because, honestly, she didn't know what it was she really thought. Was her husband really Dart Man?

She still didn't know, but she did reach one conclusion: If it was him, she wasn't going to rat him out. "I think I heard about it on the radio at work. I'm a CPA." Irrelevant, she knew, but throwing it out. Attempting accreditation.

Four eyebrows going up again, but the Hispanic-looking one suddenly appearing bored. Believing her. Smelling the truth. Ready to move on.

The Irish-looking one, harder to convince. "This Dart Man's been riding around on a red mountain bike like that one. Would you know anything about that?"

Her moments of doubt, gone. Firm and committed now, toughening up under the scrutiny, employing a new approach to the Irish-looking one. Seeing him now as an IRS agent, a certain type that she had dealt with countless times at countless audits—the suspicious ones who were looking for the big bust, disappointed that she was clean, driven to stretch out the probe when there was no reason to.

"I know nothing about that. I only know that someone's going to get a present of a free hunk-of-junk bike in the morning and my husband's going to get a new one—a shiny safe one he'll eventually get attached to." Shrugging nonchalantly. Lobbing light humor. "It might take him twenty years."

They listened, taking it all in. The Hispanic-looking one, clearly convinced. Scratching the back of his neck, shifting his gaze, scanning the park in the dark of the night. The Irish-looking one, stubbornly crossing the line. She could see it.

"Now, if there's nothing more," Elisabeth, sweetly, but with some authority. Transmitting the message that she was old enough to be their mother—not really, but close enough. "I'd like to get going."

The Hispanic-looking one nodding, stepping back, opening the path to her.

The Irish-looking one having to say something, to assert his authority: "Go ahead. Get going." As if it were an order.

Elisabeth, controlling her walk back to the car. Her hand on the door handle, looking back at them. Seeing them getting into their flashing car behind hers.

Elisabeth, driving away orderly. Obeying speed limits down Fifth Avenue, checking her rearview mirror every few seconds. Gratified that no one was following her, relaxing. Rolling back the tape, replaying the scene. Her brush with the law.

Maybe it would be funny in the retelling after all.

Settling more deeply into the driver's seat, relaxing. Taking a deep breath. Looking forward to the Williamsburg Bridge.

Where she let loose: laughing, speeding, blasting music, singing, bobbing in the driver's seat. Her chest and stomach pressing into the taut seat belt, her left hand belting out the beat on the steering wheel. Bursting with pleasure, relief, disbelief at her own actions, her big caper.

Giddiness all the way home.

TWENTY-FOUR

THE NEXT MORNING, Elisabeth back in a business suit. Her teenage attire, retired during office hours, slung over the back of the low silk chair in the bedroom, awaiting her return, which she would do. When Michael pulled up his drawers, so would she.

The first morning after her escapade was awful, starting with a painful rising. Fifteen minutes after the alarm went off, her cheek, still pressed deeply into the pillow, her stomach, down, one arm hanging over the side of the bed, nearly touching the floor. Then Josh broke in, rousing her, informing her that her alarm had been going for fifteen minutes and that she had better get up or he would miss the bus. They all would. Where was their breakfast?

Somehow Elisabeth made it. She got their breakfasts, got them on the bus, got to work, vowing to cut out her nighttime madness. Rubbing her tired eyes. Fretful. Today was Monday. Richard rode his bike downtown. Elisabeth, plagued by guilt and worry. He would call to tell her. How could she talk to him? What would she say when he told her? Her naughty little secret. Dreading his call, trying to focus on someone else's taxes.

By lunchtime she was relieved that she had made it through the morning. Two open, untouched Chinese food containers on her desk, a set of chopsticks poking out of one. Up to her chin in tax returns but not attending to any. Instead, her eyes on her computer. Gazing at the screen, her head cocked, drinking in pictures of cocker spaniel puppies.

Afraid of his call. Half hoping it would come so she could get it over with. Counting the moments, mentally tracking his day. Switching to Shetland sheepdogs. Sampling possible responses for when Richard told her the news about his bike.

Because now that she sat in the light of day, she could hardly believe what she had done.

D AISY, ALONE. THE FAMILY, GONE. The boys went to school in a whirlwind. Richard left before Daisy awoke, but she couldn't help hearing Elisabeth blowing through the house like a fast-moving hurricane. The whole morning was combustible because of Elisabeth's oversleeping, sprinting to catch up. But now it was quiet, and Daisy was alone in the garden.

The sun, beaming down radiantly in glorious hues of gold, a sight sorely missing in Liverpool. Daisy, with nothing else to do, lingering outdoors in the beautiful gardens and exquisite landscaping. Walking slowly along the perimeter of border flowers, the foxgloves, lilies, and geraniums, inspecting the flowers, fingering them, smelling them. Ambling over and around the full property: two acres. Watching the colorful birds of many different species skirting around the trees, busy in their lives. Daisy, testing herself by identifying the trees: several apple trees, a cherry tree, a magnificent Japanese maple, a giant ash in a far corner of the back property, close to a walnut tree, a sassafras, and several magnolias.

Back into the house to make herself a cup of tea. Then back out with it, sipping it on a low-slung chair by the pool, listening to the different calls of the birds, a wide variety; some were similar to home, some were new. Hearing a distant fire bell ringing, lawn mowers, leaf blowers, occasionally the faraway rumbling of trucks and closer sounds of passing cars.

In the afternoon she went to her room, opened her suitcase, and pulled out the letters. Treating them with care, she brought them back out to the garden to look again at his picture and reread the old letters from New York.

While in New York.

A T 6:30, ELISABETH, pulling into Ann's driveway, parking. Getting out.

Walking into the house, a lot on her mind. Richard had not called all day, meaning that the news of his bike would happen face-to-face rather than via the safer, more desirable method of over the phone.

Suddenly barreled down by Michael, his iPod slung around his neck, unplugged, wearing his droopy jeans. Frantic. Telling her not to have her usual gab with her mother. He had to get home.

Elisabeth, perplexed, annoyed, telling him he would have to wait. She had to get his brothers together and say hello to her mother. Michael, huffy, impatient, following her into the kitchen, the tips of his feet crashing into the heels of hers.

Ann was busy, scrubbing the kitchen counter. Scrubbing, with oomph. Frown lines circumnavigating her face. Elisabeth, greeting her. Michael, hurrying Elisabeth along, pressing her to get a move on. Elisabeth, unable to get an unbroken sentence out to her mother, asking Michael where the fire was.

"I have to get home to Daisy."

"Daisy?" Elisabeth's eyes widening, not hiding her surprise. Realizing then that she hadn't given Daisy a thought all day. Scrambling to remember if she even knew what Daisy had planned to do. Casting back to the morning, when she had overslept and flown out of the house. She hadn't even exchanged a word with Daisy. Daisy had spent the whole day without interacting with a single member of the house. What must she think?

"Yeah, Daisy," Michael, in a tone of voice that implied, "You got a problem with that?"

Elisabeth, looking at her mother. She could see all manner of emotions in her face but could read only half. She didn't want to attempt the other half.

Michael, shifting his weight from foot to foot. Fidgeting with his iPod, saying, "Can we get going?"

"Go get your brothers. I'll be right there." Elisabeth, turning to her mother as he left the room. "Where'd that come from?"

Ann, "I thought you'd know. Fast friends, indeed." Sarcastic. Haughty.

Elisabeth, shaking her head. "I have no idea. The truth is, I'm sorry to say, that I forgot all about Daisy. I feel terrible."

"Don't. Why'd she even come anyway? When is she leaving?"

"I don't know. Didn't she just get here?"

"Michael hardly ate dinner. He didn't talk. He didn't listen to music. He read right through it, saying he had to study. His textbook was practically on his dinner plate." Like it was an accusation of the highest order. The next words spit out more fiercely. "Apparently he made some deal with Daisy that he'd do well on all his tests."

It was hard to say which woman felt worse.

Ann, "I made his favorite dinner. I spent all day on those barbecued ribs. He barely touched them."

Michael, flying back into the kitchen, his brothers in tow. "We'll be in the car. Hurry."

Mother and daughter, locking eyes. KO'd by someone a quarter their size. A fraction of their weight.

•   •   •

ELISABETH, SUCKING IT in on the car ride home.

Pulling into her driveway feeling terrible, embarrassed that she was able to give a houseguest, a cousin, so little thought. Cringing at what Daisy must be thinking. Guessing she must be disappointed and disgusted.

Michael, bolting out of the car before it was even in Park. Up the porch steps two at a time. Josh and David were slower, struggling to lift their heavy unzipped backpacks off the car floor. Both boys yanking too hard, their notebooks, workbooks, and textbooks spilling out all over the car floor. Then somehow lunch boxes, mixed up. Both boys steadfastly refusing to carry in his brother's.

The argument, finally ending. Elisabeth, following Josh and David up the porch steps. Telling herself that tomorrow she would make proper arrangements for Daisy. Today was just a consequence of her oversleeping. Tonight she would stay in her bed and get some sleep. Tomorrow would be a better day in every way.

Following them into the house. Seeing something different in the family room. Continuing into the kitchen, seeing something different there, too: flowers. In vases, placed all over the room. On tabletops. Counters. Windowsills. Elisabeth, blinking twice, stunned.

Daisy, sitting on a high stool at the counter, carefully watching Elisabeth's reaction. "I hope you like it. Please don't mind that I went at your garden with clippers. I only took flowers you had plenty of, of course—some geraniums, butterfly weed, and Iceland poppies in the vase here and over there. In that vase some blue bugles, musk roses, and violets. You have so many beautiful wildflowers, I couldn't resist helping myself," smiling guiltily, "to your sneezeworts, your gorgeous oxeye daisies and your poppies. Most of them couldn't even be seen outside. There were all in the back, hidden by high shrubs." Looking for a reaction. Not getting any.

Daisy, her delicate neck wrinkled and stretched, her head held high, looking over at Elisabeth with sympathetic eyes. "Oh, you've had a long day, haven't you? How about I make you a nice hot cup of tea?"

Elisabeth was not moving, not speaking. Only standing there at the kitchen counter, blinking, in a light blue knit top and a string of pearls with matching pearl earrings. Dark blue puffy crescents rose out of sunken hollows under both eyes. Where her eyelashes met her eyes was rung in deep red. Her mouth sagged, and its outside corners were flanked by parentheses. She looked tired, careworn, and beaten—the offer of a cup of tea was the least Daisy could do.

Elisabeth, declining. Shaking her head. Wanting to get out of there. Wondering if she had hit bottom yet.

"I like the flowers, Daisy." Michael, noticing how stumped his mother was. His arms were thrust straight down, his hands balled in his low front pockets, standing there, rocking back and forth from toe to heel. "It looks good in here." A look at his mother, a tone of voice as if to say, "For a change."

Elisabeth, glancing from the kitchen into the living room. Flowers were in there, too, changing the room that had been put together by a host of interior designers. The elaborate living room furniture, window treatments, and Persian rugs were all top quality, all enormously expensive, all put together by someone else. The whole house was redone when David started kindergarten four years ago. Elisabeth and Richard had agreed that the time had come to upgrade to more mature, sophisticated, formal living areas. The last of the children was in school, so it was time to lose the playroom look. But Elisabeth had been without time or confidence to do it herself. Looking at it now, she was able to appreciate how tasteful it was, but how unreflective of them. She didn't even want it. She should sell it all on eBay and go back to the comfortable college dorm room, playroom, or ski lodge look.

Turning her attention back to Daisy, smiling, saying, "It does look nice in here. Thank you so much, Daisy. I'm sorry we weren't home for dinner. I hope you've been able to find something to eat."

"Oh, don't worry about me." Daisy, making the under suggestion of the year. "I'm fine. I had a gorgeous day, gorgeous." She had managed to make do. She had several cups of tea, and scrounging around in the refrigerator had yielded a few hard-boiled eggs and a package of American cheese that she had sampled, carefully unpeeling the cellophane. She had never had it before, not even when she was almost marrying an American. Despite a small stomach growling, she had been content all day. Eagerly anticipating getting closer to that American she had almost married.

"Oh, good." Elisabeth, showing guilt to the door. At least for the moment. Reminding herself to ask her mother later why she hadn't invited Daisy for dinner with her and the boys. Maybe Daisy would have eaten those barbecued ribs. "I just need a minute to change out of my work clothes." Looking at Michael who was still in low-flung jeans. Making a point of noticing.

"Come on, Ma. Quit it already."

"I'll stop dressing like you do when you do." Elisabeth, prancing out the door.

Michael, rolling his eyes, watching her go.

Daisy, turning to Michael. "I believe you and I have some business to discuss."

"I did okay on the test. I can do better. I begged my teacher to let me take another tomorrow. She hasn't decided yet, but I'm going to study tonight either way. Will you tell me anyway? I did do better than on the last test. Who are you tracking down?"

Daisy, looking him over. He had a guarded, eager expression, trying hard not to give anything away. But he was a breeze to read nonetheless. Daisy, seeking her own boys in him, catching glimpses, recollecting their thirteen-year-old lives. Finding commonalities—the thirteen-ness. It was there. She could see it.

"I will tell you, of course I will. I'm happy to. Should I wait for your brothers and parents?"

A wave of his hand making it clear where he stood.

So Daisy beckoned Michael, patting the top of the counter stool beside her.

Michael, getting on it, bending his knees all the way, slipping his big feet on the high top rung. Listening. Daisy, talking. Telling him everything. The past flowing out of her mouth and into his young ears, open wide and waiting.

Michael's head, spinning with the details. When she finished, he popped off the stool and pulled on her hand that had so little weight to it. Yanking her to her feet. Marching her out of the kitchen.

"His name is Michael, like mine?" That, making him happy. "Baker? We'll find him on the computer. We can probably find him tonight. Come on. You might be able to talk to him before bedtime!"

Daisy's hand, rising to her collarbone, her arthritic fingers spread out like a bumpy fan. Allowing herself to be pulled down the hall, shuffling hurriedly over the hardwood floor in low-heeled shoes. Permitting him to pull a chair over for her at the computer. Getting excited herself as it blinked on, listening as Michael tossed out plans. They would start by googling *Michael Baker*.

Daisy's heart, pounding.

Michael, keying in *Michael Baker*, typing faster than Daisy anticipated. He was very efficient, like a secretary in the old days, in the days when no thirteen-year-old boy would ever have been caught dead typing.

He got 10,840,000 results.

Michael, frowning. "His name is too common. Do you know his middle name?"

"Leonard."

Michael, entering it. Got 6,010,000 results, including thousands regarding a murderer with the same name in Minneapolis. Michael, frowning again. Working on new approaches when his mother walked in. Her baggy jeans, riding low, biting a nail, her hair spilling untidily forward.

An overflowing laundry basket resting on her left hip, her arm around it like a friend. Telling Michael to get started on his homework.

Making Daisy feel guilty.

"No, Mom. I've got to do this. A few more minutes."

"What's 'this'?" Elisabeth, asking.

Michael, bubbling over, telling her. Elisabeth, eyeing Daisy as he spoke. For confirmation. Daisy, nodding. David, at the piano doing scales. Elisabeth, finally learning why Daisy had come.

"I want to help her find him," Michael, finishing up.

"Do you want his help?" Elisabeth, asking Daisy.

"I would like that very much, if it were possible." Daisy, gracefully and gratefully.

"Fine." Elisabeth. "I'll help, too—but not much longer tonight. It is a school night. I've got to go over David's math homework and test Josh on his Spanish. He has a test tomorrow."

"And tomorrow, Mom, I want to come straight home and not go to Grandma's. We can start right after school. You'll be here, won't you, Daisy?"

Daisy, nodding, unable to imagine where else she could be.

Elisabeth, saying, "It's okay with me if you get your homework done and if Daisy doesn't mind." Thinking her mother was going to have a cow when she heard.

"Mind? It would be my great pleasure." Daisy, responding.

Michael, thinking, "That's telling her."

Very satisfied.

TWENTY-FIVE

RICHARD, WEARY, WALKING in the front door close to eleven. Putting down his briefcase, pouring himself a drink, noting that the level of Cointreau in the bottle had gone down. Picturing Daisy sipping a glass, speculating that the family had been graced with another night of stories. Wishing he had been there.

The house was quiet. He turned on the TV, flipping briefly through the channels as if they were pages of a magazine, making his way through his drink. He would have these few minutes before going upstairs and telling Elisabeth what had happened. He had tried calling several times throughout the day to tell her. But couldn't reach her.

She was awake when he walked in. Sitting on the bed, leaning back against a tall pile of pillows, a laptop propped up on blankets over her stretched legs. Saying, "Hey" to him but not looking up from the screen. Busy on the computer. Richard, sympathetic that she still had taxes to deal with.

But Elisabeth wasn't doing taxes. She was scrolling through images of Old English sheepdog puppies. Hiding behind them.

Richard, loosening his red and blue tie with his forefinger, undoing it in small, incremental, right and left movements. His head, moving in the same rhythm in opposite directions. The sound of silk shifting silk. Elisabeth, pressing the arrow down key, moving the screen slowly so as not to miss a puppy, hearing, "You're never going to believe what happened today."

"Oh?" Showing only a minimal amount of interest.

Richard, "Somebody stole my bike."

"No!" Acting totally surprised.

"Yeah. Right out of the garage. They took the lock and everything."

"How'd they do that?" Acting incredulous. Her eyes wide.

"Damned if I know. It was made of kryptonite. The attendant claims he saw nothing." Richard, taking his usual great care placing his tie on the rack. The rest of the house could be in shambles for all he cared, but not his suits, ties, shirts. Those he babied, keeping them picture perfect.

"No kidding." Elisabeth, in all seriousness, as if trying to imagine such a thing. Saving for later, for private moments for many years to come, the deep introspection and speculation about how she could have done what she had done. Now she was just working at keeping guilt and shame at bay and the bit of laughter that went with it.

Richard, sitting on the edge of the bed, affecting the mattress beneath her. Untying his shoe. Pulling it off from the heel. The sound of a sock slipping out of a tight, stiff space. The heat of his foot, released into the air. Richard, rolling down his sock, picking the tip out of his toes, saying, "The attendant has no idea when it happened, but the man before him, on the six p.m. to one a.m. shift, said he was pretty sure that it was there when he was. The next guy didn't see anybody taking it. You'd think it would take some time to cut through kryptonite. You'd think it would make noise and draw attention. You'd think someone might notice." The sound of his other shoe coming off. A trace scent of leather.

"You would," Elisabeth, agreeing. Needing a place to hide. Finding one. Reaching over and picking up her glass of red wine from the bedside table. Her fourth. Downing it. Wiping a runaway drip off the side of the glass with her tongue, the last drop.

Richard, standing up, undoing his belt, yanking it fast through the belt loops like a subway train making no local stops. Throwing it on the bed. It kept its coil.

Looking at Elisabeth as he unbuttoned his shirt, stretching his neck and jaw, moving his head out of the way so he could get to the top button. "It blows not having a bike. I had to take the subway downtown. What a nightmare. I haven't done that in over seventeen years."

Elisabeth couldn't go on. Putting her hand to her forehead, announcing, "I have a terrible headache." Turning to the bedside table. Clicking off the light. The back of her head falling abruptly onto the pillow, closing her eyes.

Leaving Richard puzzled. His tailored white shirt untucked, his fingers manipulating the fourth shirt button. Blinking at her suddenness. "I'm sorry, Lizzie. You should have told me sooner."

"It just came on." Rolling over, pressing her hip into the mattress. Roosting in. Knowing that the four glasses of wine would make her stay in bed. That she wouldn't be able to fly through the streets of Manhattan and shoot gleefully over the Williamsburg Bridge. Drifting off to sleep, picturing who might be gliding down the hot city sidewalks on her husband's bike. Thinking about Daisy and her World War II soldier, about her finding him and seeing him again after sixty years.

Two rooms away, Michael, too, falling asleep, Daisy's story on his mind—how she had a watch in *his* house that was inscribed by Arthur Rubinstein! How she had had an American boyfriend, a World War II soldier, and that he, Michael, was going to track him down.

Richard finished undressing. Lining up the press in the legs of the navy blue pants, balancing the jacket evenly over the wooden hanger, putting both pieces in together in the closet in the dark.

TWENTY-SIX

L
OUD VOICES IN HIS HEAD telling him not to, but there he was,
doing it anyway.

Dennis's long fingers clenching the ballpoint. Like it or not, it
was done. The contract for the purchase of a huge house in Chessex was
signed. It was legal. He had been won over by his wife; she had pulled
out and made use of every tool and every strategy in her possession. She
should have been a politician. No one else he knew came close to matching her powers of persuasion. Dennis eventually agreed that they could
do it without the involvement of his mother. He had sold all the stock,
emptied the bank accounts, liquidated the mutual funds, and cleared out
the nest egg.

Emitting a slow, deep breath as he put down the pen. Looking across
the table, a few beads of sweat glistening his upper lip.

Amanda, smiling back at him. Wearing a yellow top, red lipstick,
dangling silver earrings. Her hair was tied back; her blue eyes, dreamy.
Her long arm stretched out to place a cool hand over the top of his sweaty
one. His fingertips, leaking perspiration. Marks on the wood were the
moist imprints of his hand. Her clear, pale hand resting over his.

Dennis, looking out the window at the rain that was steadily falling.

He would like to call his mother but didn't have the number with him. Wondering how he would get it, his thoughts interrupted by the estate agent with the big mustache. Saying something before sliding the contract across the table to Amanda, who signed in big, dark, bold, swirling letters.

TWENTY-SEVEN

THE INTERNET YIELDED no real results. Michael Baker was way too common a name, as was Michael L. Baker and even Michael Leonard Baker. Michael, Daisy, Josh, David, and even Pete, when he was around, spent long hours huddled around the computer every afternoon after school. This left Ann with just the other grandchildren, begrudging Daisy her visit, her time. Wishing she would go back already.

Elisabeth's days were spent in quiet guilt. Nights she was deep under the covers, her back to Richard. There were no more midnight rides. Anxiously waiting to hear that Dart Man had struck again, hoping to hear that Richard was cleared. So far, nothing. Morning after morning she sat with feet planted in low-heeled pumps on the floor under her desk, spreadsheets on the screen, but she was staring across the room, seeing the empty night highway unfolding before her. Hearing her own voice belting out songs over the stereo, seeing the colored lights of the city, windows rolled down, smelling the aroma of millions of lives. And the view from the bridge, all gone—like Richard's two tires, handlebar, narrow black leather seat.

Now from him, stories about the subway. Complaints. Vows to replace his bike as soon as he got a minute. Tales from below. Of straphangers. Vermin. Dirt. Delays.

◆ ◆ ◆

A JOINT DECISION. To start the search at square one.

The address in Brooklyn: 1]440 Second Street. Brooklyn, an easy driving distance. Michael Baker could still live there. He could. An argument over who would go. Elisabeth, thinking just her and Daisy.

Michael, insisting on going, too. Mapquesting the directions. Printing them out.

Elisabeth, still refusing. It was the weekend before his week of Regents exams. Surely he should use the time to study, not driving to Brooklyn on what was more than likely a fool's errand.

Michael, arguing hard. He wanted to go. If Michael Baker was there, he wanted to meet him. He ran to get his backpack, came back feeling indomitable. Showing his mother that he had done an extra-credit research paper for his European History teacher about Liverpool during World War II. His class had studied only London, but Liverpool was a key player, too. With Daisy's help, and in between utilizing people-finder Web sites, Michael had pumped out a paper about Liverpool. Showing his mother. He had gotten an A.

TWENTY-EIGHT

THE THREE OF THEM, en route to 11440 Second Street, Brooklyn, New York. Early Saturday morning. Zipping by the Brooklyn Museum, the enormous Brooklyn Library, the Brooklyn Zoo, the Brooklyn Botanic Gardens. Hordes of people.

Elisabeth, making a left onto Prospect Park West, the main boulevard. People, promenading. Babies in strollers, dogs on leashes. A gorgeous, lush park, very much like Central Park, on one side; it had been designed by the same team, Olmstead and Vaux, after they had finished in Manhattan. Magnificent architecture, buildings more than a hundred years old. Nineteenth-century brownstones four stories high; flowers spilling abundantly out of window boxes; bikes, skateboards, Rollerblades; children jumping rope, drawings made with thick pastel-colored chalk on the sidewalks.

Daisy, in the front seat. Her heart, pumping rapidly as they neared the address.

Michael, in the back, reading the directions and the history of that section of Brooklyn: Park Slope. Flipping through the chapter on the Brooklyn Bridge. Showing pictures. Elisabeth, nearing Second Street, scanning the curb for parking spots that didn't exist.

Richard, at work on a Saturday. David and Josh were at friends' houses, playing computer games. Pete was on third base, hoping to turn the game around. Ann was at the hairdresser, complaining nonstop about Daisy to the woman who was coloring her hair.

After sixteen rotations around the block, a spot opened up when an old Volkswagen pulled out. Elisabeth, ramming the SUV into the spot. It was so tight between the car in front and the car behind that she and Michael couldn't get over to Daisy on the sidewalk. They had to talk to Daisy over the top of the car as they confirmed which way to walk, finally heading uphill. Elisabeth was not alone with her bumper-to-bumper parking. They had to walk more than half a block before Elisabeth and Michael found enough space between two parked cars to cross over to the sidewalk.

A few minutes later they found the address. It was the top building on Second Street, just off the main boulevard, Prospect Park West. A four-floor brownstone with double glass doors. The numbers 11440 were painted on the glass in gold, outlined in black. The same gold and black paint ran around the boundary of the glass doors.

A directory, listing six names. Daisy, holding her breath as Michael read the names.

No Baker. Michael, looking at Daisy, expecting disappointment, but he found Daisy smiling. Saying, "Oh, come now, Michael, we didn't really expect that he'd still be here. We knew it wasn't going to be that easy."

Michael, "I guess." Scratching the back of his left shoulder, his elbow poking straight at Daisy, bobbing up and down in rhythm.

"Should we ring a bell?" Elisabeth, asking. "While we're here, maybe we should talk to the super." She was wearing Richard's Levis, down low like Michael's. She had begun reaching for them automatically, putting them on without thinking. One foot was on a higher brownstone step than the other. The back of her hand was on the top of her knee, palm upward, fingers relaxed, cupped, and idle.

Daisy, nodding. The bottom of her beige pleated skirt billowed around her calves in the soft breeze, a breeze that brought with it the mixed smell of window box flowers. Flowers were everywhere in this neighborhood, seemingly at every window and on every step. A hotdog vendor had set up across the boulevard at one of the entrances to Prospect Park, selling water, ices, ice-cream pops, hot pretzels. The sun, bright, strong, and intense, shot rays through the medium-sized maple trees lining the sidewalk. It was a fragmented ray by the time it hit the brownstone steps, creating moving patterns of shadow and light on all three of them.

Cars were speeding along the three lanes of the boulevard. An occasional one turning down the street, looking for a parking spot. A small red-haired woman in a lime green T-shirt walked alongside a huge black scruffy dog. The top of the dog's head, reaching almost to her shoulder.

Michael, answering, saying, "Definitely, we should talk to the super. Maybe he knows something."

Daisy, nodding. "Let's."

So they did. Michael, reading the directory of names alongside the buzzers, saying, "It looks like this is the super—Brian F. Davis."

Looking at the others for the go-ahead, his finger poised above the bell. Daisy and Elisabeth, nodding. Michael, ringing. They waited, shifting their weight around, listening to the breeze through the leaves, the call of birds, the sound of a basketball bouncing at some distance. Children. A sweaty man about Richard's age on the opposite sidewalk, wheeling his bike down the hill. A pang of guilt rippling through Elisabeth. Elisabeth pushing that pang right out of her body.

They heard someone approaching—thongs on creaky hardwood floors—before the door swung open. A latch, slipping across. A man of medium height, weight, build, and age, holding a wooden spoon with something brown and gloppy on it, looking at them. Loose denim shorts and a black shirt. Probing dark eyes under thick eyebrows. A crooked wide nose, not precisely centered over thick lips, dark uncombed hair, too long on the top, short around the ears. The beginnings of tomorrow's stubble were visible today, polka-dotting the bumpy contours of his lower face and neck.

"Mr. Davis?" Elisabeth, asking.

"Yes?" Ready to turn down any request. To send them packing. One hand, resting on the doorknob, the other holding the spoon. Preparing to shut them out.

"We're looking for someone." Michael, saying.

The man's eyes on Michael. Considering him.

"We're hoping you can help us." Daisy, adding. "We'd really appreciate it."

The man, turning to Daisy. Then back to Michael, not understanding her accent.

"We're looking for someone who lived in this building in 1945." Elisabeth.

The man, looking at Elisabeth. Blinking. Repeating, "1945."

"We know it's a long shot," Elisabeth, conceding. "We thought we'd try. This is the last known address of the man we're looking for."

Brian Davis repeating it, "1945."

"It's ridiculous, we know." Daisy, adding a little self-deprecating chuckle.

"No," Brian Davis, snapping, a rough edge to his deep voice. Surprising them, the three automatically stiffening. "What is ridiculous is that there may be someone here who *can* help you." His left hand, dropping from the doorknob, falling to his side, indicating that he wouldn't be shutting the door in their faces after all. "One of my tenants has been here since 1938."

Daisy, grasping the information, becoming weak at the knees. Was there really someone here who had known Michael Baker? Could it be possible?

"No kidding." Elisabeth. Impressed.

"No kidding." Brian Davis, repeating, sharply. Again his voice, loaded with unconcealed harshness—but not toward them. "Hulda Kheist, third floor, since 1938."

Somewhere down the street a car horn was honking. A tall black man, skating elegantly past down the hill on Rollerblades, his pale blue T-shirt pressed against his firm stomach and chest. The breeze suddenly picking up, stirring the leaves. Daisy's skirt flapping against her thin legs. She reached for Michael, taking the back of his upper arm, holding it because of the sudden wind. And the news. She hadn't expected either.

Nor had Michael expected the news. Or that Daisy would need his arm. Looking at her, touched that she had reached for him.

"What wonderful news," Elisabeth, saying. "She may really be able to help us."

"Wonderful for you, maybe," Brian Davis, spitting out, "but not for me since she pays only $278 a month and basically has done so since I bought this building fourteen years ago." Getting agitated. The hand holding the gloppy spoon traveling up the door frame, resting against it high over his head. One foot, toes down on the top of the other, creating a triangle in the space between his legs. "They told me when I bought this rent-controlled building that its being rent controlled wouldn't be a problem, that the woman in apartment three was seventy-eight-years old and that when she went, I'd be able to bring her apartment up to current market value. She has a beautiful floor-through with views of Prospect Park that would rake in a fortune. I'd just have to live in the basement apartment until then. Then when I rented hers out, I'd be able to afford to move upstairs to the second floor, to what's half the size of hers, pulling in $4,500 a month. Instead, I've been holed up for fourteen years. Fourteen years! Living like a rat underground while she and her bird live in total luxury for $278 a month! I'm forty-one years old and stuck in a hole in the ground waiting for Mrs. Hulda Kheist to go, one way or another."

Momentary silence. Elisabeth, wondering how many times he had told his story over the years. It had to be beyond count. A young woman in a blue floppy hat was walking by the apartment, heading down the hill, humming what sounded like Beethoven's Ninth, pushing an empty shopping cart. One wheel was squeaking. Distracting them.

"She taunts me. Tells me she's going to live to be a hundred because of all the Swiss muesli she eats. I hear that, and I can't help thinking of this story I heard on the radio—1010 Wins. You know it?"

Daisy and Michael, shaking their heads.

"I know it." Elisabeth.

"'You give us ten minutes, we'll give you the world'—that's their motto. It's news radio. Anyway, I heard once that there was this old guy, seventy-one-years old, who was caught strangling his ninety-four-year-old mother in her nursing home bed. Caught red-handed, his fingers tight around her throat. Why? He was tired of waiting for his inheritance. He was stuck in a sinkhole of poverty, drowning in bills, about to be thrown out on the street with no place to live, and there's his mother, barely functioning, spending thousands of dollars a day to live another day of life she's barely living—money that would otherwise be going to him." Shaking his head. "I really felt for that guy. He ended up in jail, the poor schlub." Daisy, Elisabeth, and Michael, standing uncomfortably, looking wordlessly at him. "It's a wonder you don't hear more stories like that, I'm telling you." Staring at the concrete below their feet, contemplating the unfairness of life.

"Oh." Daisy, after a minute. Breaking the silence, "That is something. And is she here, this Mrs. Kheist?"

"No. It's Saturday morning. She gets her hair done and then gets her groceries. She'll be back within the hour probably. If you want to come into my dump and wait, you can, or you can go over to the park or maybe down to Seventh Avenue to get something to eat."

"Thank you, Mr. Davis." Daisy, politely. "I think we'll go over to the park for a bit. If you see Mrs. Kheist, please let her know we'll be back in an hour." Turning to Elisabeth. "Is that okay?"

Elisabeth, "Fine. Let's walk over to the park."

Daisy, turning back to Brian, saying "Thanks." Noticing that he was eyeing Elisabeth's wardrobe choice. Daisy had grown used to seeing Elisabeth in those jeans but remembered her first impression of them. She could imagine what Brian was thinking. Starting down the steps after Elisabeth, her hand lightly attached to Michael's proud arm. Saying, "If it's all the same to you, Elisabeth"—tentative words coming out in a rush—"I did see some rather nice shops just down the street. Perhaps we could pop in."

Elisabeth's eyes flickering. "Shops? Yes. I saw them, too. Yes, let's go."

"You don't mind, Michael?" Daisy, asking.

"No." Although he did.

They turned around, moving together on the sidewalk down the hill.

B Y THE TIME they returned to 11440 Second Street, they were all weighed down with shopping bags. And something else. New. On Elisabeth. And Michael.

Jeans that fit, that didn't have enough extra material to sail to China. Both were relieved to see the other in different clothes.

Michael, placing his finger on Hulda Kheist's bell. Silently checking with Daisy. She nodded a go-ahead, and he pushed it, alerting the woman in apartment three that someone down below wanted her.

The woman in apartment three looked up from the TV, startled. It had been a long time since she had heard the bell. Figuring it was a mistake, returning her attention to CNN.

Down below, Michael, saying, "Do you think she's back?"

"We've been gone more than an hour." Elisabeth.

"Maybe it takes her a little while. Let's give her another minute and try again."

Giving her another minute then trying again.

The woman in apartment three beginning to consider that it might not be a mistake. Starting to get up off the old couch, pushing herself up with hands pressing into the worn moss green fabric. A plane, passing in front of the sun, momentarily darkening the otherwise sun-drenched room. Wide front windows overlooking Second Street, and sunlight spilling across the floor, creating a healthy environment for the many green leafy potted plants that were spread across windowsills, providing for a very happy parakeet.

"Try again," Daisy, whispering to Michael. Under the rumbling of the plane overhead, Michael, ringing again.

The woman in apartment three, shuffling to the front door. Her back, slightly hunched, her head thrust forward from the neck. Her knobby finger, pushing on the intercom. "Hello?"

"Hello?" Daisy. Her voice, too high-pitched to travel well. Too excited. "Uh, hello?" If possible, her voice even higher the second time. Two sparrows were engaged in a loud, lively conversation in the neighbor's front garden. Daisy, turning to Elisabeth, tapping the top of her forearm. "Maybe you should talk."

Elisabeth, stepping closer to the intercom. Her mouth, not far from the dented, tarnished silver plate. "Uh, hello. My name is Elisabeth Jetty." Politely, in her best CPA voice, wearing her brand-new, one-hour-old, snappy, beige summer linens: loose drawstring pants, khaki-colored cotton and linen top, and brown leather-strapped flat sandals. "I'm here with my son and cousin who is visiting from England. We were hoping we could talk to you about someone we're trying to find who used to live in this building."

The woman in apartment three, letting the words make their way slowly through her. Her heart pumping harder at the possibility that this might be a Saturday worth noting, something to remember, something that was not routine.

"Oh? I will buzz you up." An accent of some kind shaping her words.

The buzzer, sounding. Michael, pushing the heavy glass door. Crossing through the echoey dark-wood-paneled front hall, less grand than in earlier days, and up the stairs, each hoping they wouldn't see Brian Davis again. They didn't. They ran the smooth dark oak banister under their hands, listening to the creaking of the wood. Passing a steel gray door on the second floor, plastered with sheets of a child's drawings, mostly flowers, top-corner-page suns, and long bright yellow rays. Continuing up to the third floor, Daisy, leaning on Michael's arm. Michael, thinking, "See, good thing I'm here." Daisy, thinking, "Such a nice lad. It's a good thing he's here."

Arriving on the third floor. Standing in a small cluster in front of the steel gray door not plastered with children's drawings. The woman in apartment three, looking at them through the peephole. Finding them wholly unthreatening, opening the door. Saying, "Hello."

Elisabeth, employing the voice she had used below, "Mrs. Kheist? Thank you for seeing us. I'm Elisabeth Jetty. This is my son, Michael, and this is Daisy Phillips from Liverpool." Her words, resonating louder in the cavernous hallway.

The woman, nodding again. "Nice to meet you. I'm Hulda Kheist. Won't you come in?" Stepping back so they could get past her and into the apartment: Michael first, then Elisabeth, then Daisy.

Hulda, motioning them over to the couch. They sat down, three in a row, rather too closely at first. They had to shuffle apart a bit. The three of them, exhaling, facing Hulda expectantly, with knees soldered together, palms touching palms.

Michael hadn't sat that upright since his days in the high chair when he would slobber over apple sauce and baby food and finger his Cheerios. Feeling strange, he looked past Hulda Kheist to anywhere else in the room. His eyes settling on a large green bird with the best view in the place: perched high on a wooden horizontal bar in front of the window. The bird was riveted on them, eating seeds from a silver bowl under the perch.

Not only did Michael feel strange, he looked strange. Elisabeth, staring at him across her shoulder for a good long minute. Getting to know him, this different him. Seeing how his face was maturing. A new look in his eye; there now but not before. The slow, inexorable march to manhood seemed recently and quite suddenly to be picking up the pace.

Daisy sat poised with all her attention on Hulda, her heart thumping, sitting so close to this connection to her alternate life.

Hulda, lowering herself slowly into the large velvet armchair. Michael, staring at her, wondering how old she was. Hulda, sitting regally, her head held high, facing them diagonally. She had dyed, permed light brown hair, a high forehead; lantern jaw; small, quick, dark eyes; scrawny neck; weak shoulders under a flimsy lacy white robe.

The room was large and had graying white walls, last painted in days gone by but clean and not peeling. The room also had very high ceilings, and the window that overlooked Second Street was wide enough for a pack of elephants to fit through, shoulder to shoulder. It spanned almost the entire wall and was where the bird sat. Opposite the couch was a high, wide fireplace that had been built when the apartment was built, in the late 1890s. It remained unchanged through the decades. Thickly glazed dark green tile formed the boundary of the opening and part of the surrounding wall and floor.

In short, the apartment did have the potential to be utterly smashing. It was a truly authentic real estate gem.

Brian Davis's frustration, silently spotting the air. Dripping on them.

"Forgive me for being in a housecoat," Hulda, saying. "I don't often have visitors."

Nodding kindly. Telling her not to worry.

"So," Hulda, clapping the palms of her hands on her knees, "what can I do for you?" Her accent was from somewhere in Europe. Germany? Poland? Sweden?

Daisy, speaking. "I'm looking for a man who lived in this building until 1945. His name was Michael Baker. He lived here with his parents."

A heavy silence, Hulda ingesting Daisy's words. The others, waiting quietly. The bird, chirping. Michael, turning his head to watch it. Daisy and Elisabeth, keeping their eyes on Hulda, as if watching the wheels slowly creaking behind her eyes.

"Baker," Hulda, repeating softly. Tapping her huge forehead with the tip of a very old finger. "Let me think—1945. I moved in here in 1938, so it would have been seven years after that." Squeezing her eyes shut. "The children were in primary school."

"Here," Daisy, leaping forward on the couch. Opening her purse, pulling something out of it, a creased white envelope. "I have a picture of him."

Michael and Elisabeth, surprised to hear that, trying to catch a glimpse of him as the picture was passed over the coffee table faceup and into Hulda's shaky hand.

Hulda, taking glasses with thick black frames out of a pocket in her housecoat, looking down at the picture in her lap. A young, handsome serviceman in a stiff army hat. Broad shoulders, a straight nose that rounded at the bottom, a serious expression in his eyes, gazing back at the camera. Hulda's thoughts, moving in reverse, skidding through time. Hoping the picture would trigger something—create an individual out of a generic army face. But Hulda could find no personality exhibited in the picture, nothing to latch on to, nothing to distinguish him.

Hulda, thinking and thinking. Then saying, through a sorrowful mouth: "I'm sorry. I don't remember him. There were soldiers all over Brooklyn. I'm so sorry." Handing back the picture.

Daisy, Elisabeth, Michael, a trio of silence.

Hulda, "And you came all this way. Hoping I'd remember him?"

Daisy, nodding. "I have something of his, given to me sixty years ago, that I'd like to return to him or any children if he's gone. We were hoping you'd remember him because I'm afraid we don't have much else to go by."

"How did you come to know to ask me?" Hulda, wondering.

"We started with the landlord."

"Oh, dear," Hulda, saying. A sober silence. Brian Davis, with his scowl and dripping wooden spoon, suddenly conjured into the room by all four of them, wavering like a ghost before them. Somewhere outside, a dog barking. "I'm relieved that he was helpful. That's not always the case."

A moment passing. Brian, fading away.

"Maybe if you saw Michael Baker's handwriting?" Daisy, fumbling. Handing Hulda the envelope. Hulda, taking it, turning her attention to it.

Gazing down at it, smiling, saying, "Oh, yes." Hope crashing in on the three on the couch who were holding their breath. "I remember those stamps." Fingering the outline with a thick, crooked finger.

Hope, shot down, apparent on their faces. Hulda, not blind to it, feeling bad. "Can I offer you something? A cup of tea?"

Elisabeth, declining.

Michael, declining.

Daisy, saying, "Yes. That would be very nice, thank you."

Hulda, very happy to oblige. "I'll put the kettle on." Standing up on thin bowlegs, shuffling in worn red slippers across the oak floor to the small kitchen.

"He played the piano." Michael, surprising Daisy and his mother, turning all the way around on the sofa to face Hulda. "He was a piano prodigy." Using an expression formerly used by others about him. "He had a watch engraved by Arthur Rubinstein. Maybe you remember that?"

Hulda, stopping to think, holding the kettle in her hand. "Piano," shaking her head. "There were so many in this building. Do you know what floor he was on?"

Daisy, considering. She had seen so many envelopes with the return address over that short period of their love, trying vainly to picture them. Did any of them include his apartment number? She had left all but two of the envelopes at home in Liverpool. The one with her was no help and the other was in her suitcase at Elisabeth's.

Daisy, shaking her head. "I don't think he ever included an apartment number, but I do have one more envelope here on Long Island. I can check when we get back to their house."

Elisabeth, saying to Daisy, "Do you remember his parents' names?"

"Good question." Daisy, thinking. A long way back. She was sure she had once known the answer, but not anymore. "I'll have to think about it. Maybe with some luck it will come back to me."

"That would be good," Hulda, turning on the flame under the kettle. Opening a cupboard, taking out two dainty china teacups, asking Daisy how she liked her tea. "I suppose I'd be more likely to remember the parents' names or what they did for a living or maybe what they looked like. Can you remember anything about them?"

Daisy, scratching through the veneer of memories, trying to reach deeper. Half a minute later, saying, "His father worked in the newspaper business and liked to fish. His mother read a lot of books and played the piano. She played on Sundays at church. Michael was very proud of that. I don't know what they looked like. I never met them."

Hulda, concentrating, shaking her head. The kettle whistled.

Over tea, seated at a small square table under the open kitchen window, thick summer heat filling the room, Daisy told Hulda about herself and how she had come to know Michael Baker. She hoped that giving her details would trigger a memory—his cherry lollipops, his card tricks, the way he couldn't sing and couldn't hold a tune but could play the piano like none other. He liked to hum and whistle. He might have had a cat. Daisy thought so but wasn't sure. She thought she remembered his mentioning they had a cat. He liked Maltesers Candies and English marmalade; he had taken two-dozen jars from Dunkirk's back to New York with him. Daisy, finishing her thoughts, sitting back in her chair, feet together, back straight.

Every eye fixed on Hulda, searching for—hoping for—sparks of recognition.

Nothing. She pushed a plate of cookies toward Michael. Urged him to have one.

He did. Chewing it slowly, telling her the cookies were great.

Hulda, her small eyes shining from a very wrinkled face, saying, "They're called Mailaenderli. It was my mother's recipe and her mother's before her."

Michael, eating. "What's his name?" Pointing toward the bird.

"Yodeli."

"Yodeli?"

Hulda, nodding. "Yodeli Kheist."

"What kind is he?"

"A Quaker Parrot, twenty-two years old. My late husband named him."

"He just sits there? He doesn't fly away?"

"He has no flight wings. They get snipped by the vet."

"Cool," Michael. "Can I touch him?"

Hulda, nodding. "Come with me."

Michael, following her to Yodeli. Watching excitedly as she pet the top of the bird's head, stroking his long wings, whispering soft, cooing, loving words in another language. After a moment, picking up Michael's hand, holding it, bringing it slowly to the watchful bird, letting Michael touch it gently—its head and green feathers. Yodeli stiffened but allowed it. Michael, holding his breath. Elisabeth and Daisy, twisting in their seats at the kitchen table to watch. Hulda, continuing to whisper unrecognizable words in a singsong voice.

"Where are you from?" Daisy, asking. "If you don't mind my asking."

"Not at all," Hulda, saying. "That's Swiss-German I'm speaking. I'm an old Swiss girl from outside Zurich, a village called Neerach."

"Is that why he's called Yodeli?" Michael, asking, tentatively petting it. "Can he yodel?"

Hulda, laughing. "We tried for years. We used to play yodeling albums, hoping he'd pick it up." Shaking her head. "He never did."

"I've been to Switzerland many times," Daisy, saying. "It is a gorgeous country, just gorgeous."

"It is," Hulda, saying, naming cantons she thought the most beautiful. Alps. Lakes. Villages. Cities.

Michael, continuing with the bird. Turning to his mother. "Mom, can we get one?" Young again. A child's plea.

Elisabeth, not responding.

Michael, repeating the question. Gently petting it, cooing at the bird, studying it up close, looking into its black eyes. Remaining with it even after Hulda returned to the table, slowly lowering herself back into her kitchen chair, talking to Daisy.

Elisabeth, not answering Michael. Feeling grouchy, left out. All this talk about places she had never been. England—Daisy, repeating how awful the weather was and how baffled she was that anyone would want to visit. Switzerland—Hulda, declaring the weather in Switzerland was equally awful to that of England, but the food was better. Segueing into further talk about other places they had both been in Europe.

Elisabeth, frowning, plunking her chin gruffly into the palm of her hand, with her elbow impolitely on the table. Questioning herself: Why was it that she had never been to Europe? She had always wanted to go. Grouchy now about how all her dreams had been ignored for twenty years, swallowed up by children. The two older women, spiraling backward. Elisabeth, catapulting forward, picturing herself in a conversation when she was Hulda's age. What would she be able to say about her life other than that she had raised five children? That she had once stolen her husband's bike and left it in Central Park at two in the morning? That she had been a good CPA? That she had never lived anywhere other than Port Washington and was living out her days five miles from where she grew up? That she had never used a passport because she had traveled only to Mexico, Canada, and the Caribbean, where she hadn't needed one? That after being a reproductive powerhouse she was moving toward menopause at an age when some women were still having babies?

Elisabeth, going from irritated to irate. Mad and getting madder—at herself, at Richard, at their narrow, little Manhattan–Long Island–centric lives. It was a great big world out there. Why had she put up with seeing so little of it? Vowing then and there that things were going to change. They would go to Europe this summer. All this time they had been spending money on the wrong things. They should sell the living room furniture, sit on crates, buy tickets, see the world. Instead of obsessing over Richard's bike, they should take a bike tour of Europe.

Elisabeth, tuning back into what Hulda was saying, how much she missed the Alps.

"I've been in this country since 1938. It is my adopted home and has been good to me. I love it here and always have, but I've never stopped missing the Alps. I can't. Mountains are in my blood, my soul. They are a permanently missing piece of my heart." Smiling, she remembered something. "Albert knew how I felt. He used to console me by saying that we lived in the highest building on the street, the top of the hill."

"Haven't you ever gone back to Switzerland?" Michael, asking. "To visit?"

"Oh, yes, of course, but not in twenty years. I'm ninety-three years old." Looking at him, at his earnest young face that had cookie crumbs on his upper lip. "My wonderful husband, Albert, has been dead twenty-one years. Two of my children, bless their souls, have passed away. I have another son living in Venezuela and many grandchildren, some in California, some in Arizona, and some in Venezuela. My friends are all gone. I have family in Switzerland, of course, but no one I've kept in touch with.

Who am I going to travel with? Who am I going to stay with? I'm afraid I'm not as lucky or young or as brave as you, Mrs. Phillips," turning to Daisy, "I could never go back now, but even when I was younger, fitter, and stronger, when I was your age, I was too cowardly to travel alone. And now, of course, it's too late. I'll never see the Alps again. I admire your courage."

Daisy, waving away the compliment. Remembering her own recent upset about not being able to travel without Paul. Knowing just how Hulda felt.

"Circumstances," Daisy, saying humbly, "and being lucky to have family here whom I didn't even know a few short weeks ago and who have been so generous to me. I am very lucky and very glad I came." Looking over at Elisabeth and Michael. Smiling in appreciation.

Hulda, pouring Daisy another cup of tea. Chatting on about how she met Albert, how he spent summers in Switzerland visiting his paternal grandfather, and how he had proposed in her parents' doorway— nervous, stuttering, and clutching a bucket spilling over with Granny Smith apples from his grandfather's tree. He had stripped the tree of the best apples to present to her, making his grandfather apoplectic and Hulda secretly laugh because her family had an apple tree of their own that yielded more apples than they knew what to do with.

Daisy, sipping her tea, listening happily, becoming more resigned incrementally with each passing minute until full surrender and acceptance. They would be getting no information. Exploring the dark caverns of Hulda's mind, probing musty spaces with flashlights had yielded nothing. They had empty hands and empty buckets. They were no closer to Michael Baker except that they now shared a view with him of Second Street in Park Slope, Brooklyn.

They soon got ready to leave, thanking Hulda. She had tears in her eyes, dabbing at them with the lowest knuckle of her bent pointer finger, saying no, she should be thanking them. Michael, saying many good-byes to the bird. At the door Hulda, slipping something into his hand, totally surprising him: Mailaenderli cookies wrapped in paper towels.

An exchange of phone numbers. Promises on both sides to call if either remembered anything more.

TWENTY-NINE

Moving day. Liverpool, England. The sun, shining brightly. Clouds far from sight. Dennis, taking that as a good sign.

Sweaty in his pale pink shirt and rumpled gray pants, guiding the moving men, terrified that they would poke a hole in one of his canvasses after he had hired the cheapest outfit he could find. Now near tears as they moved his art collection—his prized possessions, all that he cared about—out of the house and into the moving van. Feeling overwhelmed, a sudden swooning attachment to the house and to Liverpool, thickening as the day wore on—as the house lightened and the truck got heavier.

Yesterday was his last day of work. He had cleared out his office, touching things that hadn't been touched in decades. He pulled old favorite books, magazines, and flyers off the shelves, dismantling a life there. He had given notice three weeks ago, announcing to shocked stares and open mouths that he would be leaving, moving away. He wished them well, his successor and the others at their desks, computers, workstations, water coolers. All activity momentarily ceased, all faces turned toward him.

They wished him well, too. Saying they were sorry to see him go, that they were looking forward to reading his new book when it came out. They would be sure to look for it. Did he have any idea of when that would be?

Dennis shook his head. Smiling with coffee cup in hand, shifting his weight, adjusting the waist of his trousers at the belt buckle, under his small paunch. A reflex.

Driving out of the company car park for the last time, filled with doubts, many and varied, and uncertainties, vast and powerful. Had he done the stupidest thing imaginable in giving up his job? In believing in Amanda and her financial predictions of a rosy future? His knuckles were white on the steering wheel. His teeth were clamped together. His jaw was locked and his eyebrows down. The radio was on but ignored. He told himself that one had to take risks in life, reassured himself that everything was going to be all right, that he was, in fact, lucky to be able to make such a move. He was going to love the sea air, and it really *was* going to provide him with a new book idea.

He also believed, besides, that the magazine was going under, that all magazines of his kind were. It was better to leave voluntarily. He wasn't getting any younger, and if he was going to make a move, now was the time.

Amanda, flittering around the house exuberantly, dressed down, uncharacteristically, in cut-off jeans, sneakers. Dashing off to get her hair done at her tried and trusted hairdresser. Allowing her time to find a good replacement in Chessex so that she didn't start off with her hair in need of an appointment and no idea where to get one. She made the hairdresser the last thing she did in Liverpool, a city she had never liked.

It was almost six in the evening before the van was finally packed. They pulled out of the driveway for the last time, in two separate cars. Dennis, exhausted, grateful that his mother wasn't there, fearing what the vision of the two of them pulling away might do to her. It should take nearly five hours to get to their new house, where they would sleep on the floor. The moving van, with all their possessions, would arrive the next day.

Amanda, saying they should spend the night somewhere else. They should celebrate their new lives in a four-poster bed under top-quality Egyptian cotton in a fancy roses-and-violets wallpapered hotel with heavy burgundy drapery and ornate chandeliers, overlooking water. They could uncork champagne bottles from the minibar.

Dennis, putting his foot down wearily. They would celebrate their new lives under scratchy polyester sleeping bags. They would unscrew bottled ale from their positions on their new highly varnished floorboards.

THIRTY

SILENCE IN THE CAR. Daisy, Elisabeth, and Michael pulling away from the curb, heading down Second Street.

Broken by Michael: "Maybe we can invite Hulda for dinner on holidays. And Sundays."

Elisabeth, nodding absently. Saying it was a good idea. Watching the road, full of pedestrians milling on sidewalks, curbs, crosswalks, crossing the street with or without a green crossing light. Making sure not to crash into any of them. About to remind Michael that the deal was that he study on the way home, but when she glanced into the mirror, she saw she didn't have to. He was back there reading his textbook, deep in concentration. Elisabeth, needing to look again. It was true. He was studying. Elisabeth, afraid to say a word.

Daisy, sitting in the front seat, nervously thumbing her purse strap with the flat fleshy part of her thumb. Elisabeth, taking a sideways look at her at a red light, assuming she was upset that they had gotten nowhere. Not guessing that Daisy was deeply stewing. Reviewing Hulda's life: living alone at ninety-three. Having a landlord counting the minutes, licking his chops at the thought of her death or one-way-ticket hospitalization.

Hulda had admired Daisy's courage. Daisy, thinking Hulda was the brave one.

Also thinking about what her own life might have been in a floor-through apartment on Second Street with Hulda and Albert Kheist as neighbors. She and Hulda would have missed their homelands but embraced their American lives, American husbands. A New York life with Prospect Park, flowers in window boxes, nineteenth-century brownstones, and shops down the hill.

Inside her, a strange feeling with no name.

THIRTY-ONE

A N HOUR AND FIFTEEN MINUTES of talk about Daisy. Truth be told, Daisy bashing.

Ann paid the hairdresser, tipped her generously, keeping her eyes averted because of the clumsiness of the money pass. Fixing her attention on the lone plant in the gold-glazed pot with its long, broad, dark green leaves. It was set in the front window and bent toward the hot June sun. Ann tipped the one who had washed her hair and swept her split ends off the floor. She said her good-byes throughout the store, including the regulars in various stages of hair transformation—some with color glopped on flattened hair, some under hair dryers, some under scissors. She tipped the workers well, those who spent their days dwelling in the falsely sweet scents of hair tonics. She left the store with a more confident step than the one she'd had on the way in. She always did.

A short walk back to the car, across a busy summer sidewalk. Back in the driver's seat, feeling awful about her stinging words and the allegations she had leveled against Daisy. Her words spoken above the noise of hair dryers and surrounding female voices. Now the words, coming back to haunt her. Surely she must have said something nice about Daisy. Ann, thinking back to the hour and a half with Henryka, rerunning the conversation. Hoping she'd recall something, some passable snippet, some comment she had said that wasn't awful.

Picturing Henryka, standing with the light brown hair dye, laying it on thick. Picturing herself and her complaints about Daisy, laying them on thick. Ann, feeling thoroughly ashamed. It was all so unlike her. Who was this new dreadful Ann?

Pulling out of the parking spot feeling like a heel. Peeking over her left shoulder with one hand on the wheel and the other pressed to her lips, keeping her mouth shut tight. After twenty-four years with the same hairdresser, Ann was used to her as a confessional. But now feeling terribly sorry that she had. How could she have said those things, some of them not even true? Daisy wasn't luring Ann's grandsons over to Elisabeth's after school with home-baked goodies. Daisy wasn't smiling coolly when they came to her instead of Ann. Daisy wasn't saying unkind things to them about Ann. Ann knew that but had said so anyway. She had thrown them in as embellishments.

Feeling dirty. Sitting at a red light, shaking her head as if to send all the mean words flying out of her ears. Wishing the morning undone—not the hair, which seemed to have come out especially nice, but the garbage that had come out of her mouth.

Suddenly aware of how dirty her minivan was with pretzels, crumbs of unknown origin, small plastic toys, Pokémon cards spread across the floor like carpeting, plus an apple core and three small juice boxes in cup holders. Turning the car around, heading for the car wash, the one where they let you sit in the car as it went through. Usually she had one, two, or many children with her. They all loved it, issuing squeals of excitement. This time she would go through it alone.

She paid the dark-haired man with the dripping rag, the one who helped guide her wheels onto the track and told her when to shift into neutral. She paid him more than he asked for, telling him to keep the change. Here, as in the hairdresser's, she was a very generous tipper.

Sitting back, leaning her head against the headrest, relaxing, letting the car wash carry her through, cleansing her. Suds slopped on every window. Long, heavy, vertical blue slats pierced through, slapping the front, top, and sides of the minivan with giant rotating brushes. Hard water rushing in from every direction.

Ann, loving the intensity. Feeling safe behind the windows and doors, impregnable in her fortress before the calming, almost soothing follow-up: the application of the hot wax.

And then it was over. Gliding the minivan out on tracks, back into the sunshine of the day. She was asked to get out, to stand aside while four young men went in four separate doors with vacuum hoses, detergents, and torn rags to clean the interior, to make it shine.

Ann, standing on the sidelines, blinking in the glaring sunlight, watching. Letting the young ones do the work, sucking out the grime and dirt with their long rubber hoses. Making her respectable again. Disappearing were the dried, twisted Wendy's french fries that had been wedged under the seat and the little tinfoil balls of chocolate Kisses tucked in the seat back. Her life being cleansed.

Back in the car, feeling better, more orderly. Back to thoughts of Daisy. Forgiving herself now for her transgressions, ready to start anew. Tonight was a planned dinner at Elisabeth's. They would be back from their trip to Brooklyn and eager to tell all that had transpired. And she would be there, Ann would, with a bouquet of flowers for Daisy and well wishes for success in whatever it was she was searching for. It was something about a watch and a Brooklyn soldier. She hadn't followed all that Michael had said when he spelled out his reasons for not going to her house after school.

Ann, stopping at a florist for a big, beautiful bunch of flowers wrapped in tasteful paper, a bouquet so big that she had to hold it with two hands. In her house she laid it across the kitchen counter. Picturing herself presenting it to Daisy as a peace offering, an apology of sorts for her appalling behavior. Most of it was unknown to Daisy, but, nonetheless, it would be an apology and a plea to start again. Offering up a new

Ann, one interested in the arrival, continuing presence, and well-being of Daisy.

Leaving the kitchen. Finding her son-in-law and his brother in her garage. Her son-in-law had a circular saw, his brother was holding the two-by-four that was being cut. Tremendous noise, wood dust flying, settling on their denim jeans and the garage floor. Ann, standing in the doorway, fingering her gold chain necklace, chatting pleasantly, offering coffee, but they refused.

Hurrying back to the kitchen to make herself coffee, her eyes going immediately to the bouquet. Feeling good about turning over a new leaf—with flowers. She couldn't wait to give them to Daisy. She might even make a little joke about daisies for Daisy, as if Daisy hadn't already heard every daisy joke imaginable. Brewing her coffee, turning on the TV, making a few phone calls. Sipping from her large mug on the re-cliner in the lived-in living room, picturing herself dressing for dinner. Picturing the night at Elisabeth's, happy to be there with everyone gath-ered around her at the table, talking in their usual way—the way they used to before Daisy got there. That picture morphing seamlessly into the bunch of them gathered around Daisy, listening to Daisy, fixated on her as they had been since her arrival. Leaving Ann sidelined, cast away—as Daisy's mother had done to her before.

Taking a deep breath, swallowing the rest of the coffee, even the dark, thick, slimy stuff on the bottom. Picking up the remote. Changing the channel, absently, more in her head than out. Trying to bring back the first scenario, the one where she was the headliner and Daisy listened quietly. But the unwelcome scenario kept creeping back in as though someone had a remote to Ann's mind and effortlessly changed back to the All Daisy, All the Time channel.

Standing up. Returning to the kitchen. Putting the dirty mug under the faucet in the sink. Rinsing it, setting it on the drying rack. Visions of Daisy, more popular than ever, dancing through her mind. Everyone would be discussing the day's trip, with inside jokes and stories about

Brooklyn. Ann, becoming upset, unable to shake the feeling that Daisy didn't deserve it, that no child of her aunt Meredith deserved such happiness.

Ann, feeling cross, picking up the bouquet. Tearing off the tasteful paper. Hoisting a crystal vase onto the table. Neatly placing the long-stemmed explosion of color in a spectacular way. Standing back, admiring the arrangement. Then picking up the phone to let Elisabeth know that because of a dreadful headache, she wouldn't be able to make the dinner.

THIRTY-TWO

ELISABETH, LEAPING OUT OF BED. Monday morning. Sensing it. A feeling nine weeks behind schedule had finally returned. Racing into the bathroom, certain it was back.

She was wrong.

Elisabeth, slumping over the sink, brushing her teeth. Running a brush through her hair, making her scalp tingle. Throwing on her work clothes with not so much as a glance in the mirror. Not even bothering with makeup.

Thinking about Dart Man—worrying. Not escaping her notice that he had not struck again since she had stolen Richard's bike. Making her more unsure than ever before. Going back and forth in her mind, she realized that the absence of darts could be unrelated to Richard's lacking wheels. Elisabeth, thinking, frowning. If he never shot another dart, she would never know for sure—for the rest of her life—what the truth was. Hurrying down the stairs, ludicrously hoping that Dart Man would strike again, just one more time.

In the kitchen, Elisabeth, running through another Monday morning of kids and breakfast. Daisy, raising her voice above the din, offering to make Elisabeth a quick cup of tea. Elisabeth, saying she would drive through Dunkin' Donuts on her way to work. Daisy, wishing Michael well on his first Regents exam. Elisabeth, listening, stunned, guilty. She had forgotten that the Regents was today. Watching in astonishment, Michael allowing Daisy to give him a sweet good luck peck on his forehead. Michael, hurrying out the door and onto the school bus.

Daisy, in a pastel skirt set, standing in the doorway, waving goodbye to all of them, Elisabeth included. Then all were gone. Quiet in the house. Daisy, lingering in the kitchen before making up her mind to do something radical.

Turning on the computer to pick up where she and Michael had left off, the long, slow slog of searching for the right Michael Baker out of hundreds of thousands. Trying to get military records and death certificates in New York. Daisy, proud that she was able to remember how to get back to where she and Michael had left off before Michael had to hurry off to study. Daisy, poking one finger at a time on the keyboard. Remembering where the Enter button was, remembering how to use the mouse and when to use it.

Thinking if only Dennis could see her now.

Two weeks in New York, and she was already a thoroughly modern Millie.

THIRTY-THREE

THE PHONE, RINGING. WEDNESDAY NIGHT. Dennis and Amanda were not home to hear it. They were on the coast for the first time since moving day. Things had finally settled down enough at home to allow them this treat. Their gazes were locked over the water. Even at that hour, the sun was still running high in the sky. Sprinkling golden rays over them. All was peace and serenity.

Dennis, surprisingly calm. He had never been to this sea before but would be back, for this incredible slice of earth was fewer than five minutes from where he now lived. He found himself dizzy by it. It was deeply shocking to him that this profoundly stirring vision could be his in this new way of life. The two had spent the last twenty minutes standing elbow to elbow and shoulder to shoulder in virtual silence, drinking in the peace and the stunning beauty of what lay before them, behind them, and to their sides. Hearing only the lapping of the unfolding waves and the busy sea birds.

Dennis, removing his pensive eye's grip on the sea. Turning to the top of Amanda's head, the side of her face. Watching the gentle breeze lift and part her hair. His fingers doing the same. His sandals, squishing rocky sand. Reaching down to kiss her damp lips, saying, "Thank you for all this."

Amanda, smiling up at him, lips apart, her pretty teeth revealed, her eyes shining. Saying, "I knew you would love it." Picking up his hand, putting it to her lips. Kissing it, running the tip of her finger slowly along the contours of his thumb.

"I do." Enjoying that she was tickling his thumb. The subtle feeling reached a long way. "And, really," his voice getting lazy, "we ought to be okay financially if we can just get through the first year or two being very frugal. No major purchases. That shouldn't be too hard. The house already has everything we need. We'll just have to have plenty of meals with little more than potatoes, lettuce, and pasta."

Amanda, shrugging softly. "I don't mind. We'll have all this." Gesturing toward the sea. "Who cares about fine food?"

"Good," Dennis, responding, agreeing with her. "And I'll start my book soon." Wondering when. "Maybe I'll look around for part-time work, maybe something at the college."

"I know you don't want to hear it," Amanda, nuzzling close, her hand on the inside of his upper arm and her cheek on his shoulder, "but I'll remind you again. Your mother is sitting on a pot of gold, most of which will eventually be ours. She has only the one grandchild. Remember that."

Dennis, refusing to let anything interfere with his deeply felt peace. Too content to summon the energy for anger or reprimands.

Not knowing that at that moment the phone was ringing in their new house that they weren't there to answer. Allowing them to forestall their learning the big news. They wouldn't hear the message from Lenny until later that evening: his announcement that Sarah was the one, that they were getting married as soon as Daisy got home from the United States. Lenny, asking Dennis for their mother's phone number in New York. Chomping at the bit to tell her all the news: that she was getting a new daughter-in-law. And three new stepgrandchildren.

THIRTY-FOUR

DART MAN, CAUGHT RED-HANDED.

Launching a dart. At 10:17 a.m. on East Thirty-ninth Street and Third Avenue. From a red mountain bike. It was a risky move because people knew about him. People were on the lookout. He struck earlier than usual but was seen, chased, and caught by a Korean grocery store owner who was stacking tangerines in orderly rows. He saw Dart Man making his escape, thought quickly, and rolled a barrel of fresh-cut flowers into his path, causing Dart Man to swerve, hit a lamp-post, crash, and land on his back, feet in the air. The heroic Korean grocery store owner managed to hold him down until the police arrived.

Dart Man had finally fallen. He was a white, twenty-two-year-old, skinny, pointy-chinned redhead, an out-of-work actor from the Midwest whose only fame had come, and would come, from terrorizing the city for thirty-three days.

Elisabeth, hearing the news on the radio. Feeling relief. And humiliation. It made her want her bed, piles of pillows, heavy blankets—a place to hide.

Instead, performing an act of penance. At lunchtime, dashing out of her office, into her car, off to a bike store. Discussing pros and cons with the young, overweight, very personable salesman. Explaining what she wanted. Listening to his advice. Together, choosing a bike.

Guilt made the purchase. Guilt signed the credit card screen with the tethered stylus. Guilt bought the most expensive bike in the store.

E LISABETH, ALL SMILES when Richard got home. At ten after ten.

He found her in the kitchen, ironing the white shirt that Pete would need for graduation. Richard, going upstairs to change out of his suit, to say hello to the boys, and to hear from Michael that the Regents was a breeze. Passing through the hallway, finding Daisy, exchanging pleasantries with her, asking for an update on her search.

Daisy, beaming, remarking casually that she was doing her *own* Google search and was undeterred despite continuing to come up empty.

Richard, back in the kitchen. Elisabeth, still on the white button-down shirt. Putting the iron down, asking Richard to follow her—which he did, first stopping at the refrigerator for a beer.

"You're never going to believe who I met today," Richard saying, popping the top off the bottle then putting the bottle opener on the kitchen counter above the open drawer. Following Elisabeth out of the kitchen.

"Who?" Elisabeth, asking, more interested in presenting her surprise than in the answer. She was excited, thinking that in the end she had done the right thing. It had been time to put the other bike to rest anyway.

Richard, "Heather Clarke. Remember her?"

Elisabeth, stopping in her tracks. Remember her? She was the closest thing to a super model their high school had ever known, the most popular girl in the school, hands down. She was an original. Everyone knew her. Half would have loved to hate her if only she hadn't been as nice as she was beautiful and smart. Elisabeth knew Richard had lusted for her as much as everyone else did.

Elisabeth, saying flatly, "Didn't she marry a billionaire?"

Richard, nodding. His eyes bright, looking inward. Remembering the encounter. "Yeah, but she's divorced now. She said she got a very generous settlement and the apartment on Park Avenue. She looks terrific, almost the same as she did in high school."

Elisabeth, glumly assuming that Heather was still on a perfectly precise twenty-eight-day schedule.

"She has two daughters." Richard, saying, his eyes fuzzy and soft around the edges, reliving the conversation. "One is at Harvard, and the other is away at boarding school."

"How nice for her."

"She seemed as sweet as ever. She's involved in philanthropy and is putting together a charity for underprivileged children."

Elisabeth, thinking, "Enough already," but saying, "I have a surprise for you, Richard. You're going to love it." Trying to bring her former eagerness back. Throwing open the door to the garage, darting in to get the bike.

Richard, saying, "I met her on the subway."

Elisabeth, stopping. The garage floor, cold under her bare feet. Her hands, dropping heavily to her sides. Enthusiasm for the bike bleeding out of her. He met her on the subway? *On the subway!* Elisabeth, remembering what had put him on the subway. Not wanting to dwell on the irony.

Richard, noticing the bike. Taking steps toward it, smiling. "Hey, that's nice. You bought that for me?" Looking at her, surprised and happy.

Elisabeth, nodding. But, it was no longer fun.

"It's nice." Running his hand over it. "I guess my other bike was getting kind of old." Smiling at her. Leaning over the top of the bike to kiss her forehead. "Thanks. This was very nice of you." Then, "Heather said her husband left her for a trophy woman. Can you imagine that? Leaving Heather for a better-looking woman?"

Elisabeth, an edge to her voice, "I'm glad you like the bike. We can drive it into the city this weekend and make a day of it. Take Daisy to the Empire State Building. She hasn't been to Manhattan yet. And you'd better get a better lock—double kryptonite this time, maybe even triple."

Richard, responding, "Are you kidding? I wouldn't take this bike into the city. It would be stolen the first night. And, besides, I like the subway. It's very convenient. Heather and I made plans to meet every Monday and Thursday."

Elisabeth, her face in free fall.

THIRTY-FIVE

DAISY, HANGING UP the Jettys' phone. Staring down at her lap, busily fingering a nonproblematic nub in her creamy peach skirt. Her chair was pulled out, angled from the kitchen table. Her feet were flat on the floor, back stiff, and erect as usual. Daisy, absorbing the news. Shocked. Lenny? Remarrying? Sensing eyes on her, looking up. Josh, in a *Star Wars* clone trooper costume, was standing at the refrigerator, about to open it. Turning to her, asking through the mask if something was wrong. Daisy, shaking her head. Telling him that she had just received surprising news from home.

Elisabeth, coming into the kitchen at that moment, dragging the vacuum—just in time to overhear their exchange. Asking if the news was good.

Daisy, so stunned that she was almost unable to string together the words. "My son Lenny is getting married." Sounding quizzical, as if she were passing along a silly rumor.

Elisabeth, holding off vacuuming. Hurrying to Daisy at the table to warmly express her good feelings. At various times Daisy had filled Elisabeth in on her family, leaving Elisabeth with a degree of ownership large enough to feel joy at the news. Asking when.

Daisy, saying it would take place as soon as she got home. Thinking about Sarah. Seeking to elicit new information about her future daughter-in-law from the one frozen image in her memory bank. There were three blank spaces for the three new stepgrandchildren—girls eleven, fourteen, and seventeen, Chloe, Carrie, and Christine. A dizzy head for Daisy. Three blank spaces. Three blank faces. New grandchildren. A new daughter-in-law. Lenny, a married man.

The *Star Wars* clone trooper had poured himself orange juice and was almost finished when a surprise attack sacked him from behind. David, currently Darth Vader, caused the clone trooper to spill his juice all over the counter and floor. Loud, angry, boisterous screams—David with laughter, Josh with anger. Elisabeth, with paper towels, to supplement the lousy cleanup from David.

All of it stirring Daisy. Sucking her out of Liverpool, back to Long Island, back to the kitchen table.

Standing up. Straightening her skirt with the palms of her hands. Clearing her throat and raising her voice to speak over the maelstrom. "I should be going home."

Six alarmed eyes suddenly on her. Josh, immediately running, screaming the news to Michael, who was seated at the computer in the next room, sifting through the hundreds of thousands of Michael Bakers to find "the one."

Elisabeth, stooped, soaking up the juice from the floor. Crouching over the sticky area, looking up at Daisy, saying that she couldn't go because she hadn't found Michael Baker yet. Pushing herself up off the floor, moving the hair off her forehead with her wrist.

"I know." Daisy, saying, her voice sad. Reflective. "But they want to get married. I shouldn't keep them waiting."

"What?" Michael, charging into the room like a bull, straight to Daisy, his arms crossed defiantly over his chest. Demanding an answer. "What? You're going?"

Daisy looked at Michael, then Josh, then David, and then Elisabeth, the four standing before her, waiting for the answer, poised to pounce.

Daisy, wobbling slightly on skinny ankles, tears of sincere affection springing to her eyes.

"I'm sorry, Michael, I know you've been working very hard to find him, but what if we never do? There's a good chance he's already dead. And if we can't find *him*, we'd never be able to find any children he might have had. I tried. We tried. I'm truly glad we did. I am indebted to you, all of you," looking into each face, "forever. But I should be getting back home now for Lenny."

Nobody speaking.

"You can't go yet," Michael. "I might be getting somewhere now."

Elisabeth, who was so proud of him, asking, "How many more Michael Bakers are there?"

Michael, grimacing. His face, a vision of youthful flexibility. Reddening. "I don't know exactly." Meaning hundreds of thousands.

He looked beaten. Daisy wanted to hug him, but instead Elisabeth did. Pulling him into her arms, placing her warm maternal lips on his bare forehead. Michael, allowing her in, stiffly, for a second, then pushing her off, saying, "Please, Daisy, don't go."

"I'm sorry, Michael, believe me. It will be very difficult for me to leave here—you, your family, and our goal—but it looks as if I must." Her voice, soft, matching the expression in her eyes.

"When will you go?" Elisabeth, asking, feeling a sadness and a sudden rush of loss that she never would have expected, coming through in her voice.

"I'll see if I can get on a flight today."

Again, no one speaking. Josh, taking off his clone trooper helmet, his face sweaty. "Today? That's so soon."

"It's just not right, Daisy." Michael, angry. "I just finished my last Regents—which I studied for because of you! I'm totally done with school now. Summer vacation has started. I'll have all day long to continue the search. You can't leave now!"

Daisy, exhaling, her shoulders sinking, uttering, "I'm sorry, Michael." Falling back down into the hard-backed chair. Looking wistful, her kind light blue eyes, wet. "I'll tell you what. I'll leave the watch with you for you to continue the search. If you find him, you can send it to him. Or if you don't, you can keep it for yourself. I'm sure it's very valuable even without its being engraved by Arthur Rubinstein."

A quick inhale from Josh and David. Looking at Michael as if he were the luckiest kid on earth. Michael's eyes, brightening, the surprise of the words working their way through. But lasting only a minute before darkening again. Clouding over. Because as appealing as the idea was, it was not what he wanted. He wanted Daisy to stay. He wanted to find Michael Baker.

They all did. They all stared sullenly at Daisy. A heaviness in the air.

"Are you sure you have to leave today?" Elisabeth, asking, tossing the sticky sponge into the sink, the wet paper towels into the trash. "We were planning another day with my sisters. We were thinking we'd all go on the Circle Line, the boat that goes around Manhattan, and then stay in the city for dinner. I'm sure Richard would love having dinner in the city with you." Thinking he might love it even more in a subway car.

Forcing herself to snap out of it, making herself stop. Richard loved her as much as ever. Nothing had changed outside of her own head.

Daisy, regretfully repeating that she really had to go. Sudden thoughts of her house and of keeping it herself. Lenny had told her that Dennis and Amanda had made the move and that Dennis had actually sounded quite happy until Lenny mentioned the wedding. He also said that Sarah was wondering when Daisy would be getting back, that they were both quite eager to tie the knot. Telling Daisy he would be calling back in an hour to see if she had return-flight information by then.

Michael, saying, "Thanks for the watch, Daisy, but it's not what I wanted." Stomping off. Josh and David, arguing over who got to use the computer now that Michael would be off the Internet. Elisabeth, saying neither; she needed it to arrange Daisy's flight.

Daisy, following Elisabeth out of the kitchen to the computer.

Elisabeth, tapping away at the keyboard. Daisy, watching Elisabeth intently, thinking she might have been able to do it herself at this point, marveling at the miracle of the Internet—how easily she was rebooked and how quickly.

It was done. She was booked on an evening flight. Arrangements were made for her to be picked up at 6:00 next morning at the Manchester Airport.

Red suitcases were repacked, zipped tightly, standing upright in the living room.

D AISY, OUT ON THE DECK, sipping tea she had just made. Naturally she had offered to make a cup for the others, and naturally they all declined. She would be returning to England without ever having served anyone a single cup.

She sat silently, enjoying the last look at the incredibly gorgeous property. The sweet smell of honeysuckle was pungent around her. The brightly colored flowers seemed to be enjoying themselves. Some new summer perennials were making their appearance, beginning their romp with the late spring varieties. The familiar and unfamiliar birds chattered and zoomed from one specimen tree to some other utterly majestic one. There was the sun, the weather, the bees, and an assortment of other sinister-looking flying things that Daisy chose to ignore, refusing to crumble in terror at the sight of any of them. She inhaled and exhaled slowly and deeply. The setting called for relaxation, asking only that from its viewers, but not for lack of trying or desire, Daisy was not relaxed. Instead, she was filled with so many mixed emotions, she couldn't possibly relax. She needed to be alone, to sort through them.

She was going to miss the boys; that much was certain. She would miss the boys and the family more than she ever could have imagined.

She had grown to love it here in a short time, being back amid the joys of living with a family: the daily beat of life, the promise of new days, the energy of children, the fulfillment of others sharing the same calendar. Richard was exhausted and rarely around but was as nice as can be. Elisabeth was mixed up, goofy, overwrought, and overwhelmed. She had been slow to start in those early days after the airport, with her mysterious disappearances deep in the night—which still remained a mystery although the activity itself appeared to have ceased—but she was very sweet, sympathetic, and kindhearted, and did her best. Pete, the high school senior, talked of girls and sports and would be off to college in the fall. Steve was the only one Daisy had never met; he was expected home within days. Daisy was disappointed that they wouldn't overlap. And there was sweet Michael with all his noble attempts and determination, a different child entirely from the one who had picked her up at the airport. And Josh and David who had played for her night after night as she sipped her Cointreau in the living room, listening to them at the piano, interrupted more and more lately by Michael's racing in with a Michael Baker question, a comment, or an update, never tiring of the quest. He tried so hard.

And now, despite all this, Daisy was going home. Dennis was now gone, living five hours away, and Lenny was soon to be married. Still, she had her house, her garden, her lawn, her friends. She loved them all. She did. But.

Daisy, pondering. Still pondering out on the deck when into the house walked Ann. Having heard the news, coming to see Daisy off. Standing in the family room, keys hanging from one hand, her bag slung over her shoulder. Hurrying over to the couch to kiss Josh and David while they were watching a movie. They let her, obediently, although it was clear they were totally involved in *Star Wars*. Ann, asking them where their mother was. Two hands pointing upstairs, mumbling, "Vacuuming." Ann, asking about Daisy. Two hands pointing out to the deck.

Ann, going off to find her daughter. Coming up from behind,

unheard over the vacuum, Ann tapped Elisabeth on the shoulder, shocking her. Elisabeth, flying out of her shoes. Turning off the vacuum with the tip of her toe.

Ann, leaning in conspiratorially, ready for a naughty snicker: "So she's finally going, huh? You must be ready to uncork champagne."

Elisabeth, feeling indignation collecting in her throat. Her mother's behavior over the last few weeks was shameful. Daisy had taken the hearts of Elisabeth's family's by storm, but Ann hadn't been anywhere near enough to witness it.

"Actually, Mom," Elisabeth, saying, her voice not shielding her feelings, "we're all begging her to stay." Annoyed enough to add: "I guess you didn't get the memo."

Ann, unusually rebuffed, drawing her head in like a turtle's. Looking at Elisabeth. Needing to replant herself. Not yet sure what to feel other than astonishment and—no stranger to her lately—left out.

Elisabeth, adding, "Why don't you go talk to her while I finish. Since she's leaving today, it might be a good time to find out why she came in the first place."

Turning her back on her mother, toeing the vacuum back to life again, returning to the thoughts her mother had interrupted: the world of Heather Clarke, well-toned society gal. Wondering what her life must be like, Elisabeth suffering through the cold splash of her own inadequacies. She had Googled Heather, had seen pictures.

Ann, standing there, chastised, bewildered, with no idea why or when Elisabeth's feelings for Daisy had changed so radically. She had no idea when Elisabeth had crossed a line, leaving Ann in a field of one. Turning, without a word, disappearing to find Daisy.

Ann, sliding open the glass doors, stepping out into the brilliant sunshine. There was no breeze to speak of. Gigantic, tall, puffy white clouds dotted the sky. Daisy was sitting at the table on the deck, looking serious, grave, and sober, contemplating the gigantic ash tree thirty feet away. She lit up when Ann stepped out, offering her a greeting of great warmth. She held nothing against her. Daisy didn't have a judgmental or critical bone in her body. She'd excised them long ago when it became clear that her mother was made up of little else.

Ann, lumbering over to the table, pulling out a chair. Sitting down.

Daisy, smiling. Saying a cheerful, "Good morning." Asking Ann if she could get her a cup of tea, gesturing to her own. Ann, shaking her head, murmuring a polite "No, thank you." On her very best behavior, keeping a cork wedged tightly in place. The two, embarking on a polite conversation about the weather. Ann, explaining that usually the humidity this time of year was intolerable but that Daisy had gotten lucky. They talked about the landscaping, Ann only pretending interest when Daisy compared English and American shrubbery.

Ann, saying that she'd like that cup after all, but coffee, not tea. Asking Daisy if she minded if she just ran in to make herself a cup.

Daisy didn't mind. She got up herself, using the opportunity to make herself more tea.

Following Ann back into the kitchen. Putting the kettle on. The two women, standing in silence, watching the kettle heat up.

The silence, becoming awkward. Neither woman knew what to say. Finally, with difficulty, Ann, saying, "Before you go, Daisy, I owe you at least this." Daisy, curious, nodding. Ann, taking a deep breath. "I know I haven't been very nice to you. I'm sorry. I just can't help it. Every time I try to move us into the future, the past keeps coming in and knocking my good intentions out of the way."

Daisy, blinking at her. "The past?"

"Look," Ann, saying, "let's just be honest here."

Daisy, "Yes, of course, but I haven't the slightest idea what you're talking about. I'm sorry."

Ann, eyeing her warily, saying, "I'm talking, of course, about what your mother did to me, to us—me and my mother." Swallowing. "It still makes me sick to think about it." Taking hold of her stomach.

Daisy, stupefied. "My mother?"

"Yes, your mother."

"What my mother did to you? How could she have done anything to you? You've never even met."

Ann, studying her closely. "You really have no idea?"

Daisy, mystified, shaking her head. "All I know about you is that your mother used to send us sugar, flour, and rice during the war."

Ann, "And some thanks she got for doing it."

The kettle, reaching its boil. Whistling. Bringing their attention back to it. Both going to turn off the flame at the same time. Daisy, getting there first.

"Why? What did my mother do to you? I honestly don't know what you're talking about."

"You don't know that when I was six my father left us? He ran off with another woman, leaving me and my mother with nothing."

Daisy, shaking her head. This was news to her.

"You don't know that my mother, an immigrant in this country, with no family here other than his, had to sell what little we had to buy us passage back to Liverpool? That we went back with only what we had on our backs? You don't know that when we got there, your mother—my mother's older and only sister, the only family she had—turned us away? That she wouldn't open her doors to us but instead made your father take us back to the docks, dumping us there in the cold and fog. That he told my mother that your mother said that she'd made her bed when she married an American, and that now she and her 'fat daughter' had to lie in it." Ann, taking a breath.

Daisy, aghast, horrified. Her mouth, hanging open. Finally she was getting Ann. Finally she was understanding. "Oh, no." Feebly. "I'm so sorry, Ann. My mother was a terrible person, really she was." Shaking her head. "I didn't know any of that, none of it. I never even heard that your mother came back." Daisy, reaching out to pat Ann's shoulder. "It must be awful just to look at me. I'm so sorry. And here I was with no idea."

Ann, "If that's the case, then I should be the one apologizing to you. I'm so sorry. I assumed you knew. I thought for sure you would have heard. You were a teenager at the time."

"When was this?"

"I was in first grade. It was May, 1945."

Pieces slipping together. "No wonder." Daisy, pouring the water into her teacup and Ann's coffee carafe. "My mother and I were not speaking at that time. I had fallen in love with an American soldier, you see, and my mother wouldn't let me love him. She hated Michael. She hated me for loving him. She tried to break off our courtship. She cheered when he stopped writing to me. I've always believed that she had something to do with stopping his letters but could never see how. For all the crying I did, she never once showed me an ounce of sympathy or kindness." And then, saying it, saying it aloud without shame: "I hated her."

Ann, "Maybe that was why she was so violent about my mother's marital disaster involving an American."

"Or why she was so opposed to her daughter's talking about marrying one."

Both women, sifting new information.

"I hope you believe me," said Daisy. "It's the truth. I knew nothing of what you just told me."

Ann, "Goodness, I'm so sorry then. I owe you a huge apology for my behavior while you've been here. I tried to be nice, I really did, but I couldn't do it. The bile would rise in my throat, and I'd have to turn away. I hope you'll forgive me."

"Of course I do." Daisy, taking Ann's hand in hers. Creating a new reality for themselves. "Come, let's sit at the table and have our coffee and tea. We have a lot of catching up to do and very little time to do it. I'm going home tonight, as you've heard."

Ann, "I'm so sorry I let your whole visit go by before bringing it up. What an idiot I am. I could shoot myself." Allowing herself to be led by hand to the table.

Daisy, pulling a chair out for her. Scurrying back for their cups, saying, "Well, don't do that. We have the whole rest of our lives to mend things."

Ann, watching Daisy balancing the cups, saying, "Let me help."

Daisy, hurriedly saying, "No, no. You just sit right where you are. Let everything inside you settle while I devote myself to trying to undo in some small way the cruelty of my mother—not that I ever can." Placing the cups on the table. Settling across from Ann.

Ann, watching Daisy. Reaching over and squeezing her hand. "It won't be difficult to start loving you now."

The phone, ringing. Neither making a move to get it, assuming that someone else would. Still ringing. Ann, shouting for Josh or David to get it, guessing that Elisabeth couldn't hear it over the vacuum. Neither Josh nor David, who usually raced for it, moved. No one upstairs was getting it, either. Ann, calling the boys again, louder.

The machine, picking it up.

Daisy and Ann, sitting right there, with no choice but to listen to the noises and gibberish coming out of the answering machine. High-pitched, excitable, inscrutable. Grabbing their whole attention. Daisy and Ann, both sitting at the table in someone else's kitchen, listening. Eyes locked. Stifling an urge to laugh together. Team players at last.

What was that, anyway, coming over the machine? Damned if either of them knew—until one of them did.

Daisy, almost dropping her teacup. Lurching out of her chair, spilling hot tea on her hand and the front of her dress. Racing across the room to grab the receiver. Barely registering the pain from the tea, pressing the receiver to her ear, saying, "Hulda?"

There was some confusion until Hulda realized that she was no longer leaving a message, that in fact it was a human ear on the other end of the line—Daisy's, no less, the very person she had been hoping to speak to. Hulda, excitedly, "I remembered something! Something came to me. Something I remember now."

Daisy's stomach, stirring. Catching up to the surprise of hearing

Hulda on the phone, dying to hear what she would say. Daisy, concentrating, not letting Elisabeth's sudden appearance in the room distract her. Ann, telling Elisabeth who was on the phone, someone named Hulda.

Elisabeth, exclaiming, "Hulda!" Wide-eyed and excited, briefly filling Ann in, in short staccato sentences.

"What?" Daisy, asking.

Hulda, saying, "I remembered the family. They lived on the second floor." Hulda's voice high, screechy, very excited. "The son was a pianist and a soldier. Michael. Very handsome, now that I think of it."

Daisy's stomach, lurching. A tidal wave cresting in her throat.

"I remember now that he said he had a sweetheart in England he'd be going back for as soon as he could afford it."

"That was me!"

"Yes," Hulda, saying, having already figured that out. "So, listen. There was a terrible tragedy, very sad. His parents died in a restaurant fire on Fourteenth Street in the city. George and Maria, I remember them now. I looked and found pictures and newspaper articles about the fire. I've been going through my closets ever since you left. I'm sorry it took so long. I have so many photographs and scrap papers and memorabilia and junk." Chuckling self-effacingly. "But I remembered that this happened and thought it could be them."

"Oh, my," Daisy, picturing Michael. Such a terrible thing. "When did it happen? Does the newspaper say?"

"I have it right here on my lap . . . July 16, 1945."

"That's when he stopped writing to me! My last letter is dated July 15. *That* must be why!" Not because he had stopped loving me! *Not because he had stopped loving me.* Daisy's heart, pounding in her chest.

Hulda, speaking again, "It says here he was just coming from a doctor's appointment, apparently on his way to join them, when he saw the fire. He ran into the restaurant through flames to save them, injuring himself."

"Oh, no," Daisy, crying. "What happened to him?"

"It doesn't say. It only says 'injuring himself.' It says the injuries put his plans to be a concert pianist in doubt. In fact, that's the title of the article: Tragic Fire Fells Parents and Dashes Hopes of Heroic Son, a Rising Musical Star."

Daisy, having to sit down. Wobbling over to the counter stool, allowing herself to fall into it. Saying, "I'm sorry." Her voice, faint. Her head, in her hand, her palm shielding her eyes. Tears, years of tears, welling up. "I just need a minute." A minute to close a hole sixty years open.

"That's okay," Hulda, saying. "I have all day. I'm only going to be putting my closet back together again. I can't even close the door now." Giggling good-heartedly. "Wait, there's another article here. I haven't read it yet. I ran right to the phone. Let me see . . ."

Silence over the phone as Hulda read and Daisy wept. Telling herself it was silly to cry over something sixty years old. She tried to stop, tried not to let it overpower her, but tears kept coming.

Elisabeth, going to Daisy. Wrapping her in her arms. Daisy, reaching up, holding Elisabeth's forearm. Ann, grabbing hold of Daisy, too.

"Does the other article say anything?" Daisy, asking, her voice shaky.

"The headline is 'Heroic Son Released from Hospital to Ruined Dreams.' It's dated July 28, 1945. It says he's being released from the hospital and that injuries sustained in his attempt to save his parents make it unlikely that he'll ever be able to play the piano professionally again. It goes on to list all the competitions he won all over the world and how he had played for Arthur Rubinstein when he was sixteen. It says Mr. Rubinstein was so taken with Michael that he presented him with a watch which he'd inscribed. It ends by saying he plans to leave New York. He's going to his aunt Lucille and uncle William in Littleton, New Hampshire."

"New Hampshire?"

"That's what it says. That's good information. Littleton, New Hampshire."

"Thank you so much, Hulda. You've been gorgeous, just gorgeous. I don't know how to thank you."

"You don't have to. I'm thrilled to be of some use. Just let me know if you find him. I'll be rooting for you."

"Of course, of course," Daisy, assuring her.

Closing comments. Daisy and Hulda saying good-bye, promising to stay in touch. Daisy, giving Hulda her address and phone number in Liverpool, saying she'd be sure to call her once she got back to England.

Hanging up. Turning to Elisabeth. "I need your Michael."

DAISY, ELISABETH, MICHAEL, and Ann, leaning over one another's hunched shoulders, eyes on the computer screen silently and tensely. Michael, keying in *Michael Baker New Hampshire*.

Bingo. It reduced the number to 249,000, even including thirteen phone book results: thirteen addresses, and thirteen phone numbers.

Daisy had a major decision to make, and it took her less than half a minute to reach it. Asking Michael to go back to the Web site where they had arranged her flight.

Asking him to cancel her ticket.

Michael, bursting into smiles. Getting right on it.

Elisabeth, noticing Ann rubbing Daisy's back affectionately. Elisabeth, saying, "Well, it's about time, Mom."

Ann, replying, "I couldn't agree more."

Daisy, smiling. Picking up the phone. Dialing Lenny.

THEY CALLED THE thirteen Michael Bakers with phone numbers in New Hampshire. Daisy's hand, shaking. Asking for Michael Baker. No luck.

Some of the Michael Bakers answered the phone. None of them was a Michael Leonard. None of them knew a Michael Leonard. Other Michael Bakers called back later in the day. None of them was "the one," either.

Elisabeth and Daisy, pulling out an atlas. Looking up New Hampshire. Finding Littleton in the White Mountains. Studying surrounding towns.

Michael and Ann, scrolling down through the other 248,999 *Michael Baker New Hampshire* Google entries, looking for something, anything, that might indicate a man in his early eighties.

Busy all afternoon until Daisy insisted they take a break and celebrate the New Hampshire find with a trip to Ben & Jerry's. Insisting on buying ice cream for all and even a pint to take home for Richard, who couldn't join them, having unexpectedly gone into the office on a Saturday. Elisabeth, declining the cone—thinking of Heather Clarke's waistline. Taking herself next door instead, to a hairdresser. Directing the stylists to make it right, whatever it took. Returning home an hour and a half later with short, short hair of a lighter shade. Tossing out the anchorwoman/professional CPA look for a funkier look, an anti–Heather Clarke society gal with long curly hair glam look. Giving herself a new look. Missing her midnight rides, her loose baggy jeans, her period. But not letting it get her down, not with her brand-new look.

Hoping Richard would like it.

All of them back home again. Back to the computer. Michael Leonard Baker, Littleton, New Hampshire. No further luck. Nothing on the Internet. No property tax bills. No court records.

New ideas, bouncing around. A check of death records in New Hampshire yielded no results, which could mean almost anything. A call to the Veterans Administration in New Hampshire. No one picked up the phone.

Michael, saying they had to go there. To ask in the post office. To ask around town, grocery stores, nursing homes, senior apartments.

The idea of traveling there taking flight, even though it was such a long shot. He could be dead or living somewhere else. He might have left New Hampshire decades ago. He might never have actually gone.

But. He could be alive. He could be there.

Making plans to go. Discussions. Maps. Hotels. Schedules.

ICHARD SAID HE LOVED HER hair. Said she looked great, said he meant it. Said it again. Also said he met Heather on the way home, that it wasn't unusual for her to be at Penn Station on a weekend. She was going out to her house in the Hamptons, which is where she left her car. Heather said she was worried her plans for the charity might be falling through, in which case she'd be looking for something new. He told her about an opening in the Private Foundation Department of his office. She said it sounded perfect and gave him a kiss on the cheek.

Elisabeth, deciding to watch Richard closely to see if he was washing around a spot on his cheek.

THIRTY-SIX

D EEP IN THE NIGHT. Daisy awake, unable to sleep. The result of the information from Hulda in the newspaper clippings. Daisy, in the dark of the night, pacing her room. She had tried to sleep but couldn't. Only tossing and turning and staring at the ceiling. Trolling her mind, reliving July 1945, looking through the prism of time with new information. Pouring concrete into blank, unfinished spaces with all that she now knew.

Above all, facing Michael's pain, picturing her handsome young soldier, seeing the horrors of July 1945 through his eyes, and living the tragedy. How hard it must have been. How young he was. How could life have been so cruel to him, to come home from war to that? And she, blithely unaware, was an ocean away, angry at him, indignant, insulted. If only she had known, she would have gone to him, unwanted or not. Did he know that? Why hadn't he asked? Why didn't he send word? She would have gone in a heartbeat with her mother's blessing or without.

It would have been without.

◆ ◆ ◆

S UNDAY AFTERNOON, MORE PLANS for New Hampshire. Lengthy discussions. Strong opinions. Deliberations. Attempts at determining when to go, how to go, and who should go. Certainly Elisabeth, but she would have to put in for vacation time. Certainly Michael. But what about Pete, Josh, David, and Ann? Ann, saying she'd love to but couldn't possibly. Because of her grandchildren, she had to be home. And Steve, who was due home from college just that day, naturally wouldn't go. And Richard, who could surely use a vacation but couldn't take one just then. He told Elisabeth she should go and enjoy herself. Raising her suspicions. Asking him again if he really liked her hair.

Daisy, overcome with gratitude. Asking to use the phone, to thank Hulda again. Getting her on the fourth ring. Filling her in. Hearing Yodeli in the background, mixing with street sounds of Brooklyn.

Hulda, very pleased to hear that they were going to New Hampshire. Excited. Asking questions. Discussing.

Daisy, listening, her eyes growing wide. Turning to the others. "Hulda wants to come with us."

M ONDAY MORNING, ELISABETH, in her new funky hairdo, her overnight bag packed, doing something radical. Michael on her bed, watching, listening, doubting that she would really go through with it, that she would really call in sick. It was something she had hardly ever done, even when she was short of being at death's door. When the boys were small, she was always afraid to call in sick when she really wasn't sick, fearing that one day she would really be sick or one of the boys would be, and her days would be gone. And vacation days were not something to lean on. They had to be limited to holidays, or the boys would seriously know their grandmother better than their mother. And this year she would have to save vacation days to help settle Pete into college in August. So, with vacation days always in demand, she had to be very prudent with sick days and always had been—until now.

Ninety degrees before 9:00 a.m. Humidity, equally high, the skies a gloomy gray, but nobody cared. Anticipation lifting spirits. Elisabeth, picking up the phone. Michael, watching. Elisabeth, spilling the lie, dribbling it into the mouthpiece, saying she was too ill to go in. Michael, cheering silently. The secretary, saying to feel better, sounding sympathetic. Elisabeth, hanging up, sitting down on her bed. High-fiving Michael. Yee-ha! A minivacation!

Bubbling with excitement, the trio—Daisy, Michael, and Elisabeth—going to New Hampshire, a first for all of them.

The car, packed. Small overnight bags. Wheels, starting to roll over gravel, backing out slowly. Michael, in the front with the Mapquest directions, seven bags of potato chips, three boxes of Chips Ahoy—Costco sized—and enough water to cause a catastrophic flood. Elisabeth had carrots and celery. Daisy had her teabags.

Waves of good-bye. Josh and David pressing their mouths up to Elisabeth's window, pretending to cry. Elisabeth, rolling down the window, calling them on it. The boys smiling, admitting they were faking. Blown kisses as the car slowly backed out of the driveway.

Then Daisy, calling out: "Wait! One last thing, if you don't mind." Opening the SUV door. Hurrying back into the house.

The car, idling.

Daisy, hurrying back out with the bottle of Cointreau. Slipping into the car, smiling. "If I'm going to be face-to-face with Michael Baker tonight, I might be wanting a drink."

Fifty minutes later Michael, ringing Hulda's doorbell. Elisabeth and Daisy were double-parked in front. No spots available as far as the eye could see. Heat, assaulting the sidewalks and streets.

The return buzz coming almost immediately. Michael pulling open the glass exterior door, stepping inside. Hit by an enticing aroma. The scent was everywhere, saturating the humid air. His appetite kicking in. Hoping it was coming from Hulda's. Remembering those cookies. But nearing her floor, the scent, diminishing. Oh, well.

Hulda, waiting at the door. Letting him in. Michael, carrying on a quick conversation with Yodeli. Hulda, showing him what he should carry down to the car: her small canvas overnight bag and several tins.

Asking him, "You like cupcakes?" Michael, nodding. "You like carrot cake?" More nodding. Hulda, grinning proudly. "Wait till you taste these."

Those *plus* three-dozen Mailaenderli cookies plus apricot tarts plus raspberry torts. Michael, thrilled, "You did enough baking for a week!" Pointing at the bird with his chin as he moved toward the door. "Is Yodeli going to be okay by himself?"

"He won't like it, but he'll be okay for one night." Hulda, picking up her purse, taking the plastic container of tarts and torts. Taking a deep breath. About to follow Michael out, pausing and turning back. Michael, standing in her doorway, watching her go back to Yodeli. Kissing him good-bye. Patting the top of his head with her free hand. Telling him to be a good bird while she was gone. Even saying, "I love you."

Michael, waiting in the hall while she locked the door. Looking at the painting on the wall. Not on a canvas but on the wall. It was of mountains, the Alps, and was about seven feet wide and four feet high, on the wall adjacent to her door. He had noticed it the first time they came up. They all had—it was impossible to miss—but no one had asked about it. Now he did. "What's with the painting?"

Hulda, still busy with the locks, double locks, triple locks. Without turning to look saying, "The Jungfraujoch. Albert did it for our first wedding anniversary in 1939." The sound of strong metal sliding. Clicking in. The last lock, in place. Hulda, turning to look at the painting. Contemplating it, as though for the first time, her old eyes becoming misty behind her glasses. "I was so missing home when I came back to this. Albert wanted it to be permanent, so he painted it right on the wall. It was nervy, I know, but he was young and in love. It drives the owner of the building, Mr. Davis—I think you met him—crazy." Michael, nodding. "He's been threatening to paint over it for years, saying the minute I'm gone, he's going to paint right over it. He says he has a bucket of white paint and a paintbrush ready. It will be a pleasure, he screams. He doesn't much care for me, you know. He wants my kitchen."

Starting down the stairs, Hulda, moving spryly for her age but slower by far than Michael. He walked patiently, keeping to her pace. Asking her what that incredible smell was.

"Mr. Davis is a chef."

"Really? In a restaurant? That creepy guy?"

Hulda, snickering, finding pleasure in his words. "No. 'that creepy guy' is a podiatrist. He cooks for fun. The place always smells good. During the holidays he puts out some of his dishes here"—pointing as they neared it—"on this table. He is a marvelous cook. A miserable person but a marvelous cook."

Michael, looking at the table. There was mail on it now—newspapers, flyers, magazines. Picturing it with plates of hot, delicious food on cold, snowy, Christmastime days. Thinking it must be very cozy in there with all the dark, heavy wood; old-fashioned, low-hanging light fixtures; and century-old wooden stairs and banisters. Imagining various tenants coming together and lingering with one another for a change. Picturing Brian Davis in a good mood: sharing his food, smiling at his tenants, and maybe even being nice to Hulda for just those few hours each year.

Michael, opening the heavy front door for Hulda. Hulda, stepping out into the humidity of the day, starting over to the air-conditioned SUV. Michael, helping her in, then getting in the front seat. All of them waving good-byes to Yodeli. Hulda, looking back lovingly at the brownstone's façade as they started down Second Street.

Daisy, again picturing her life there.

THIRTY-SEVEN

DENNIS, HANGING UP THE PHONE, shutting off Lenny's exuberance, having just heard the latest installment on his mother's return. Now postponed indefinitely. Thinking she must be having a good time in New York. It was crazy in his line of work that he had never been there. Maybe someday he would go. He was aware, though, that his relocation had just pushed "someday" further into the future.

Monday evening. Why he hadn't realized that Amanda would be spending more time with her mother once they had moved within shouting distance of each other eluded him. It was after six, tea time. He was alone in a huge house. Still mostly unpacked, he had been working non-stop the whole of the previous long week—and solo most of the time. Dennis, thinking back to how Amanda couldn't wait to buy the house and to get in it. Now it seemed that she couldn't wait to get out. Sighing. Assuming that she would be home soon. If he put off the sausages long enough, she might be back in time to join him. He wasn't that hungry anyway.

Pouring himself a drink. Sitting down in the enormous living room facing the wide windows. Too tired to unpack another box, too distracted to read, too frayed to think about how he should be coming up with plans to find work.

Drawing in a long, deep mouthful of ale. Closing his eyes, letting it settle on his tongue, slide slowly down his throat. Listening to the unbroken quiet.

Thinking that as long as Amanda wasn't out shopping, he didn't really care that she was hardly ever home.

THIRTY-EIGHT

MANHATTAN. OVER THE WILLIAMSBURG BRIDGE—in traffic, of course. Elisabeth, recalling those nights a few short weeks ago when she was able to fly across the bridge. Missing those nights. That feeling of being alive. Thinking back wistfully, knowing she would probably never do it again.

A new feeling striking her. Occurring to her as she sat in her SUV in bumper-to-bumper traffic. Noticing that she was feeling a surge of being alive similar to the ones she'd had on those nights. Right then and there. Elisabeth, looking out over the East River below, and the city before them, with its buildings and its beauty and its tens of millions of separate lives. It was daylight now, full of mystery and energy and the continual unfolding of private lives.

It slowly dawned on her that she didn't need the night and the open roads and the speedometer needle flickering at seventy, although that had all been wonderful. She had mystery and energy and private lives unfolding right there in the car, in the form of her son, who was almost unrecognizable from the boy a month ago. Replaying in her head how he had jumped out of the car at Hulda's without being asked, to help this slow old lady down three flights. Elisabeth, glancing at him in the passenger seat now, seeing him content with his books and maps.

Shifting her attention to the rearview mirror, to her traveling companions. Daisy and Hulda, content back there, smiles on their faces, chatting about their lives. Elisabeth was now a part of those lives, a main character in this act as they were now in hers. Who would have thought a little while ago that she would be part of something like this, whatever it was that was about to transpire. People popped up in one another's books in the most unexpected ways.

Finally getting over the bridge, traffic easing. Elisabeth, turning north to cross Manhattan at Thirty-fourth Street because she wanted a page in her book where she got to show—and watch—a seventy-seven-year-old woman laying eyes on the Empire State Building for the very first time.

DAISY, THRILLED BY THE Empire State Building and the other nameless and less famous skyscrapers. Gushing at all of it—the streets, signs, vendors, and people of New York. Enjoying her breeze through Manhattan. Elisabeth, apologizing more than once for not having taken her in before, saying it was terrible, promising they would when they got back from New Hampshire, and that they would also do the Circle Line ferry, a double-decker bus tour, a Broadway show, and Chinatown. Michael, interrupting to ask if they knew that Liverpool was the home of Europe's oldest Chinatown, a fact remembered from his research paper. They did not. Thanking him for telling them. Elisabeth, promising Daisy that they would see Soho, Little Italy, Central Park, and a sunset over the Hudson River.

Daisy, nodding. It all sounded wonderful. Those were the very things she had hoped to see in New York, but what she had actually found was far better: Elisabeth's family. Elisabeth. Richard. The boys. And finally Ann. Hands down, they were all she needed.

◆ ◆ ◆

ONNECTICUT WAS PRETTY, lush, leafy, well moving. Mostly. Some snarled traffic around Stamford and again around Yale.

Massachusetts, lovely. Traffic-free. They took a break at a rest stop somewhere outside of Worcester to stretch their legs and backs. Michael, letting Hulda lean on him, not minding Daisy on his other arm. Crossing the hot, sticky parking lot with an old lady on each arm. Everyone needing to use the bathroom.

Normally Michael would have begged relentlessly for a Mrs. Fields chocolate chip cookie. Elisabeth, mentioning how surprised she was that he had not. Michael, squinting against the glare of the sun off the car fenders, saying, "Not half as surprised as I am that you called in sick. Besides, you must be kidding about Mrs. Fields when I have Mrs. Kheist's."

Hulda, overhearing, smiling. Her eyes, shining. What higher compliment could she ask for?

ORTHERN MASSACHUSETTS. DAISY, telling them about the flood in her basement, about fixing the shower head, about being on a ladder for eleven hours, about mowing her own lawn. No one could believe it. Michael, more impressed than ever.

Hulda, telling them that three months ago she had wallpapered her own bathroom. She said that years ago Albert had insisted on painting it green but she had always hated the color. She saw some man on HGTV wallpaper a room and thought she might be able to do it herself. She went down to Seventh Avenue, picked out something she really liked, and did it successfully. It took almost a week, but she had done it.

Ninety-three years old and she had wallpapered her own bathroom. Now she was thinking of doing the other, the one Albert had insisted on painting red. Red? A red bathroom? Whoever heard of such a thing? Hulda, laughing. That was Albert.

Elisabeth, thinking she had nothing to add. She didn't mow her own lawns or fix her own shower heads. She had never gotten stranded on a ladder for eleven hours and never wallpapered a bathroom. She hired people to do those things. All she did were tax returns and drive her kids around. She never did anything worth mentioning. Except maybe this trip.

THE NEW HAMPSHIRE BORDER. Much hoopla—until doubt set in about the wisdom of the trip and the chances of finding him. Being so blindly hopeful, they had allowed themselves only one overnight to do it. It was a needle in a haystack, a wild-goose chase.

Continuing north on I-93, getting quieter in the car. Getting hillier outside. The same clusters of big-box stores flanked the highway during the last 250 miles, but now they were set against increasingly hilly backgrounds. As the hills got bigger, Hulda's heart pumped faster. Mile after mile north, the only sound was from Hulda.

Passing Concord. Passing the lakes region. The White Mountains appearing before them in the distance, towering blue. Passing exits. The blue changing, defining itself. Cars thinning out on the road. Anything but jeeps and SUVs bailing out one by one. The blue of the mountains becoming green. Grand trees.

Then even grander when the peak of the great Mount Washington came into view. Michael, reading from an atlas. Mount Washington was the tallest mountain in the Northeast. All of them, setting their attention on it, the mightiest peak among the mighty.

Almost losing Hulda in a swoon. Sounds from her throat pouring forth with unrestrained pleasure, leaving Michael thinking that there was a world of emotion he had yet to discover, levels he had never reached—although maybe he came close once when he played Chopin. Hulda's hands trembled with emotion. Tears in her eyes as she urged everyone to look, look, look! They already were. Seeing mountains, majestic mountains. Look. How like Switzerland! Not as high, of course. They were not her beloved Alps but, still, they were exquisite mountains. Asking, "Please, could you stop the car at the next scenic overlook?"

They did. Hulda, stumbling out of it almost before it was fully stopped. Leaning against the car, gazing, in black shoes, stockings drooping around her ankles, causing brown rings around them. Her pastel paisley dress fell crookedly below the knees; it dipped lower over the right one and crumpled more on the left side. Her hands were clasped in front of her, her fingers twitching with excitement. Facing the mountains, the midday sun warming her face. Breathing in deeply. Saying, "Fresh mountain air!" Spoken exuberantly through lips stretched in a smile. Inhaling again, taking it in slowly through her nose as if appreciating each molecule individually. Taking it all in, all the mountain air, all that was available, into her lungs.

The others, watching her. Enjoying her joy. The sight of Hulda sucking in the mountains wrapped around them, comforting them like fleece.

Then, all too soon for Hulda, the others were eager to get going again. Daisy, feeling the pull of Littleton. Elisabeth was fine either way, going on or staying a bit longer. Feeling strangely content. Not having to think about the next moment. Feeling the peace of not needing to know the time. She was able to live in the moment for the moment, having unbroken minutes to devote to an appreciation of the mountains and the beauty of the earth.

Quiet in the car. The sound of asphalt under their wheels, air slipping past the windows. Hulda, saying, "You know, Michael, you won't be my age for another eighty years. Can you imagine? Eighty years from now—almost into the next century." Hulda, gazing at him. Michael, twisting around in the front passenger seat to look at her in the back. Hulda, continuing, "And if you remember me when you're my age, eighty years from now, then a part of me, some essence of me, would have stretched almost two hundred years, from my birth to you at age ninety-three."

Michael, emitting a contemplative "Whoah."

Hulda, looking earnestly into his eyes. "So, Michael, please do this: Promise to remember me."

Michael, saying easily, "I promise." Smiling. "I promise to remember you when I'm ninety-three—and your bird, your cookies, and this trip. I'll take you with me all the way to the year 2100."

"Good," Hulda, saying, feeling satisfied. Leaning back in the back-seat. "Thank you."

Michael, twisting more, almost all the way around, to Daisy behind him. "I'll remember you, too, Daisy, even if you're not as old. You're still a spring chicken." Daisy, chuckling, a high-pitched *yoo-hoo-hoo*. Michael, turning to Elisabeth. "And you, of course, Mom, I'll remember you wearing Dad's pants. That'll be my only memory of you."

Elisabeth, reaching across the front seat console. Hitting him with the back of her hand on his skinny chest.

Michael, laughing, hitting her back. Then turning again to Hulda, saying, "So, what's it like to be ninety-three?"

Hulda, thinking. A mile going by, then two, then, "I think as you get older you become more of who you always were. You become a more concentrated version of yourself. You really learn who you are, why you're unique, who you've always been. Everybody always talks about the teenage years as being the years concerned with figuring such things out, but those years are nothing compared to these. And if you're lucky enough to be in generally good health as I am, then it's quite nice. Things fall away as we age, making you really appreciate what remains." Elisabeth, thinking, "Don't I know it." "There's a winnowing away of nonessentials, sometimes essentials, it's true, but what remains is your core, your essence, the real 'you,' and you realize you're still you without what you've lost as long as you still have all your marbles—or most of them anyway." Uttering a light laugh. "I'm happy for every day on earth but won't be sorry when I go. Each day brings me closer to Albert and my children and my parents."

Finishing, looking satisfied with her answer.

The car, quiet. Everyone thinking about it.

Until passing a sign saying LITTLETON. Then everyone talking at once, jabbering, breaking the mood they had fallen into after Hulda's little talk. They were there.

Littleton, New Hampshire.

THIRTY-NINE

THEY FOUND A MOTEL first thing. No problem, they had many to choose from. The one they picked was the unanimous choice beyond question and without discussion: The Swiss Hut.

Pulling into the parking lot. Spilling out of four SUV doors. Watching Hulda gazing at it. Who would have guessed? A Swiss chalet against a mountainous backdrop. It had two flagpoles, two flags: a Swiss one flapping in the same breeze as the American one. It also had exposed exterior dark wood beams against white plaster and red geraniums leaping out of window boxes. Hulda clapped her hands together in the parking lot, a single clap. Exclaiming, "Just like home!" Giddy with glee.

They were all excited, hurrying to check in. A Swiss hotel portended well, a harbinger of further success. They gathered around the front counter, asking the promising-looking woman if she knew a Michael Baker in town.

The woman, repeating the name. After a beat shaking her head. Saying she knew plenty of Michaels and plenty of Bakers but no Michael Baker. Asking her how long she had lived there. Her answer: thirty-five years. Asking her if she had known a Lucille and William. They didn't know the last name but they were Michael Baker's aunt and uncle, so their name could have been Baker. The woman, repeating, "William and

Lucille." Putting the flat of her pointer finger on the flat of her lips, tapping it three times, then saying no. It didn't ring any bells.

They thanked her, got the keys—which were more like credit cards
than keys—and found the two consecutive rooms, one for Daisy and Hulda
and one for Elisabeth and Michael. They went in. Dropped their things.

Then hit the road—first the post office, which was easy to find on
the main road through town. The woman behind the counter looked
almost exactly like the woman at the hotel. They could have been sisters,
but they weren't. Michael asked. She had the same gray hair, the same
bifocals on her nose, the same healthy-looking pink-toned, barely wrinkled skin, and the same casual, open demeanor.

She also had the same answer: no Michael Baker. Now or lately or
never? The woman, saying she had been working in the post office for
twenty-seven years and couldn't remember a Michael Baker. Saying this
with authority, but they wouldn't take no for an answer. They told her
why they had come, all contributing morsels of information. Layering it
for her: why they believed he would be there and how important it was to
find him. Gesturing toward Daisy, explaining that she had come all the
way from England to find him.

The woman, shaking her head. Saying she wished she could help.
Suggesting they speak to Harry Gates over at the firehouse. His family
had been living in town more than a hundred years. He might know.

They thanked her. Heads down. Feet shuffling heavily. Tongues tut-
tutting. They had jointly believed the post office was their best shot, because if he lived in the town, he would get mail, and the post office
woman should know. Elisabeth and Michael, trying to comfort Daisy,
telling her it was better to hear nothing than that he was dead.

Daisy, remaining cheerful.

Racing over to the firehouse, leaving Hulda on a street bench. No
racing for Hulda. She was happy to sit and wait for them and look at the
mountains.

The others clustered together inside the large garage of the firehouse that smelled like oil and wax polish. Asking for Harry Gates, only to be told he had gone home and wouldn't be in again until Thursday. Daisy, asking him about a Michael Baker. The firefighter, looking down quizzically at her. Elisabeth, taking over. The man, shaking his head, saying, "Nope." He couldn't recall any Michael Baker.

It wasn't looking good.

Continuing on—asking at grocery stores, liquor stores, hardware stores. Daisy, pointing out the washer she had used to replace her shower head. Talking seriously, turning it around in her hand, showing them the grooves. Elisabeth and Michael, paying close attention, nodding, an air of bewilderment surrounding them.

Leaving the hardware store. Back on the street. Asking at the movie theater, the gas stations. Showing people the military picture, providing what information they had.

Getting nowhere. Asking at restaurants, waiters, busboys, owners. No luck.

Picking up Hulda. Returning to the motel shortly before sunset.

MICHAEL, IN THE POOL, splashing alone in the water. The sun was low, tall mountains were all around them. Summer bugs buzzed, sounds of laughter could be heard from the parking lot. The three women watched Michael cannonball, dive, kick, and swim as they discussed the situation. They all had more or less come to the same conclusion: Michael Baker wasn't there. He was not to be found. He had probably moved away years ago—if he had ever been there at all. He could be anywhere in the United States or anywhere beyond.

Even Daisy was no longer positive, but she was not sorry. "This trip has still been a huge success, not just to Long Island, but here, too. Look at how lovely it is. I would never have come here otherwise."

They agreed. The beauty of the area shed itself over them. Hulda, oriented toward the mountains from her lounge chair, zoned out in an appreciative stare, dreamily, hardly speaking. Elisabeth and Daisy, chatting aimlessly. Elisabeth, her pants rolled up, her feet in the pool. With arms straight, shoulders thrust forward, the palms of her hands flat on the concrete, her fingers curled over the edge of the pool, slowly stirring the warm pool water. Looking over her shoulder at Daisy on a chaise lounge, asking her questions about her family, her sons—Dennis and Lenny—trying to figure out what their relationship was to her. Arriving at second cousins and sticking to it. Asking Daisy about her husband, Paul, her parents, and her sister, Doreen. Wanting to know everything about everyone, living and dead.

Daisy, explaining the family tree. Michael, swimming up, leaning out of the pool on the underside of his arms. Daisy, telling of dead ancestors, of two great-uncles who went down with the *Titanic,* and how her grandfather, Ann's grandfather, had worked on merchant ships in World War II. He had been awarded a medal for his service by the queen.

"The actual queen?" Michael, exclaiming.

"The actual queen," Daisy, assuring him. Then turning to Elisabeth with a look of shock. "Your mother never told you any of this?"

Elisabeth, shaking her head. Seeing now how bizarre that was. "She hardly ever talks about her English side, almost never, actually, and only an occasional word about her mother. She doesn't talk much about her father's side, either. She really only talks about my father's family."

Michael, swerving the conversation back to the *Titanic* to find out more about the relatives who went down with the ship. Daisy, happily regaling him with family folklore. She was more pleased than ever now that she had learned Ann had not carried the stories on. Feeling that, if nothing else, the trip had done that: enabled the stories to cross the Atlantic to take on new life here.

Elisabeth did not want to change a thing about the moment and did not even want to call home. She was content to assume that things were fine there or they would call her. Dropping her head back, feeling the ends of her short hair brushing the back of her neck, the lowering sun on her face, and the perfect temperature of the water up to her knees. Closing her eyes, drifting away on the absence of anxieties.

Each of them basking in contentment, despite their lack of success. Trying to stretch the moments, to stuff them so full of meaning and beauty and detail and peace that time would naturally expand as a result.

FORTY

Elisabeth, up bright and early to watch the sun come over the mountains. Taking advantage of having just the one son. Being able to focus on nothing but him. Lying on their sides, facing each other in opposite beds, neither getting up other than to draw open the draperies to the breathtaking view. Talking leisurely together. Elisabeth, listening closely. There were no distractions, not even in her head. Getting to know him better, this new Michael, covering ground on the road to adulthood.

Elisabeth, lingering over coffee—tea for Daisy and Hulda—outside at the pool. Michael was back in the water for a quick dip before breakfast. Complimentary donuts. Michael ate three. Elisabeth did not say a word but let him enjoy himself, licking his fingers clean with a noisy sucking sound. Normally she would never let him eat so much junk or make so much noise. There must have been something in the air.

Nine a.m. Back in the car, pulling out. They had a list of nursing homes, retirement communities, and assisted-living residences. They also had directions to the long-term rehab at Littleton Hospital and a map.

By three in the afternoon they had left no Littleton stone unturned. They had talked to at least half the residents, including a handful of

Gateses: Harry's son, a daughter, a nephew, and two nieces. Not a single person knew a Michael Baker.

They had struck out, but you would never know it looking at them.

HULDA WITH ONE last request before going home: Could they please take the cog railway up to the top of Mount Washington?

She didn't have to ask twice. All heads bobbing yes.

The road was long and flat, straight through the valley. It was late in the day to be arriving. Most people were already done and down, heading back to their cars.

They got out, looking up. The sky was perfectly clear. The temperature, still in the high eighties, a touch of humidity. People milling around the museum and the concession stand, large groups in the shadow of the mountain. Green, green grass. Dandelions. Kids lapping up vendor-bought ice cream or sitting on the enormous unused tractor. Once a working tractor, now there for show, for atmosphere, for ambience. The grounds smelled of fresh grass and flowers.

Hulda, in heaven.

Going into the small museum for a quick walk-through. Learning about the inner workings of the cog train, how it could go up such a steep grade. A display of the original train, more than a hundred years old. The placard proudly proclaiming that the cog railway at Mount Washington was operational before Switzerland's first cog railway. Hulda, getting a kick out of that.

Buying tickets to the top. Finding seats. Michael, alone in the back. The others, up front near the driver.

The railway, a light load so late in the day. The trip to the top, thirty-five minutes, with the train sometimes angled so steeply that Elisabeth joked they were all going to end up in Michael's lap. The mountain terrain changing as they ascended. Grass giving way to rock. Trees thinning until they reached the tree line, then disappearing altogether. Strange high-altitude bugs entered through the open windows—yellow and black ladybug-like things buzzing around, landing on them, on the glass, on seat backs. That part, unpleasant, but tolerated without complaint because of the excitement of nearing the top.

Gears under their feet, churning. The driver making jokes about having bad brakes.

Finally, the summit. Hulda, breathing deeply before stepping out onto the mountain. Holding the metal door frame with a trembling hand, saying, "Albert's watching me. I can feel his eyes on me." Eagerly stepping out into the thin air, the brilliant sunshine.

Strolling away from the cog railway toward the steps to the highest spot, the observation deck. All of them enjoying the view.

Michael, looking at Hulda, saying, "Any minute now she's going to break into song. We'll all be hearing that the hills are alive with the sound of music."

Hulda, chuckling. Saying she just might at that.

Walking past the restaurant, a small crowd inside. Stopping at the kiosk, all of them buying postcards. Up the steps to the observation deck. To the highest point in eastern North America. Up there, Hulda hugging them each in turn, her cheek pressing into theirs. Thanking them through tears. Crying that she never thought she would make it to the top of a mountain again. She had given up hope, but they had made the impossible come true. She could die happily now.

Benches ran along the perimeter of the observation deck. Hulda and Daisy, sitting down, winded, needing to rest. Michael, plunking down, too.

Elisabeth, grabbing him by his shirt. Saying, "Come on, Michael. Let's go explore."

Michael, surprised to hear such words from his mother. Jumping up, ambling down the deck steps ahead of her. Elisabeth, running to keep up.

Hulda and Daisy, settling back in a shared silence, each in her own private paradise. Hulda, busily writing out the postcards. Daisy, thinking of home. Gazing out over the surrounding mountain peaks and remembering happy times in the French and Swiss Alps with Paul. Thinking she could feel his eyes on her, too. Thinking about Lenny getting married and Dennis and Amanda living far away. Feeling a nervousness regarding maintaining the house by herself. What if Dennis was right—especially now that Lenny was remarrying? Maybe she should sell the house, not to move into The Carillion but maybe into a little apartment like Hulda's. An apartment would simplify things. It would eliminate the issue of gardening.

But it would also eliminate the garden. Daisy loved her garden. Sighing. No closer to knowing what to do than before she had left Liverpool.

Michael and Elisabeth, trolling around the top of the mountain, starting down various hiking trails but not going far. Talking about how awesome it would be to actually hike up from the bottom to the top. Michael, saying, "If Dad could ever take a vacation again, we should come back here. He'd love it."

"So would Josh and David," Elisabeth, adding. "Pete and Steve, too. We should come back here in early August before they leave for college. It's only a six-hour drive." Elisabeth, thinking she'd better get herself on an exercise machine first—and fast.

Hiking around, spinning family plans. Eventually deciding it must be time to head back.

Finding it was actually past time to head back. Out of earshot, they had not heard the many shouts of the employees that the last train was departing momentarily. Daisy and Hulda, already at the bottom of the observation deck steps waiting for them. Panicked that they would miss the last train down. Both in an old lady tizzy.

Michael, pleading for a bottle of water, saying he'd be quick getting one from the kiosk. Elisabeth, thrusting two dollar bills in his hand, telling him to hurry.

Michael actually made it to the train before them, such was Hulda's pace this late in the day. Standing at the doors with a sly smile and a bottle of water in hand, telling them to get a move on. Holding the door open as his mother whipped in past him, with Daisy right behind. The two looking around for a seat, heading toward the front. Hulda, slowly bringing up the rear, handing Michael her purse to hold. Michael, looking from front to back for a seat, trying to decide whether to be in the front near his mother and Daisy or at the back as he had been on the way up. Deciding on the front, heading that way, thinking it would have the better views. The people in the half-full car, talking quietly, pointing out things outside the windows, taking last-minute pictures.

The doors closing. The cog train starting down the mountain. The driver again making jokes about bad brakes.

Halfway down the mountain, Daisy, suddenly startled. Looking around. Alarmed. Saying, "Where's Hulda?"

The three of them shaken, peering into every face, no Hulda. Sweat springing up. Notifying the driver that they had left an old lady behind. *How could they?*

The driver, shrugging his shoulders, saying, "These things happen. There's not much we can do about it now. I'll radio up when we get to the bottom."

None of them speaking. Staring wordlessly out the window for the torturous duration down.

THE DRIVER, RADIOING up from the bottom, talking to Charley at the top. Telling him they had left a Hulda Kheist behind. Charley had been managing the mountain for thirty-seven years. He had seen this before—usually kids and sometimes old people, but not usually that old: ninety-three! Not to worry. She was probably in the restaurant. She could come down with the crew.

Elisabeth, Daisy, and Michael, with Hulda's purse on his lap, sitting on a bench in front of the display tractor. Going over the circumstances of entering the cog train. All of them feeling guilty. Hoping she wouldn't be mad at them.

Thirty minutes later the radio crackling on. Charley, telling the driver that Hulda was not in the restaurant, in the ladies room, at the kiosk, or on the observation deck. In short, they couldn't find her. They would keep looking.

Sullen faces on the bench. Daisy, saying, "Goodness, this is terrible." Elisabeth and Michael, nodding.

M ORE CRACKLING FROM THE RADIO and then a voice: "Stuart, we have a situation here. We can't find her. She's not anywhere we've looked. My people have to come down. They need to go home. I don't often do this, but can you ask her family to come up and look? I'll stay and take them down. You can bring the crew back down with you."

Hurrying on board. Starting up. No jokes about bad brakes this time.

C HARLEY WAITING FOR THEM at the top. The crew ambling past them into the cog train. Starting down almost immediately. Daisy, Elisabeth, and Michael, introducing themselves to Charley. Charley, asking them if they thought there was any chance that Hulda had started down the mountain on her own on one of the many trails. Would she be likely to do such a thing?

Shaking their heads. Elisabeth, saying, "She's in good shape, amazing for ninety-three, and she did grow up in Switzerland, so it is possible but unlikely."

"Well, she has to be somewhere," Charley, saying. "Why don't we spread out and call her name. Maybe she got confused. If she hears your voices, that will help." Singling out Daisy, saying, "Now don't you go wandering off alone."

"I'll stay with her," Michael, promising.

"Lucky thing it's June twenty-first," Charley, saying. "We can use the extra sunlight."

"Shouldn't we call the police?" Elisabeth, asking.

"They won't come to the top to find someone who has been missing less than two hours. No way." Shaking his head with conviction. "Now, why don't we fan out? Everyone go off in a different direction. There are several trails down. Don't go too far or too long. I don't need any of you getting lost unescorted on the mountain with no staff but me. Technically, we shouldn't even be doing this."

Nodding their thanks, setting off.

Finding nothing. Hulda had disappeared into thin air.

FORTY-ONE

BARELY SLEEPING A WINK. Tossing and turning and up talking in the dark. At around three, turning the light back on. The three of them rotating through roles, moving from blaming themselves to counseling the others.

In The Swiss Hut—them, their overnight bags, and Hulda's purse.

They had come down from the mountain in near darkness after three fruitless hours of searching. Daisy's knees were weak from fatigue and threatened to go out from under her. Charley finally called the police. They said what Charley said they would: They couldn't do anything that night. It was too soon and too dangerous to send up search teams or helicopters into the mountain at that hour because of updrafts and limited visibility.

Elisabeth phoned Richard to tell him they would have to spend another night. Richard, who had been called out from a meeting, consoled her and told her not to worry, that he would go back to the meeting and inform everyone that he had to go. He would be on the next train home to take the boys off Ann's hands. He would get the boys together and go out for Chinese food. Satisfied, Elisabeth hung up and went back to worrying with Daisy and Michael. The three of them tried to imagine what Hulda was doing up there on the mountain alone in the dark.

Charley had promised to get a search team together to assemble at first light in the morning. So there they were, counting the minutes until daybreak.

THEY WERE AMONG the first to arrive at the mountain, well before it opened to tourists. Charley handed the lead to the captain of the police, Captain Miller. Word had begun to get around that a search party was being formed. People trickled in to offer their time and their hearts. Daisy, Elisabeth, and Michael were asked to be on hand to field questions that might arise in addition to what they had already told the police. A crowd formed, the cog train filled, taking special search units to the top where they would scour the area before fanning out to work their way down. Regular people were being organized at the bottom to work their way up. There were search helicopters and dogs that had sniffed Hulda's garments from her overnight bag. They would find her, Daisy, Michael, and Elisabeth were assured. Captain Miller, placing his rough hand on Daisy's shoulder.

The three of them mingling with the people who had come to help. Joining them in the circle that had formed around the police. Listening to the policeman with the bullhorn saying, "Pick a path and start up slowly. Look both right and left off the path, for Hulda can be anywhere. There is no guarantee she's on a path or even near one. She's ninety-three." Repeating that. "Ninety-three."

People breaking into small groups, talking in hushed voices. No laughter.

The three of them staying back to make themselves available to answer any questions, then slowly spreading out on their own. Sticking together, picking a path—one of many—to start up. Not that they thought they would make it to the top. It was an eight-hour walk for those in good shape, six for the stars, and four for the superstars.

Daisy was exhausted from all the walking the night before, plus she had had a sleepless night. Ordinarily she would take to keeping off her feet, but this was not ordinary. She continued walking, stopping often to rest, taking a break on every bench they came to.

The weather, suddenly changing. Clouds hustling in, unseen until they were overhead, knocking out the sun. The air, already heavy with humidity, thickening, turning a dreary day more dreary.

A group of two men and two women, all members of the National Ski Patrol during winter months, overtaking them on the path although they had just started out. Reaching them in fifteen minutes. It had taken Daisy, Elisabeth, and Michael over an hour. A quick exchange of information. Daisy, thanking them for volunteering. They said they were happy to and continued on, propelled up the mountain on strong ski legs—unlike Daisy, who was winded, perspiring, and nearly hobbling but insisting that she was fine, saying it was Hulda they had to worry about.

Elisabeth, worrying about both, wondering if they should turn around, go back to the bottom, check in with Captain Miller, get Daisy some water and a place to sit.

Doing all that. Back on the bench at the bottom, Daisy, saying, "This is awful." Coated in perspiration, red in the face. "How could this have happened?" Asking for the hundredth time.

"What are we going to do?" Elisabeth, small twigs undetected in her cropped hair. Exhausted herself.

No one answering.

Michael, in between them, his face falling into his palms. "Maybe she'll hear the cog train and go back up to get it."

The people around them had a purpose. Everyone there was there for the search. "I wonder if anything will change when it opens to the public. Do they ask everyone to help or not mention it at all?" Elisabeth, inquiring.

Neither Daisy nor Michael answering. They didn't know the answer and were too tired to speculate. They could only sit and stare at the people with not an ounce of strength left to give. All of them, totally spent, needing a fresh burst of energy. Michael, going to buy a supply of water bottles and giant Snickers bars from the vending machines. Returning, handing them out. Eating and drinking, but still needing more of a boost.

Getting more of a boost. From a certain face in the crowd.

Daisy's arm flying to Michael, with an unwrapped Snickers bar in her hand, Snickers residue smudged on her lower lip.

Michael, turning to her. Seeing her face. Following her eyes watching the people heading for the open cog train. Looking as if she had just spotted Hulda. Michael, saying jokingly, "What? Did Hulda join her own search team?"

Daisy, not laughing with him. Saying, "Look, over there." Pointing. Words squeezed tightly through unmoving breath.

Elisabeth and Michael, eyeing the crowd. Seeing, not too far away, a tall, robust old man with a younger woman, maybe fifty, at his side, her hands wrapped around his left forearm. Both of them were boarding the cog train, moving in step with the group through the open doors of the car.

Elisabeth, "What, Daisy?"

"That could be him."

Elisabeth, "Him who?" Suddenly getting it. "You mean Michael Baker?"

Michael, excited. "Really?"

Daisy, her voice shaky, saying, "It could be. I'm not sure."

Michael, urgently, "Quick. Let's go ask before he gets away." Pulling on Daisy, yanking her off the bench to her feet.

Elisabeth, getting up, too. The three racing across the grass to the train. Groups of people were in their way, some walking, some stalled. Michael, pulling Daisy, trying to get her to go faster. Daisy, moving as fast as her thin legs would take her, trying to see through the crowd. Losing sight of him. Hurrying, wondering if it could be. Could it really be? Could they really have found him? Was that really him, or was she just exhausted and seeing things? Was he just a tall old man?

Michael, saying a little more loudly, "Come on, Daisy, faster."

Daisy was moving faster than she had in half a century, but not fast enough. The doors on the cog were starting to close.

Michael, saying more urgently, "Come on, Daisy."

Daisy, panting, red in the face. "I can't go any faster."

Elisabeth, looking at her. Worried. "Take it easy, Michael. It's not worth a heart attack."

Michael, yelling, "But the doors are closing!" Letting go of her. Taking off. Running up to the train. The doors closed, the train beginning to depart. Michael, peering into the crowded car. Finding the man. Shouting, "Are you Michael Baker?" Feeling the old man's eyes on him. Getting no reaction.

The woman with him, shaking her head, calling through the closed window, "No, sorry."

The wheels of the train slowly turning, beginning its journey up the mountain. Michael, hurrying alongside it, keeping pace with it, ignoring the woman. His eyes were on only the man. Shouting, "Did you ever play the piano?"

The woman, sliding a window down, leaning her head out, saying, "Please leave my father alone. We're here to help in the search." Pulling her head in.

Michael, suddenly indignant, running alongside the train. "You don't have to tell me about the search! We *are* the search. Hulda came here with *us*. And we came here to find *you*!" Pointing at the old man. Michael, jogging, trying to keep up with the train. Running over uneven terrain. Knocked off balance by the tip of a boulder implanted in the mountainside. Stumbling. Falling. Hitting the ground. Looking up, watching the train moving away. Screaming at it in desperation: "Daisy Phillips is looking for you. She's right there." Pointing at Daisy some yards back. Daisy, panting, leaning on Elisabeth. The two stumbling over the grass, making their way toward him. Michael, scrambling up from the ground, cleaning himself off. Suddenly tired. Suddenly wanting to go home. Suddenly done with the whole darn thing.

The train gone, the three returning to the bench. Daisy, apologizing. Doubting it was him. Feeling guilty for causing trouble. Noticing the change in Michael's face. How young he looked, how tired, how unhappy.

Daisy, handing him another Snickers bar. Finishing her own.

E IGHT MORE HOURS. No closer to a resolution. Breaking for dinner, leaving the mountain. Eating heartily, feeling guilty about their lusty appetites and their pleasure in the food. Asking themselves again what they should do. How could this have happened? Where could Hulda be? And what if they didn't find her after dinner?

Back again to the mountain, dreading another nightfall.

Nothing found. Search units, people, and dogs were dismissed for the night.

Elisabeth, making several more phone calls to Richard, to the children, and to her mother, explaining that they needed another night.

Rolling wearily into The Swiss Hut. Hand-washing their undergarments, hanging them over the shower rail to dry. Hoping the phone would ring with good news.

Fast asleep by nine.

N O CALLS. UP by first light. Rubbing sleep from their eyes. A heaviness in their bodies. Dragging through their ablutions.

And then it hit Michael. Suddenly. While brushing his teeth over the cream-colored porcelain sink, staring at himself in the fluorescent-lit mirror. One word popping into his head: Yodeli.

Flying out of the bathroom. Frantic. Demanding that they go: They had to save Yodeli! Hulda was probably worried sick about him. She had left only enough food and water for one night, and it had been three. They had better get going.

Elisabeth and Daisy stopped folding their pajamas. Turning to look at each other. Both saying, "What do you think?"

Michael, pleading with them. Throwing his pajamas and toothbrush into his overnight bag. Screaming that they had to go. Elisabeth, suggesting that they call Brian Davis and ask him to go into Hulda's apartment to feed the bird. Michael, exploding, charging her with idiocy. Saying that Brian Davis would never do it, he would never do a thing for Hulda, and she should know that.

Elisabeth and Daisy, thinking a minute. Talking it over. Finally agreeing that going to Yodeli was the right thing to do, that Hulda would say there were enough people on the mountain to help her but no one was helping Yodeli.

Elisabeth, making a phone call to the police. Explaining to Captain Miller that they had to get back. Leaving all her relevant contact information with him. Thanking him enormously for his help, saying they would be in touch.

Pulling out of the parking lot of The Swiss Hut, another mission on their minds.

FORTY-TWO

THERE DIDN'T SEEM to be anything more to be said. Hulda's empty seat was the loudest thing in the car. It was a terrible feeling, leaving the mountains behind. Leaving Hulda behind. If not for the goal of helping Yodeli, they might not have been able to do it.

They needed to. They needed to get back. For the boys and Richard and Ann, who had been picking up the slack, and Elisabeth's job.

BACK IN BROOKLYN. Not far from Hulda's apartment. Daisy, asking how they were going to get into it.

"No problem," Michael, reminding them. "I have that bag she gave me. She must have her keys in there." Reaching down between his feet. Picking it up. Hesitating before opening it, fingering the latch. "It's okay, right?"

Assuring him it was. He was just going to get her keys.

But that wasn't what happened. Because right there at the top of the bag was something addressed to him. And to Daisy. And to Elisabeth— postcards from Mount Washington. Written out at the top of the mountain from a bench on the observation deck while Daisy sat nearby in the bright sunlight and Michael and Elisabeth ambled around.

Postcards written to them.

"Oh, no." Michael, reading. "Oh, no. Mom?" His voice, younger.

Elisabeth, looking over at him but keeping an eye on the bustling Brooklyn street ahead. "Michael, what is it?"

A bad feeling creeping in.

Daisy, leaning forward from the backseat, her hand on the side of Michael's seat.

His voice shaky, Michael, saying, "Mom, pull over."

Elisabeth, a sideways glance at him. Pulling over to the side of the road. There was nowhere to park. Double-parking, using her emergency flashers, blinking rhythmically. Turning to Michael. The postcards. Nodding for him to go on.

Beginning in a wobbly voice: "Dear Daisy, Elisabeth, and Michael. I don't know when you'll be reading this, but by the time you do, I will certainly be missing—for hours or days, I don't know. Or maybe I will have already been found, found how I want to be found—as a part of the mountain. I hope you will forgive me the grief and inconvenience I have caused you in doing what I did. I am doing what I want to do—ending my days with Albert's name on my lips and those of my children and parents, how and when and where of my choosing."

Michael, flipping to the second postcard. "You three have made my wishes come true, for there is no glory in dying alone in a Brooklyn apartment with the landlord celebrating at my last gasp. But there is in returning to a place like my parents knew and their parents before them. You have allowed me to end my time on earth at a place so reminiscent of my beginning.

"Please, if I could ask, get in touch with my son in Venezuela. He's number one on my speed dial."

Switching to the third postcard, Michael, reading, "Elisabeth, please take my recipe book and always make the Mailaenderli cookies for sweet Michael. Michael, I would like you to take Yodeli. Maybe you'll be able to get him to yodel! And Daisy, what can I say other than thank you. Your spirit and bravery in coming alone to New York are what started this. You gave me the guts. I'm looking at you now as I write this in the glittering sunlight. You're beautiful. I wish I could do more to help you succeed in your goal. Best of luck in reaching it.

"Love to you all, Hulda Kheist."

"Oh, no," Daisy saying, her voice cracking, her mouth dry.

"Holy shit." Elisabeth.

Silence from Michael. The three postcards spreading across his hands. Rereading them. Wrapping his young brain around them.

"She planned the whole thing," Elisabeth, realizing.

Daisy, slowly nodding. "That's why she gave Michael her purse."

In the car, silence except for the clicking of the emergency flashers. Three heads, grappling, trying to absorb. Street sounds from outside. A hot, humid day in late June. New Yorkers out in shorts, sandals, tank tops. People from all over the world. Cranky babies in strollers. Dogs pulling against their leashes, sniffing. An old woman pushing a grocery cart. A young man carrying a guitar in a big black case.

Daisy, her eyes on the postcards in Michael's hands, wondering what to think. Picturing Hulda on the mountaintop hunched over the postcards, busily writing. Picturing herself sitting right there, just a few feet away, not having any idea what Hulda was doing. Now, sitting here, not having any idea what she was feeling. Confused. Needing time. Needing it to settle inside her. Needing to sift through all her emotions. It was so big.

"We should call Captain Miller. He has to be told this." Elisabeth, taking charge.

"So she might be dead?" Michael, asking, looking at his mother. His lower lip quivering, tears in his eyes. Elisabeth, silently marveling that he hadn't already feared that. That what had been taunting her mind never entered his. She looked at him a long minute without answering. Wondering if she should let whatever process it was that had kept him from thinking the worst to continue protecting him. Should she let him off the hook, not burden him with the truth? Protect him from being uncomfortably close to death? From rubbing up against it in this way?

For Hulda had literally left him holding the bag. Cementing her hope that she and the weekend would never be forgotten.

Elisabeth, looking Michael softly in the eye. Slowly nodding her head. He had asked for the truth, she had to give it to him. "It's what she wanted." Her voice gentle, caring, loving.

Michael, biting his top lip. Tears welling up. Releasing. Crying long and hard. Full of fear and sorrow.

Elisabeth, taking him into her arms across the car's dividing console. Cradling him like a baby. Comforting him as in days gone by. Soaking in the smell of his hair, his skin, his scalp. Thinking she would continue inhaling him as long as he let her.

Finding deep contentment in the moment.

THEY HAD TO PULL themselves together. Wipe the tears from their eyes. Rescue Yodeli.

Elisabeth and Michael, breaking apart. Elisabeth, reaching for her cell phone. Michael, staring forlornly out the window. The postcards still in his hands. His eyes fixed on a sunflower in the corner of someone's garden. His thoughts six hours away.

Daisy, feeling for Michael. Her heart breaking, wanting to reach out to comfort him. But resisting it. It was Elisabeth's moment. With one eye on Michael, Elisabeth, managing to find the torn paper in her bag with Captain Miller's phone number on it. Managing to dial.

The call, answered almost immediately. Elisabeth, explaining. Captain Miller, saying the new information would change the nature of the search but not end the search. He thanked her for calling, expressed his sympathy, said they would be in touch.

Elisabeth hung up, glanced over at Michael, who was still staring out the window. Resisting the urge to rub his shoulder, not wanting to push too far.

Shifting into drive, heading for the apartment. Double-parking in front, flashers going. They got out. Michael had the keys.

On their way up the exterior front steps, Elisabeth, saying, "I hope we don't have to see that Brian Davis. Anything but sadness on his part might push me over the edge."

"I might knock him down the stairs." Michael.

"I'd take his heart out." Daisy.

"Hopefully he's at work." Elisabeth, thinking that that's where she should be. If she misses tomorrow, it would be a full week. Thinking "Holy shit, they must be pissed." Watching Michael, trying the first key. Seeing it didn't work.

Trying another. Success. Pushing the heavy front door open. Stepping inside. Instinctively inhaling. No yummy food smells. "It seems like he's not home," Michael, murmuring.

Up the stairs they went to the first landing. Passing the door with the child's drawings of flowers and the sun. Starting toward the second, hearing the sound of a door opening, a voice from below.

"Hulda? Is that you?" Brian Davis. Coming down his hall toward the stairs.

Three sets of alarmed eyes looking at one another. Michael, asking, "What do we tell him?"

No time to answer. Brian Davis, bounding up the stairs. "Where've you been, gone three nights?"

Rounding onto the first landing, slamming headlong into the space where they stood. Halting, his eyes sliding over and across each of them, remembering them. Looking in the space between them, around them. For Hulda. A moment passing before anyone spoke.

"What are you doing here? Where's Hulda?"

No one answering, shifting their weight, blinking.

Again, "Where's Hulda? I've been worried about her silly bird. I almost went in to feed the damn thing myself, but then I thought she'd hit the roof if she caught me. So where is she? When's she coming back?" Looking from face to face for an answer. "What's the matter with you guys? Cat got your tongue?"

Daisy, clearing her throat. Saying, "She's not coming back. We think she's gone."

"Gone?"

"Passed away . . . in New Hampshire." Daisy.

"No way." Brian, falling back, leaning against the wall, acting incredulously, as if it were impossible, as if she hadn't been ninety-three, and, most surprising of all, as if he cared. "How?"

"On Mount Washington. We all went to the top. She never came down. They're still searching for her up there." Elisabeth, this time.

Brian, asking, "On a mountain?" Tenderly. With feeling. "She probably loved that. Did you see the painting on the hallway wall outside her apartment? Of course you did; you'd have to be blind to miss it." Processing the news. Muddling through it. "She died on a mountain. I don't believe it."

"It's true," Elisabeth, saying. "She died on a mountain, and we have her keys. We're going up to her apartment to take the bird home with us."

"And her recipe book," Michael, adding. "And don't forget she wants us to call her son."

"She's really gone? I just can't believe it." Brian Davis, barefoot, wearing a loose white T-shirt, black shorts, rubbing his forehead, his eyes with the back of his hand. "I've imagined this day for fourteen years, and

now I'm sorry. I don't believe it. I guess I'm more of a sap than I realized."
Shaking his head, starting up the stairs, going around them to lead the
way. "The poor thing must be starving."

Daisy, Michael, and Elisabeth following him, blinking at one another
in stupefaction. Stopping at the wall-sized painting of the Alps. Holding it
in view, its new dimension.

Brian, saying, "You know, I don't even think I'm going to paint over
it. It's been here since 1938. It's more a part of the building than I am. I'm
keeping it." Then, to their astonishment, adding "It will make Hulda
happy."

Stepping out of the way so that Michael could get to the door with
the key. Michael, opening it. Going in, looking around in a state of hyper
awareness. Everything resonating with them. Feeling creepy.

Seeing the bird in its cage with an empty water bowl and an empty
food bowl. Yodeli, looking back at them with intense, distrusting coal-
black eyes until Michael brought fresh water and filled the bowl to the
top with food. Daisy and Elisabeth, tending to the other things Hulda
had requested. Brian, standing around unanchored, his hands balled in
the front pockets of his shorts. Shaking his head in disbelief.

FORTY-THREE

Home. Pulling into the driveway. Relieved.

Michael, popping out of the SUV, carefully retrieving the birdcage.

David and Josh, hearing they were home, flying out of the house, down the steps, into their mother's arms. She had never been away three nights before. Fighting over her, vying for turf on her body, both pushing the other away with his hips, arms wrapped tightly around her waist.

Elisabeth, laughing. Enjoying it.

Then Richard, in a red T-shirt, coming out onto the porch. Unshaven. Ungroomed. On a Thursday. In the early afternoon. Wonder of wonders, he had taken the day off, Josh and David having pleaded until he yielded. He broke in between David and Josh for a hug. Folding his arms around Elisabeth, murmuring that he had missed her. Sympathizing that she had gotten more than she had bargained for.

Elisabeth, in his arms, thinking how she hadn't given Heather Clarke so much as a single thought the whole time she was gone, and she wouldn't begin now that she was back. A small part of her was savvy enough to know the truth: that the Heather Clarke worry, and the Dart Man before that, was all self-induced, brought on by herself. If she rifled around inside herself for only a minute, she would figure out why.

But she didn't have to because her next trip to the bathroom was going to present her with a present in the form of an oblong red stain in her panties. Pop some corks. She still had it. But, as Hulda said, things would fall away over time. They would, and that would be one of them. But Hulda had also said that what was left hanging on would be the most important thing: her core, her essence, the person she really was. Elisabeth, smiling, hugging Richard back, thinking it was okay, thinking that everything was okay, even better than okay.

Richard, turning to greet Daisy, expressing his disappointment in her not having found Michael Baker.

Daisy, looking earnestly into his face, tending to the disarrayed hair on her forehead. Telling him that in coming here she had found so much more. Thanking him for lending her two of his dear family members for the journey. And announcing that this time it really was time for her to go. She was going to book a flight for the next day. She did not want to keep Lenny and Sarah waiting any longer.

Saying that she would leave the watch with Michael. If he wanted to continue the search, he could. If not, that was okay, too. It would be fitting for him to keep the watch.

Michael, at the moment anyway, had no interest in continuing the search. He had had enough. Struggling up the stairs with the enormous birdcage, yelling his thanks for the watch, begging Daisy to stay longer. Richard, hastening to help him with the cage, seeing that one of the legs was caught on a step.

Elisabeth, joining Michael's chorus that Daisy should stay just a little longer, to rest a few days before traveling home.

Daisy, shaking her head. It was time for her to go. Following them up the steps, into the house. To hit the computer. To book a flight. On the Internet—all by herself.

FORTY-FOUR

S HE COULDN'T DO IT. It became painfully clear within just a few
weeks that Amanda just couldn't do it.

Dennis had gotten over that he had had to do all the unpack-
ing himself. She always had a little something that caused her to run over
to her mother's. He had gotten over her tirade when she heard that Lenny
was remarrying. He had listened dutifully as she rambled on about how
his mother owes those three stepgrandchildren nothing and how Lenny's
marriage didn't have to change their inheritance prospects one bit. He
had gotten over eating dinner alone almost every night since they had
moved and that she was putting off looking for a job while she yelled that
he hadn't made more than one appointment for an interview himself.
He had gotten over all that. But there was one thing he just wouldn't be
able to get over, and Amanda managed to find it.

He had just come back from the shops where he had passed up the
fine ales although his tongue was hanging out of his mouth. He made the
case in defense of the ale to his brain, hoping his brain would send out a
message to his hand to pick up a bottle. But Dennis was strong. He
pushed his trolley past the rows of captivating bottles and picked up a
single box of pasta, a single jar of sauce, and a package of broccoli. He
headed home with a stiff upper lip, reminding himself that the beauty of

the surroundings in which he now lived was worth more than an ale sliding down his throat. He also reminded himself that Amanda was happy and that was what really mattered.

Back in the house, a pasta pot on to boil. The jar of sauce in the saucepan. The broccoli cut into florets, waiting to be sautéed in a little garlic and olive oil. Dennis, putting in a jazz CD, scrolling through job sites on the Internet, hoping to find someone who was looking for someone in his mid-fifties who'd done nothing for a decade after a splashy book publishing adventure and worked for decades editing a dying *Artifacts, Archeological Treasures, and Antiquities* magazine, an expert in seventeenth-century artifacts.

Not surprisingly, nothing popped out at him. Causing him to really want that pint of ale. Finding himself justifying having just one, telling himself that things weren't so urgent yet that he couldn't have a single pint. Turning off the computer, on his way out to grab one. Amanda, rolling into the driveway. Her long leg exiting the car before the rest of her. Standing up tall, smiling up at the house, hurrying up the walk, her heavy bag slung over her shoulder.

Charging over to Dennis, full of good cheer, taking the sides of his face in each of her hands, squeezing them together. Kissing him hard on the lips. Saying, "You're never going to guess what I just did." Kissing him again. His face was in a vice between her strong hands, being crushed from both sides into the middle. She was bouncing on the balls of her feet.

"Now, promise me you won't be upset. I know it was a little extravagant, and I know I promised not to buy anything for a year, but, oh, darling, how could I resist? It would have taken superhuman strength because it was such an amazing deal! You should be proud of me, not angry. Do you promise?" Kissing him longer and harder.

Dennis, taking a step back, worrying that his face might not come out of her kisses undented. Wanting to ask what she was going on about, but his lips were under siege. Fighting off the kiss. Asking what he feared most: "You didn't buy anything, did you?"

Amanda, pausing. Nodding. Meekly. Her teeth clenched in a guilty grin.

"Oh, no, Amanda," Dennis, saying, massaging his cheeks. They were throbbing. "You didn't. What? What did you buy?"

Amanda, becoming worried. Her good cheer being quickly replaced by fear. Realizing now that she might not be able to wriggle out of this one. Looking at Dennis's face, seeing an impatience she hadn't seen before. Taking a deep breath, pulling herself up to her full statuesque height, telling herself that he was just going to have to take this one on the chin, not her. Opening her charm full throttle, drawing her fingers through her hair, tossing her head in a beguiling way—a way that had worked wonders in the past.

Dennis, repeating the question. Tonelessly. Through a tight mouth.

Amanda, "I got us a great deal on something we've always wanted, something we've talked about for years." More hair maneuvering.

Dennis, impatient, his whole body stiffened for battle, barking out: "What?"

"A baby grand." Giggling a little guiltily now that it was out. Reaching for "coquettish" but instead getting "nervous."

"You didn't!" Dennis, really blowing his top. Veins bulging across every patch of exposed skin. "A piano! A baby grand? Are you out of your mind?"

Amanda, staring at him in horror. She had never seen anything like it from him before. Her lower lip trembled.

"Return it! You hear me? Cancel the order! We don't have the money for that!"

"I got us on a monthly installment plan, interest free! I thought you'd be excited." Weakly.

Roaring, "That's because you live in a fantasy world! There's no way anyone listening to the things I've been saying could think I'd be excited. You'd better call the credit card company right now and cancel it! I'm going out for a pint, and when I come back, you'd better tell me it's been canceled!"

Storming off. Leaving her nervously chewing on the ends of her long mane.

D ENNIS, SOME TIME LATER. One pint had slipped into four. Mounting his front steps, ready to do battle. Throwing open the door.

To an empty house and a note on the kitchen table. Saying, in scrolling, flowery handwriting:

> *Dennis,*
>
> *You owe me an apology. I think you must know that by now, having sufficiently cooled off, I hope. You had no right to blow up at me that way when all I did was try to make you happy and furnish you with the beautiful home you so deserve. I know you want a piano. You've said so many, many times. And the deal I got was really a steal. Of course you wouldn't know, running off the way you did. I'm sure later we can talk about this like two adults, and when you hear how low the monthly payment is, you'll come to the right conclusion. I'll be at my mother's. Call when you're ready to talk sensibly.*
>
> *With kisses,*
> *Amanda.*

Dennis, reading it only once. Finding that he *was* ready to talk sensibly—but not to her, to the Realtor.

Alone in the huge bed, sleeping soundly. Up at dawn. Showered. Sufficiently packed by breakfast. Locking the front door behind him. Throwing his suitcase in the car. Picking up the sign so recently stowed away on the top shelf in the garage. Taking it outside with him.

Planting it firmly in the front garden.

FOR SALE. In bright, blazing letters.

Satisfied, he stood back, rubbing his hands together, cleaning them. Washing them of the whole mess. Then getting in his car, pulling out of the driveway.

Heading for the motorway.

FORTY-FIVE

DAISY, UP AT DAWN. SHOWERED. Completely packed by break-fast. She spent the early hours sipping tea before the boys were up. Richard and Elisabeth had said their good-byes before going to bed the night before. Elisabeth had hugged and kissed Daisy, saying she wanted to bring the whole family to see her at *her* home this year. Richard, in a blue-and-white-striped robe and slippers, said that would be nice but they simply didn't have the money. He re-minded Elisabeth that now they had *two* kids in college. Elisabeth sighed and got ready to go to work. She apologized before she left that she couldn't take Daisy to the airport. She couldn't possibly take an-other day off.

Daisy told her not to worry. She leaned over and gave her a kiss on the forehead, a motherly kiss.

Now Daisy, alone in the living room, waiting for the boys to wake up, listening to the plentiful sounds of birds from beyond the sliding glass doors. Going through old photo albums, enjoying seeing the boys when they were small. Flipping pages, watching them grow. Trying to pretend that she wasn't going to miss them much. But what she had told Richard was true: She hadn't been successful in what had brought her there, but she had found so much more.

✦ ✦ ✦

ELISABETH, BACK AT HER DESK. Having dealt with the concerns for her health, the questions, and the expressions of sympathy. A summer flu? There is nothing worse. And how was she feeling now? Better? That's good.

Elisabeth, looking around her office. Her eyes sliding over the dull, light-blue walls, shelves of books, photos, and objects that covered far too many years to remember. Everything was the same, depressingly so—except the piles of tax returns, the to-do list, and the inbox. They had all gotten higher and more backed up.

Looking at the tax return on her computer screen with all its blank lines, Form 6258. An open file full of spreadsheets on her desk. Resisting the urge to X out of the tax return and log on to PuppyFinder.com just for a minute, just to get a peek at Saint Bernard puppies or English mastiffs or schnauzers. Anything would be fine. Anything would be better than Form 6258 with all those blank lines stubbornly waiting to be filled in.

Her thoughts were six hours away—on the mountains and Hulda, who was still on the mountain. She had spoken to Captain Miller a little while ago. The search was still on, the unit smaller. Volunteers had diminished to a handful of stalwart souls. He was surprised that Hulda still had not turned up. He thought she must be deep in the woods. He promised Elisabeth that they wouldn't stop until she was found.

Elisabeth, wishing she were back there on the mountain with the fresh clean air—so clean that it sparkled in the sunlight—and the clear mountain lakes and the vigorously running rivers of water cascading over smooth, colossal white rocks. The beauty of healthy nature.

Feeling sad that Daisy was going. Elisabeth, sighing, resting her chin on the inverted cup of her hand, her elbow leaning on her desk. Wishing she was back in New Hampshire. Wishing she was home. Wishing Daisy was staying longer. Wishing that they were all going back to Liverpool with her. Wishing herself anywhere but there. Resisting the urge to go on PuppyFinder.com.

Logging on to eBay instead.

Putting her living room furniture up for sale.

SHORTLY BEFORE DAISY had to go, Ann was on her way to Elisabeth's to get her. Daisy was at the table with Pete, Michael, Josh, David, and Steve, now back from college, all of them eating breakfast. Daisy, saying that if she could, she'd like to come back the following summer to see them. The boys agreeing that a whole year away was too long.

Steve, asking questions about Liverpool. Daisy, repeating stories by request.

Ann, arriving. Bringing small grandchildren with her. They raced into the kitchen, electrifying the house.

Daisy and the boys, clearing the table, placing bowls into the dishwasher. A clinking of dish against dish.

Daisy, making a final request before going. "Michael, would you please do one thing for me?"

Michael, surprised, curiosity on his face. Happy to be singled out in the room crowded with his brothers. Nodding, yes.

"It's been a long time since I've heard a Michael play the piano."

The request, settling in. Michael, shaking it off. Saying, "I'm really sorry, Daisy. Anything but that."

Daisy, deeply disappointed. Telling him so by the expression on her face.

Josh and David, taking off, fighting each other all the way to the piano. Josh won and slid onto the piano bench. Filling the room with Chopin. David, huffy, arms across his chest, falling back on the sofa.

Daisy, asking Ann if they had time to listen to one last piece from each one. Ann, saying they did. Daisy, in a big armchair, telling them she was recording their playing in her head so that she could play it back when she got home.

The phone, ringing. David, racing for it. Answering it. Bringing it to Daisy. Saying it was a man asking for her.

Daisy guessing that it was Captain Miller. "Hello?" Blinking as she listened. "What?" Blinking again. Her eyes wide in surprise. More blinking. More listening. Every face in the room on hers. "Really? All right. Hold on a moment."

Holding the phone away from her face, looking at everyone.

Saying, "Dennis has just landed in New York."

FORTY-SIX

DENNIS, SITTING IN ONE OF the blue seats in a waiting room at the airport. Looking tired, haggard. Relieved to see Daisy. Saying, first words out of his mouth, "It's a good thing you didn't sell your house."

Introductions. Dennis, thanking Ann many times over, saying he hoped he hadn't put her out.

The Belt Parkway on the car ride home. Slow but steady. Ann, calling Elisabeth.

Elisabeth, at her desk. Plodding through the tax return. Three lines were filled in on Form 6258. Ann, on the phone, telling her that Daisy canceled her flight. Telling her why.

Elisabeth, listening, getting the news. Hanging up. Feeling left out. Thinking about what she had just learned: Daisy was staying longer, and Dennis was here, a cousin, a new houseguest.

Elisabeth, trying like mad to concentrate on issues of taxation so she could get out of there at a reasonable hour. She wanted to be there when Cousin Dennis got to her house.

◆　◆　◆

ENNIS, IN THE BACKSEAT of Ann's van on the Belt Parkway, filling them in on the particulars. Daisy and Ann, shocked at Amanda. Shaking their heads. Dennis, saying he really just needed a few days to repair his battered self, that he would go home when Daisy did. Thanking Ann again. His cell phone ringing. Guessing it was Amanda.

It wasn't.

It was Lenny. Asking Dennis if he knew what was going on with their mother, when she would be getting back home. He and Sarah were really getting anxious. They didn't want to wait much longer.

Dennis, smiling, knocking Lenny for a loop. "You want to know about Mum? Why don't you ask her? She's sitting right here." Handing her the phone.

Blowing Lenny away. Dennis was in New York with their mother! Without telling him! Calling Dennis a sneak. Saying that he would be calling right back. Hanging up.

Dennis, laughing, loving Lenny's outrage.

Lenny, calling back. Daisy, answering Dennis's mobile phone. Lenny, as loud as a tuba, asking if it would be all right if he and Sarah and her children came there, too. Saying that Sarah would *love* to get married in New York, that she's absolutely besotted with the idea. Saying they could be on the first flight tomorrow if it was okay.

Daisy, asking Ann.

Ann, saying the more the merrier. Saying there was plenty of room at her house.

THIS WAS THE LAST STRAW for Elisabeth, the very last straw.

Lenny and Sarah and Sarah's children. A wedding to plan. Preparations to be made. Taking place within the next few days.

The very last straw.

Elisabeth, hanging up. X'ing out of the Form 6258 with four lines filled in. X'ing out of the screen with the schnauzer puppies, X'ing out of the English mastiff puppies, X'ing out of the Saint Bernard puppies, X'ing out of the golden doodles.

Shutting down the computer. One-thirty in the afternoon.

Picking up her bag, walking around her desk. Shutting off the light.

Her secretary asking when she could expect her back.

Elisabeth, saying, "Don't." Walking out the door.

FORTY-SEVEN

PLANS IN PLACE. There would be a wedding. That very weekend. The very next day. It was going to be an eight-minute ceremony at the Town Hall, followed by a hasty retreat back to Richard and Elisabeth's for the party.

Where high humidity would wreak havoc on the chips. High heat would wilt the fresh-cut vegetables. The lemonade would be watery, the ice would melt too quickly. Hairdos were going to fall into disrepair. Suits would be ripped off and bathing suits thrown on. Ice pops would be the hot item.

While their husbands were watching the little ones, Elisabeth and her sisters would be busy in the kitchen stripping tinfoil off catered dishes. They would be tripping through the sliding glass doors with them, before setting them up outside on the white paper tablecloths.

Sarah, the overjoyed bride, would be busy keeping an eye on her daughters, encouraging them to talk, to stop hiding behind their hair, to go ahead into the pool and have a dip, have a good time.

Dennis would fill Lenny, the overjoyed groom, in on Amanda.

Elisabeth was going to drop the twin bombs in Richard's lap: her job and their living room furniture. Both were now things of the past.

Ann would be intent on making up for lost time, hardly letting Daisy out of her sight.

And they were all going to get a personal delivery of news about Hulda from two unexpected guests. They would all learn that Hulda had been found miles away from any trail, curled around the base of a mighty pine tree with a smile on her lips.

Daisy, Elisabeth, and Michael were going to be thankful to get the news. And Dennis was going to be stupefied to find the possibility of someone new in his life. One of the two unexpected guests. A fifty-year-old concert pianist named Catherine. A Juilliard graduate, who would mention that she had almost gone to Liverpool once to treat herself to a trip to the Beatles Museum while she was performing in London, but when she found out how pricey the train fare was, she canceled the journey, unable to justify such a frivolous expenditure.

Dennis, hearing that, was going to look as if he just got knocked in the head. He was going to blink several times in rapid succession, thinking that there certainly must be two very distinct species of female. He was going to be very glad to make the acquaintance of this pretty and unmarried second kind. He would make certain that somehow he would see her again.

And Daisy would learn, as if she had ever doubted it, that her mother's coldheartedness had known no bounds. Still, on the calendar of her life in its entirety, she would have a day more than worth circling—doubly circling.

FORTY-EIGHT

FATHER AND DAUGHTER on their way to Long Island. The ride from New Hampshire, long, spotted with traffic. Frequent stops at restrooms extended the trip. Extending the time devoted to talk. An unprecedented delivery of mind-boggling information.

A crack in the past. Finally, long-held secrets slowly seeping out. Meeting the air. The father coming clean with his grown daughter, spilling facts at last that predated her birth. Hidden ever after. Until today. His mouth, moving. He could feel it. Words squeezing out. He could hear them, but it felt as if he were relating events in somebody else's life rather his own. Secrets so long tucked away, so long unshared, they had lost their meaning.

The father telling her of a horrible accident. A restaurant fire that changed everything—a name, a plan. More than one life.

Revealing another secret—that, like her, he, too, had played the piano.

His daughter's face tightening over the steering wheel, listening intently. Hearing that it was not only his left hand that had been crushed in the restaurant fire but also his dreams. He had been a child prodigy. He had won countless competitions, prestigious awards, and a gift—a silver watch inscribed by Arthur Rubinstein.

Catherine, learning this: that from his early childhood his life plan had been set, without question, for he was a prodigy. Wheels on tracks. In steady motion forward.

But then, the interruptions: The war. The army. The years away.

Including high points: England. Fellow soldiers. A grand piano where he had least expected to find one, and the young woman whose piano it was.

The best of the high points: the young woman whose piano it was. A deep love where he had least expected to find it. Then the news that he was going home. The exquisite joy that she had said yes.

And then, the derailment: the restaurant fire. The loss of his parents. The loss of musical precision in his hand. The obliteration of his plans. The sinking of certainties long held. The overwhelming grief. The breach. The crippling silence. And the loss of his love.

The revised future, no longer including Carnegie Hall, Lincoln Center, concert halls worldwide, fame and fortune, and his treasured soul mate. The revised future, a new name, Higgins, and the White Mountain National Forest road crew, and, in his later years, a Mount Washington cog train driver.

Telling Catherine now of his enduring will to pass the torch to her, his only child, over the opposition of his now deceased wife. This fierce determination had divided the marriage, creating an irrevocable chasm. His now deceased wife cried constantly that all his money went in only one direction. She resented his single-minded desire to offer their daughter the opportunity for a life he might once have had.

And now, speaking of it at last. Telling Catherine all.

Catherine, listening, bowled over. Lips trembling, trembling hands pouring sweat onto the nonporous grooves of the steering wheel. Sideways glances at her father while forcing her eyes to keep on the road. Asking him where the watch was and why she had never seen it. Admitting that she would love to, not knowing that that very afternoon she would.

Asking him why he had never told her that he had played the piano, that he was a prodigy. Asking him how he could have kept it quiet all those years that he sat through her lessons during her childhood and teenage years, maintaining his unrelenting, intense focus on her making it to Juilliard. How was it possible that he had never said a word?

Her father's face tightening. His voice becoming defensive. Saying he had wanted no pity, that that book was closed, never to be reopened. It had all been taken from him. He would never play the piano again. That was that, the way it was. He would never accept pity. He had changed his name, taking his mother's maiden name, Higgins. He had moved to the remote north woods of New Hampshire, to the small cabin he still lived in today.

Catherine, asking again about the watch. Learning that he had left it overseas and was glad he did. He had never regretted that decision, leaving it with the woman he had loved like light itself. Her name was Daisy.

Catherine, asking why Daisy never came.

Her father, shaking his head. Saying that she never responded to the urgent telegrams he had sent, six of them. There was never a word back. That long, painful silence still visible in his face. Saying that the silence was so unlike her, that he had had to assume she decided that because of the accident he no longer had anything to offer her. She must have been too afraid to give up her home, her family, and her country for such uncertainty. He was defending her still, saying it was understandable.

He had not yet learned, although he would later that afternoon, that while Daisy had watched the mail delivery like a hawk, her mother had obtained—and presumably destroyed—the telegrams.

The revelation coming to light at last: Daisy's mother's best friend worked in the telegraph office.

Catherine, her head buzzing, asking why he was telling her all this now. Did it have something to do with this trip, this car ride that he had asked her to make? Was it why he had insisted on personally delivering the information about the old woman on the mountain? And why he had told Captain Miller that he would take care of it?

Her father, nodding. "Remember the boy? The one who asked for Michael Baker?" At the time it had thrown him for a loop and rendered him speechless. A question out of nowhere, totally unexpected. A name he hadn't heard in almost sixty years.

Catherine, nodding.

Her father's voice shaky, saying it was possible that with the boy was someone he thought he would never see again. It was possible that he had seen Daisy there at the base of the mountain. It was possible she was here in America, in New York.

Catherine, silent now. Taking it all in. The news was staggeringly big. The Connecticut miles passing outside the car while inside the car, inside her head, she was thinking about love, which she had been doing more and more lately. A pang, a sharp awareness growing increasingly sharper. The ties holding her career, hitherto bound so tightly that no air could escape, were somehow loosening, creating an opening, making room for something other than music. Catherine, fifty years old, known in concert halls throughout the world, only lately beginning to wonder if she would ever find love that was able to fit snugly into the opening.

She did not yet know that before the day was through she would be presented with a possibility. In the backyard of the house to which they were heading. That there, later today, she would find what could be a start. In the form of an Englishman coming out of a bad marriage. An expert in seventeenth-century arts and artifacts, a bestselling book in his past. And, possibly, because of her, a follow-up in his future.

THE FINAL TEN MINUTES of the trip. Confusion over directions. The father, reading out loud from the paper. The daughter, making a series of wrong turns. Tension rising in the car.

The father, wondering if it was really possible that it was Daisy he had seen. Could that really have been Daisy? Could it be? Or was it all a dream, a parcel out of an old man's imagination? An old mind playing tricks on him? An outgrowth of his increasing tendency lately to look back?

Finding the address. Turning into the driveway. Car doors swinging open. The old man, gulping.

Stiff legs carrying him up the front walk. Sounds of a party out back drifting over their heads. Father and daughter, relieved that at least it meant someone was home. Both aware of the foolishness of making the trip without first calling, compromising the chances of success.

A wobbly finger pressing the bell. The old man's nerves hitting a high note not reached in decades. Feeling like an uncertain schoolboy. His knees, shaking.

Catherine, seeing the color of his face, taking his arm in her hands. Thinking how strange it was to see him this way. He had always held his emotions in check. Catherine, thinking about this woman, this Daisy, and what she must have meant to him. Hoping this trip wasn't a mistake, hoping that he would not be crushed again. After all, this Daisy had dumped him once. Catherine, flooded with worry about how risky this was and, despite that, how insistent he had been. Nothing could have stopped him from doing this, from making this journey. Catherine, thinking about the idea of love as she watched him during the long seconds between the sound of the doorbell ringing and the sound of approaching footsteps.

While her father fussed with his hair.

The door, opening. A hairy nineteen-year-old peering curiously at them. Asking if he could help them. The old man, nodding. Saying he was here to see Daisy. Was she here? He had news of Hulda Kheist.

The hairy nineteen-year-old, stepping back into the house. Inviting them to do the same. Saying he would go to get Daisy, that he would be right back.

The old man, a bundle of nerves.

◆ ◆ ◆

Steve, coming out to Daisy, sitting next to Ann. On lounge chairs, poolside. Steve, telling her that there was someone asking for her at the door, saying he had news of Hulda. Asking just for her.

Daisy, clumsily pushing herself up off the lounge chair. Steve, lending a hand. Daisy, hurrying across the lawn. Not wanting to disturb the party. Not telling anyone. Up the deck steps, across the deck, past the sliding glass doors, into the house, and across the family room.

To where two people stood, nervously waiting.

Daisy's eyes going straight to Michael. Finding his on hers. Seeing each other across the span of decades. Both taking a moment, a pause, to swallow. To register circumstances. To catch up.

Then Daisy, slowly advancing. Michael, moving toward her until they stood before each other. A busy silence.

The old man, breaking it. His voice cracking. "Daisy?"

Daisy, nodding. Not breathing. Unable to speak. Her mouth open, no language available.

"I'm Michael Baker."

Catherine Higgins's head spinning. The first time hearing him say it. Staring at her father. Digesting the name. Reconfiguring the man.

Daisy, looking at him looking at her. Their eyes traveling over each other. Absorbing the present. Matching it to the past. Reading outward emotions, searching deeper for interior ones.

Both finding in the other what each of them held in themselves. Both thinking the other still beautiful, largely unchanged.

Daisy, thinking, "Still such a handsome man."

Michael, marveling that she was just as he remembered her. Still a beauty. Still a little nugget.

Both looking, delving, retrieving. And both sensing that although they had spent a lifetime oceans away and worlds apart, somehow all along they had been keeping time.

Seconds slipping by, neither racing to catch them. Locked in a bubble as one.

Catherine, looking on in silent wonder. Sounds of the wedding party filtering in—splashing, laughing, the calling of children.

Daisy, finally, shaking with emotion, working on keeping her voice steady, asking, "Can I get you something after a such long ride? How about a nice hot cup of tea?" Fully anticipating another in a long unbroken series of noes.

Getting a big surprise. Causing goose bumps. Because there Michael was, beaming back at her. Saying. "A stiff English tea? My, that would be wonderful." Tears welling up in his eyes.

Tears also bubbling to the surface in Daisy's eyes. Her hand going to her mouth, the tips of her fingers on her lips, her heart beating irregularly. Passing along a silent nod of thanks to Hulda, who didn't know what she had done. For if Hulda hadn't requested an excursion to Mount Washington, if she hadn't gotten them all to go to the top of the mountain, and if she hadn't remained behind to do what she had done, there wouldn't have been a search party. And if there hadn't been a search party, there wouldn't be now. This incredible moment. This magical turn of events. This crystallization of time.

And Daisy wouldn't be asking Michael and Catherine, if they didn't mind, to kindly come with her into the kitchen. Michael and Catherine wouldn't be thanking her. And they wouldn't be following her out of the foyer and through the family room. Down the hall. Into the living room.

Past Yodeli, perched in front of the wide window.

And past Michael, in his soaking wet bathing suit.

Playing the piano.

DAISY PHILLIPS

MICHAEL LEONARD BAKER

request the honor of your presence

at their wedding,

July 16, 2006

at 2 p.m.

Port Washington, Long Island,

New York

ACKNOWLEDGMENTS

Words cannot fully convey my deep gratitude to my superb agent, Adam
Chromy, for his steady guidance and unwavering belief in and enthusiasm for this book. Many thanks as well to Jamie Brenner, also of Artists
and Artisans, for contributing her vast knowledge of books and understanding of stories.

I'd like to thank Dot Nicholson, my first-cousin-once-removed, for
her visit during the summer of 2007. This book would not have been
written without that visit. Expecting nothing out of the ordinary, we
found ourselves with a gem. It was her courage in coming alone to New
York, to stay with a family of strangers, that inspired me to create the
character of Daisy.

I'd also like to thank my first readers, Leonard Baker, Carol Spier,
Adele Spier, and Ellen Reiter. Many hearty thanks to my mother, Glad
McGlynn, and my sister, Cate McGlynn, for their enthusiastic repeat read-
ings and endless support. Also, to my mother-in-law, Marylin Toomey,
and my brother, John McGlynn, for their encouragement.

Thank you to J. P. Shields for his complete understanding of plumbing and basement catastrophes, and to Henry Jaglom, for saying to me
all those years ago, "You're a writer. You just don't know it yet."

My deepest thanks to Shaye Areheart, my editor and publisher—first, for giving this book a chance, then for giving it a good kick in the pants. And thank you also to Christine Kopprasch and all the others at Random House who gave it their time and enthusiasm: Kira Walton, Anna Mintz, Katie Hickey, Annsley Rosner, Patricia Shaw, and anyone else whose contributions I've benefited from but haven't had an opportunity to thank in person.

And, of course, I'd like to thank those whose daily support, encouragement, and understanding made this possible—my truly wonderful husband, Rob Toomey, and our three breathtaking sons, Jamie, John, and Owen Toomey. Thank you—my guys—for keeping time with me.

Please note: In order to provide reading groups with the most informed and thought-provoking questions possible, it is necessary to reveal important aspects of the plot of this novel—as well as the ending. If you have not finished reading *Keeping Time*, we respectfully suggest that you may want to wait before reviewing this guide.

1. Do you think Daisy's decision to travel alone to New York came to her in a flash while rolling around in the mud, or do you think it was something that had been building in her mind over time. Why?

2. What kind of relationship do you think Lenny and Dennis had growing up, with each other and with their parents?

3. Do you think Daisy would have done any traveling again if she hadn't found the watch?

4. Do you think returning the watch to its rightful owner was the sole reason Daisy chose to go to New York, or was that merely a catalyst? Was she doing it because it was the proper thing to do, or did she have a hidden desire to see the watch's owner again?

5. Why do you think Dennis was so nervous about his mother going to New York? Was it what it seemed to be on the face of it, or were his own anxieties about his marriage and pending move part of it?

6. Did Ann's response to Daisy's arrival and stay surprise you? Did you expect a different reaction from her?

7. Was it in keeping with Elisabeth's character that she agreed to have Daisy stay with her and her family when Ann was not willing to?

8. Did Daisy come into Elisabeth's life at a good time? What do you think was behind all of Elisabeth's suspicions and unrest? Did you ever think Elisabeth's fears about her husband might be true?

9. Is it typical that Elisabeth didn't want to ask Daisy why she had come and Daisy didn't want to bring it up either? Who do you think should have started that conversation? Have you ever had a similar experience on either side of that issue?

10. A certain sense of timelessness runs through the book, a linking of the generations. What elements does the author use to evoke that sense?

11. What do you suppose Daisy's life would have been like if she had given the watch to young Michael and returned to Liverpool before she did? In what way would the trip have changed her if she had gone home before finding Michael Baker? Do you think she would have stayed in her house, or packed up and moved to Chessex?

12. Discuss Hulda's role in the story.

13. There are a lot of characters in the book that have an impact on others. Whose impact is the greatest and most likely to be long-lived? Whose is the most subtle but still valuable?

14. What do you think the future holds for Daisy and Michael Baker?

ABOUT THE AUTHOR

STACEY MCGLYNN lives with her husband and three sons on Long Island. She holds an MFA from Columbia University in film. *Keeping Time* is her first novel.